Biblioasis International Translation Series
General Editor: Stephen Henighan

1. *I Wrote Stone: The Selected Poetry of Ryszard Kapuściński*
   (Poland)
   Translated by Diana Kuprel and Marek Kusiba
2. *Good Morning Comrades* by Ondjaki (Angola)
   Translated by Stephen Henighan
3. *Kahn & Engelmann* by Hans Eichner (Austria-Canada)
   Translated by Jean M. Snook
4. *Dance with Snakes* by Horacio Castellanos Moya (El Salvador)
   Translated by Lee Paula Springer
5. *Black Alley* by Mauricio Segura (Quebec)
   Translated by Dawn M. Cornelio
6. *The Accident* by Mihail Sebastian (Romania)
   Translated by Stephen Henighan
7. *Love Poems* by Jaime Sabines (Mexico)
   Translated by Colin Carberry
8. *The End of the Story* by Liliana Heker (Argentina)
   Translated by Andrea G. Labinger
9. *The Tuner of Silences* by Mia Couto (Mozambique)
   Translated by David Brookshaw
10. *For as Far as the Eye Can See* by Robert Melançon (Quebec)
    Translated by Judith Cowan
11. *Eucalyptus* by Mauricio Segura (Quebec)
    Translated by Donald Winkler
12. *Granma Nineteen and the Soviet's Secret* by Ondjaki (Angola)
    Translated by Stephen Henighan
13. *Montreal Before Spring* by Robert Melançon (Quebec)
    Translated by Donald McGrath
14. *Pensativities: Essays & Provocations* by Mia Couto
    (Mozambique)
    Translated by David Brookshaw

15. *Arvida* by Samuel Archibald (Quebec)
    Translated by Donald Winkler
16. *The Orange Grove* by Larry Tremblay (Quebec)
    Translated by Sheila Fischman
17. *The Party Wall* by Catherine Leroux (Quebec)
    Translated by Lazer Lederhendler
18. *Black Bread* by Emili Teixidor (Catalonia)
    Translated by Peter Bush
19. *Boundary* by Andrée A. Michaud (Quebec)
    Translated by Donald Winkler
20. *Red, Yellow, Green* by Alejandro Saravia (Bolivia-Canada)
    Translated by María José Giménez
21. *Bookshops: A Reader's History* by Jorge Carrión (Spain)
    Translated by Peter Bush
22. *Transparent City* by Ondjaki (Angola)
    Translated by Stephen Henighan
23. *Oscar* by Mauricio Segura (Quebec)
    Translated by Donald Winkler
24. *Madame Victoria* by Catherine Leroux (Quebec)
    Translated by Lazer Lederhendler
25. *Rain and Other Stories* by Mia Couto (Mozambique)
    Translated by Eric M. B. Becker
26. *The Dishwasher* by Stéphane Larue (Quebec)
    Translated by Pablo Strauss
27. *Mostarghia* by Maya Ombasic (Quebec)
    Translated by Donald Winkler
28. *Dead Heat* by Benedek Totth (Hungary)
    Translated by Ildikó Noémi Nagy
29. *If You Hear Me* by Pascale Quiviger (Quebec)
    Translated by Lazer Lederhendler

If You Hear Me

If You Hear Me

Pascale Quiviger

Translated from the French
by Lazer Lederhendler

Biblioasis
Windsor, Ontario

Library and Archives Canada Cataloguing in Publication

If you hear me / Pascale Quiviger ; [translated by] Lazer Lederhendler.
Other titles: Si tu m'entends. English Names: Quiviger, Pascale, 1969- author. |
Lederhendler, Lazer, translator.

Biblioasis international translation series ; 29.

Series statement: Biblioasis international translation series ; 29 | Translation of: Si tu m'entends.

Canadiana (print) 20190115432 | Canadiana (ebook) 20190115483
ISBN 9781771962711 (softcover) | ISBN 9781771962728 (ebook)

LCGFT: Psychological fiction.

LCC PS8583.U584 S313 2019 | DDC C843/.6—dc23

Edited by Stephen Henighan
Copy-edited by Emily Donaldson
Cover designed by David Drummond

Published with the generous assistance of the Canada Council for the Arts, which last year invested $153 million to bring the arts to Canadians throughout the country. Biblioasis also acknowledges the support of the Ontario Arts Council (OAC), an agency of the Government of Ontario, which last year funded 1,709 individual artists and 1,078 organizations in 204 communities across Ontario, for a total of $52.1 million, and the contribution of the Government of Ontario through the Ontario Book Publishing Tax Credit and Ontario Creates. Biblioasis also acknowledges the financial support of the Government of Canada through the National Translation Program for Book Publishing, an initiative of the Roadmap for Canada's Official Languages 2013–2018: Education, Immigration, Communities, for our translation activities.

PRINTED AND BOUND IN THE USA

Do not wait to die, but do it now. Lie down and die.
Notice what stops when you die.
Notice what wants to begin.

— Arnold Mindell

The First Hour

Hard to believe, but I'm alive.
In fact I've never been so present.
So clear.

I see everything.
Roger cursing and pacing back and forth, scolding the men one by one.

Body in the middle of the street, on the pavement, helmet lying near the head, a tool in-between—the level, cracked. Liquid seeping out from it.

Martin running over, pushing aside Max and Vidal. He kneels on the glove, places his ear close to the lips, detects nothing. Looks for the pulse on the neck—no pulse. Opens the shirt, buttons flying in every direction. The red stain, on the chest, alarms him. Several ribs are soft, possibly broken. He hesitates. Makes a decision. He lifts the chin, feels the inside of the mouth, blows air into it twice, stands back, changes position, dares to press down, hands interlocked, elbows straight. By the book. His assurance is surprising for such a shy boy.

He persists. Patiently, rhythmically.
In spite of everything, the lips, the blue nails, the white cheeks.
Roger paces up and down
anxiously watching the far end of the street, the ambulance, the ambulance, the ambulance?
Finally.
Finally, Roger yells, raising his arms skyward.
Martin steps aside
mops his forehead
goes to sit down alone, in the shade, in a corner
the paramedics unpack their equipment
lift the eyelids
one blue eye, the other black, a bad sign
insert a tube in the trachea
open a vein in the arm
what are they injecting?
adrenaline
then
there's nothing.

Nowhere.

Green room
too brightly lit.
Men, women, with gloves, masks
metal
stained sheets
murmurs.
Swollen face, shaved skull
neck in a harness
one arm in a splint.
Serum dripping drop by drop.
Each drop reflecting the fluorescent lights, snail tracks.

Green garments, their folds like mountains valleys
the weft and warp of the cotton, worn thin.

The body is young, robust, muscular, broken
familiar, but neutral
intimate, distant.
None of this belongs to me.
Not the limbs, not the face, not the threads, not the seams.
Not the air in the tube,
not the lungs.
Just barely a point of transit.
I'm up here, at the ceiling, floating
> *suspended*
> *between leaving and returning*
> *held*
> *within hazy boundaries*
> *within a slack envelope*
> *within a habit.*

Early this morning I woke up, showered, shaved, ate three slices of toast with peanut butter.

The sun was shining, for once, and I remembered to put a brownie in my lunch box.

In top shape, just one filling, no eyeglasses.

It's 11:43. That's what it says there, on the clock.

These bones aren't mine anymore, nor these tendons, these ligaments. This isn't my skin anymore.

Just barely a possible location.

An alarm sounds.

It's my turn to go fetch Bertrand from school this afternoon. I said we'd go play in the park.

Caroline always wears an ankle bracelet that tinkles like a little bell. Her cream has a scent of musk rose. She likes dark chocolate, she talks in her sleep.

_The body, down there, is the only way I have of staying with them
two hundred and six bones six litres of blood seventy kilos
this intubated body is the only life I know._

_The alarm never stops. The lines crawl, almost flat, across the
black screens. He already looks like a corpse. The waxy skin. The
immobility. The resemblance is perfect._

_Yet seen from up here, it stays ready for use by a living man.
You can tell from up here, it's plain to see._

Plain to see, a possible life, and then nothing—black black.

_It draws me upward, it buzzes, it goes fast, it goes without say-
ing. I'm not afraid. It's natural, after all, to die, why does it always
bother us so much? There's a tenderness._

The tunnel, yes, but no words to describe it.

_I'm drawn by presences. I let myself glide. It's good. It's like
giving in to a first love, on a perfect vacation day, a day of health
and a wide-open future. I'm gliding at speed_
slowly, though, s-l-o-w-l-y
until it strikes: the light
strong white unbearable
I explode without a sound.
_I spread out, to the greatest length, to the greatest breadth, in
all directions_
my thoughts pure crystal
my heart cocooned
I've just come home after a long, harrowing journey
I evaporate like a puddle in August and it's good
it's so good
and true, so very true.

Threads that bind me to the living unravel
change into coloured beads
move off into unfathomable space
driven by what?
reconciliation.

For a long time: the void

In the void I hear:
You can still choose.

Slap.
Whip. Guillotine.
I shrink.
Dark, once again, sticky.
Screwed down, nailed, heavy,
little lights come on, thunder rumbles,
I don't feel pain.

I feel the point of contact between my skull and the table, a
point where
 for a fraction of a second
 the whole universe is gathered.
 I feel my heart beginning to beat
 haphazardly
 like a horse shaking its head with a snort

Good boy, says a tired voice.

Monday, June 6, 2011
Day 1

Caroline has just come in with the groceries when they call her on her mobile from David's phone.

"Hi there, Golden Muscle," she answers.

At the other end, the response is slow.

They offer to give her a lift to the hospital. They refuse to provide details; the fact is, they don't have any. Roger Pitt, the foreman, comes to get her himself. He had to stop everything anyway, send the guys home, and have the scaffolding inspected. Besides, he feels guilty; there's nothing like a work accident to spoil his week. He drives the pickup without saying a word. Caroline looks straight ahead.

At the hospital, the receptionist guides them toward the intensive-care unit. She gestures for them to take a seat in the waiting room. They sit down as far as possible from two nuns consoling each other in a barely audible whisper. From the thermos bottle and the pile of cushions at their feet, and especially the dark rings around their eyes, Caroline infers that they spent the night here.

"You really should go get some rest! Otherwise you're going to end up there too," the receptionist urges, pointing at the large swinging doors bearing a "No Entry" sign, behind which she then disappears herself.

She returns with a curvaceous nurse, who strides directly toward Caroline and plumps down in the adjacent chair. Her name is Sue, and this is the first time she has sat down since her shift began. Getting right down to business, she fires off a series of questions about David's general health. No diabetes, no heart condition. No alcohol problem either. She promises to come back shortly and is swallowed up by the swinging doors.

The interval is filled with a hypnotic rosary that irritates and reassures Caroline at the same time. After three Sprites and a bag of ketchup-flavoured chips, Roger Pitt looks in vain for an excuse to leave.

"I have to get going, Mrs Novak. Take a cab home, ask for a receipt, the company will pay."

These are the first words he's spoken since they got out of the pickup.

A half-hour later, Sue comes back and sits down next to Caroline. She explains the situation in simple terms: David has suffered internal bleeding, a cardiac arrest, head and chest injuries. Also, a broken arm and collarbone, which, under the circumstances, are hardly worth mentioning. The attending doctor will be able to tell her more in a moment. See her husband? Of course. But not right away. Later.

Later.

Caroline's mind is blank. The shock has completely emptied it. She concentrates on the large beige wall tiles; the slightest crack turns into a living human or animal form, a hallucination.

They're torturing me, that's it! This is a torture room. I've got razor blades under my skin. Where? Somewhere under my skin.

8

This is my body—get out! They're flaying me alive. Long shreds of throat. A train rolls by, close, too close, it scrapes the rails, the cars screech, the cars reek. Is it day or night? I hear my heart, machines, orders, a saw. Dogs. A tank? Must be Nazis. Am I going to die again? They're going to kill me. A dirty, long, painful death. They want me to talk to confess to own up to snitch—I won't tell them anything. I have nothing to tell—what exactly do they want? This is a mistake. I have to defend myself. I have to stand up, to open my eyes.

Caroline decides to walk in order to activate her brain. She ambles down the corridors, goes up and down stairways, and stops at random in front of the pediatric department. She keys her in-laws' number on her cell phone. Karine answers with her sandy voice. They exchange a few brief sentences that poorly convey the magnitude of the situation. The love of their life has fallen from a scaffold. He fell just a few metres, five or six seconds, that's all; whatever the outcome, it will take them months, years to get over it.

Caroline is overwhelmed by a wave of loneliness as soon as she hangs up. She suspects that a similar wave came over Karine at the very same moment. She doesn't know her very well, but she intuits that, beneath the prominent cheekbones, the delicately arched eyebrows, the porcelain skin, under the still-striking beauty and unstinting kindness, Karine is a self-sufficient island with a fragile ecosystem. Everyone knows glaciers are melting in the north and oceans rising in the south. Islands will be the first places to get wiped off the map.

I should have been more cautious, too. Should have paid my electricity bill. Then again, it just arrived. They've slit open my guts with a kitchen knife. They want me to talk—I've got nothing to spill. They're beating my head with a rifle butt, my head, my head. They've hung me from the ceiling by the wrists and are waiting for my shoulders to pop. They shout, they laugh, they bang on pots and pans. The leather around my wrists, the metal. The leather, the metal, my head.

The train.

A man as unobtrusive as a breath of wind lands next to Caroline in the intensive-care waiting room. He crosses his legs like someone who has all day.

"You're Mrs Novak?"

"Yes."

"I'm Philippe Hamel, I'm the attending physician."

The nuns discreetly lower their eyes. There's a rare lull—all the other chairs are empty. Dr Hamel's smile is perfectly appropriate to the situation: humane, solemn, compassionate, inscribed with the word "sorry."

"Sue has already talked to you?"

"A little."

"I've come to fill you in."

"Thank you."

"Your husband sustained a ruptured spleen and a cardiac arrest at the site of the accident. He was revived in the ambulance. He was unconscious when he arrived here, with an abdominal hemorrhage as well as an accumulation of blood that was putting pressure on his brain. We removed the spleen and decompressed his brain. In the operating room he experienced a serious drop in blood pressure. Frankly, it was touch and go there, Mrs Novak. But he's a fighter, because right now all his vitals are under control."

He pauses to size up Caroline, as her face wavers between composure and angst. Should he be straight with her or soften the blow a little? He hasn't yet made up his mind when he opens his mouth, aware that any hesitation on his part could invite a host of interpretations.

"The big question mark is the progression of the cerebral edema."

"The what?"

"The swelling inside the skull. The volume of the cerebral-spinal fluid is increasing and because the skull's capacity is limited, the brain gets compressed. When Mr Novak hit the ground he wasn't wearing his helmet. That's the most obvious cause, though not the only one. The internal bleeding and the lack of oxygen during the cardiac arrest are two more possible factors."

"How long did he lack oxygen?"

"Hard to say. He got first aid at the site, but we don't have precise data before the ambulance arrived."

"In other words, it's serious."

"Yes."

"Fatal?"

Dr Hamel scratches his neck.

"Mrs Novak, at this time . . ."

"Can it be fatal, doctor?"

"It's fatal when the pressure on the brain stem is too great. Here, at the back of the head. That's where all the vital functions are located. As a rule, the pressure peaks between twenty-four and forty-eight hours. The swelling is resorbed on its own after a week or so. We've done everything that we could, Mrs Novak. He's medicated, we can perform a drainage if necessary, and he's under the care of the province's finest neurosurgeon."

"But if he survives his brain will be damaged? I mean, permanently?"

"I'd prefer to wait before making a prognosis. Let's see how he progresses."

"What do the statistics say?"

"Well, you know, an individual case and statistics are worlds apart."

Dr Hamel uncrosses his legs, a subliminal signal that he has to get back to the ICU.

"Even so, what are the statistics?"

Dr Hamel hesitates for a split second. Angst is gaining the upper hand on Caroline's face. A bad time to broach the subject of organ donations. Not that there's ever a good time, but some are worse than others. He falls back on a maxim he swears by:

"Nothing is impossible to a willing heart."

If he didn't believe this he wouldn't be on call here this week. He wouldn't be a doctor. Caroline's rejoinder takes him aback:

"No one can be expected to do the impossible."

I have to go fetch Bernard from school now. I'm going to be late. I have to get out of here before they arrest him and throw him in a cell. Before they interrogate him, too. I have to get up. Find a way to escape. I'm thirsty. I have a headache and a big hole in my stomach. That's where they got in, through the belly. Murderers. I'm so thirsty.

Sue draws the curtain to give Caroline a little privacy. The noisy, crowded, frenzied hive of intensive care transforms into a small blue nook. David is lying on a Stryker bed, a bouquet of transparent tubes attached behind his ear, his wrists restrained with leather straps. He scratches the sheets with his fingernails. His index finger is sheathed with a sensor that measures oxygen intake. His neck is in a brace, his skull is swathed in bandages, his cheek is swollen, one arm is in a plaster cast, and in his mouth is a large tube connected to a respirator that makes a sighing sound. He struggles feebly.

Caroline is afraid to move closer. The wrists strapped to the bed give her a shock. Everything else, with a little imagination, could be taken for sports injuries. But the restraints are at odds with David's whole personality.

"Is he in pain?"

"No, he's under anaesthetic."

"Why?"

Sue steers her a little farther away; she never discusses a patient's condition in their presence.

"It's a way of reducing the cerebral edema. We also want to keep him from pulling his tubes out."

"Is that why you've strapped him down?"

"He was quite agitated. That's often the case. And your husband is a strong man."

"I know."

She knows—he hugged her this morning.

"But why is he so agitated?"

"The analgesics can be hallucinogenic. The room is noisy, the treatment is invasive. It's the lesser evil, ma'am. At least he's stable."

Sue points to the monitor with an obvious look of satisfaction. Each of the four coloured lines fluctuates distinctively: pulse, arterial pressure, central venous pressure, respiratory rhythm. Each in its own way suggests that he's trying to pull through.

"We've assessed the state of his nervous system—his chances are good."

"You assessed it how? He's asleep."

"His reflexes, pupils, and so on. Would you like to spend some time with him? No more than fifteen minutes."

Their shoulders are touching. My father, mother, Caroline, Bertrand. All crowded together in my blue cell.

My mother, bloodshot eyes, wet Kleenex falling apart. Her stiff-collared black dress, patent-leather shoes, too tight. A special occasion. My father wraps an arm around her shoulders. A special occasion, clearly.

Caroline is wearing her winter coat, the one with a purple hood. All bundled up in the middle of June. Why? Who went to pick up Bertrand at school? His downy skin, big blue eyes, soil under his fingernails. Dogs running between the beds, barking, huge, growling, yellow fangs.

I'm scared.

Go away. The Nazis will catch you. Go away.

Caroline steps toward the bed. Except for the bruises, the cuts and bandages, the cast, the neck brace, the tubes, the restraints, the monitor, and the scratching on the sheets, David is still easily recognizable. His arms tanned up to the biceps, his sensual mouth, his beautiful chestnut eyebrows, forever arched in a slightly sad expression that rarely conveys his mood but makes others instinctively feel for him. Bertrand has inherited this trait. Sometimes she resents it, accusing them of winning people over on the cheap.

She takes his hand and squeezes with all her might, leaving white imprints on it. He becomes even more restless. She strokes his wrist. Silly thoughts flit across her mind: an electricity bill, a BBC documentary about the Second World War, the winter coats left at the cleaners for the past two weeks. She has trouble focusing on David; it's too hard.

She feels the pulse throbbing under her fingers. The heart carries on. Not the one on the monitor, no, the real heart, under the warm skin. She indulges in a moment of hope, but a sharp beep makes her jump. Instantly, the curtain opens. Sue, who must have been listening at the door, is followed close behind by a secretary who gently takes Caroline's arm and ushers her toward the exit.

The alarm goes off. The neighbour's car again. And owning a Jaguar in Petite-Patrie—what was he thinking? A man in green approaches. He slides the tube into my mouth. He speaks German. He's experimenting on war prisoners. He's the one who slit my belly open. He waves a pair of golden scissors, brings it closer to the tubes coming out of my neck. He cuts. He cuts all the tubes one by one. The neighbour's damned alarm—can someone shut it off? The tubes are filled with red ants. My veins are full of them now. Caroline keeps quiet—why? Why do they keep quiet? I want to move, I want to stand up, I want to leave this place.

Sue bustles around David: bolus of solutes, isotonic serum, mattress adjustment. She notes things down. She waits, eyes glued to the monitor. Having seen the Grim Reaper twice this morning, she tells herself he's lucky, after all, to be here.

The man waves his scissors. My bed starts moving. Toward the gas chamber? I can hardly breathe as it is. My mother, my father, Caroline are rooted to the spot, not doing or saying anything, and Bertrand has latched onto the blue curtain. I hear his voice, loud and clear. Too clear, too sharp.

Why are they running, Mom?

They're rushing to take Dad's heart. I've already explained.

Where does it go afterward, Dad's heart?

It'll go into someone else's life.

Someone we know?

No.

Someone we're going to know?

Probably not.

Who?

Someone who needs a new heart.

Why?

To live.

Why?

To see their children grow up, their grandchildren.

Bertrand's huge sorrow follows my bed like a cannon ball. I want to run to him. I want to save him from the horror of the camp. I want to open my eyes. They've sewn my eyelids shut. Caroline hides Bertrand under her coat. She pulls her hood down over them. Outside there's a train waiting. A freight car.

15

Where is Dad going without his heart? He didn't want to see me grow up?

My head aches. Head aches aches aches. Hang in there, David, hang in there. They're going to kill me for my organs. Which explains the hole in my stomach. They'll give my organs to their officers and their officers will eat them, roasted, braised.

My heart—I gave it to Bertrand, they can't take it.

The alarm stops sounding. Sue counts the seconds, jots down more notes on the chart already filled with numbers. The reduced reactivity and the asymmetry of the pupils, the blood pressure, the weak motor response—everything suggests the edema is rapidly worsening. She knows that David's injury is severe and that he could die this evening. She also knows he could live until he retires. In the nearby beds, sixteen other men and women are poised on the same high wire.

The waiting room has just been invaded by an Italian family, whose members all look alike. The grandmother, dressed like a Sicilian widow, immediately informs Caroline and the nuns that it's her son—he's plagued with a heart condition. Someone refers in undertones to the man's cholesterol level and his many excesses. The grandmother implores the ceiling, shaking her handbag. Then the secretary arrives. They all stand up in unison and push the grandmother to the front, so she can see her son first.

"No more than two visitors at a time. If it's for Mr Paradisi you'll have to wait a little."

"*Ma! Perché?*"

"Sorry, you'll have to wait."

She turns to Caroline:

"Everything's fine, Mrs Novak, you can go back in."

At David's bedside, only the green line has changed. It's dancing now, completely at ease on the monitor.

Everything's fine, yes.

I'm so thirsty.

Move, move, move. Let me move.

They won't stop fiddling with me. Their experiments—why me? A lab rat. The racket is unbearable. This is a nightmare; I'm going to get up and turn on the light. I'm against animal testing. I'm going to drink a glass of water. I have to start by opening my eyes. Open my eyes.

Focus, David.

Open your eyes, stretch out your hand.

Caroline takes David's work clothes and boots back home in a transparent bag that weighs more than its contents. She floats toward the exit through a warren of identical, narrow, anonymous beige corridors and, despite her effort to follow the arrows, ends up in Cardiology. It's past time to pick Bertrand up at school and she'll have to call Maxime's mother.

"No cell phones on the premises," a nurse tells her, pointing at a sign with an unequivocal message.

Caroline's throat is so dry she's unable to ask for the way out. The floor pitches like a ship's deck. She drifts on rubbery legs from Cardiology to ENT, past several bottles of antiseptic soap. *Preventing infections starts here.* The soap evaporates and leaves her skin feeling like a cool breeze, a walk along the banks of the river.

She stays there, motionless, for a long time. She thinks about all the people who saved David's life even before she knew he was in danger. The guys at the construction site, the paramedics, the surgeon, the nurses, the blood donors. She wonders how this incident could have taken place without the slightest premonition on her part.

A man in a suit rushes past her looking like someone about to leave everything behind him. She quietly follows him into the first elevator, which brings her at last to the main entrance: a café, a store with greeting cards, gifts, and balloons, a florist, a clothing shop, a pharmacy, an ATM, benches daubed with a felt pen, wheelchairs lined up against a wall, where, over the decades, their handles have left black streaks all at the same height.

In a big glass wall, sliding doors open and close automatically, exit to the left, entrance to the right. Beyond it, cars go by, and pedestrians and cyclists. A large park behaves as if nothing has happened. The mirage of a world intact.

As Caroline steps toward the doors, they seem to recede. When she finally reaches them, they stay shut. She presses her almost-pleading hand against the glass, and then she notices the slip of paper: "Out of Order."

Tuesday, June 7, 2011
Day 2

When she awakes, still huddled against one of David's socks, Caroline enjoys a split second of amnesia. Then the memory of the day before crashes down and pins her to the bed. She thinks about the explanation she gave to Bertrand last night—elliptical, unsatisfactory, like cold porridge. She makes a superhuman effort to drag herself out from under the blankets and pulls back the curtains; to her amazement, it's still summer.

Bursting into the room, Bertrand surprises her in her underwear and immediately assails her with exactly the same questions as the night before:

"Where did Dad sleep?"

"At the hospital."

"Is he coming home today?"

"No, not today."

"Can I go see him?"

"Not today, darling."

The answers are mechanical and remote. This is the only way she can keep her anxiety at bay. She just as robotically serves him orange juice and cereal, and Bertrand seizes on the opportunity to get two glasses of chocolate milk.

I'm afraid.
Animal fear. Primal
painful.
The fly before the spider
the mouse before the eagle
the gazelle before the lion
the seal before the shark
terror, hunger, flight, migration.
The fangs
the hole in the hide
the broken wing
pieces of entrails I'm going to die a bad death.
Matter, matter, matter
matter imprisoned in a gigantic matrix
mechanism of fright.
Hell.
I call for help I call
with all my strength.
Shadows
rifle butts
close in
surround me.

Caroline brushes her teeth with David's toothbrush and decides to slip on his watch, which she fished out of the plastic bag. Where he is, time probably doesn't exist. No day, no night, no sleep, no waking. She'll take charge of normality's timetable.

They miss the bus all the same and are nearly late for school. Caroline, with Bertrand latching on to her coat like a tick, snags Mrs Monette on the fly. The teacher stands there impatiently, stiff as a board.

"Bertrand," she commands with a firmness Caroline envies, "why don't you go help Jerome put the chairs in a circle."

He obeys.

"You wanted to speak to me, Mrs Novak?"

"Yes, for just a minute, Mrs Monette."

"A minute is all I have, actually."

The classroom smells of chalk and floor polish. The papier-mâché masks intended for the end-of-year show hang in the open windows directly overlooking the boulevard. Cars can be heard stopping at the pedestrian crosswalk and moving off again. Caroline's heart is in her mouth. She concentrates on her sandals, on how the linoleum holds them up and, therefore, all her weight, her whole existence.

"Bertrand's father has had an accident. He's in hospital, in intensive care."

"Oh."

Madame Monette's expression has changed, but not in any definable way. She compulsively squeezes her hands together.

"That's all I wanted to tell you. Have a good day."

Caroline smiles at Bertrand, who is holding a chair with both hands and hasn't taken his eyes off her. She has an urge to take him back home, but she stomps away.

ribs arms legs—stuck ~~*stuck*~~
day or night?
throat dry
raw
dusty. The rubble is crushing me.
Want to sleep can't sleep want to sleep.
So thirsty
buried alive

alive shit
......~~buried~~......

Dr Hamel is pressed for time this morning and has arranged for the neurosurgeon to take over with the Novak family. The neurosurgeon, meanwhile, insisted on meeting Caroline and her in-laws in his spacious office rather than the beehive of intensive care. Dr Sollers likes order and tidiness. He's a very fair-complexioned man with parchment-like skin and exceptionally slender fingers, well suited, no doubt, to his profession. His thick eyebrows, which bring to mind Charles Aznavour, are less appropriate.

He pours himself a glass of water without offering them any, then launches into a gravelly voiced monologue in quirky French peppered with *bits of English.*

"You've seen Mr Novak? Yes. Of course, he has fractures, arms, ribs, contusions to the face, produced by the impact. All this is disturbing but minor, it will heal, *no problem,*" he adds in English. "We even have encouraging news: the electrocardiogram shows that everything is *re-established* in terms of the heart, the spleen—all taken care of. The most serious issue, the subdural temporal hematoma, was here, on the left. Dr Hamel has already spoken to you about this, no? It's the accumulation of blood due to the impact, just below the surface of the skull. In such circumstances, the *must* is to act quickly, we acted quickly. I performed the craniotomy myself. However, Dr Hamel has told you of the intracranial pressure? The pressure is still persistent, but, since last night, not increased, *that's good. No surgery* possible or necessary at this *stage.* Drainage—we have already drained. As the situation improves we are going to be able to reduce the *anaesthetics.* And re-evaluate his condition. *Especially* to see if he can breathe unaided."

Dr Soller pauses to sip some water, careful not to meet the gaze of his three listeners. He assumes they look distraught.

The loved ones always look distraught. There's nothing he can do about this.

"Can our son come to visit him?" Caroline asks.

"What age?"

"Six."

"Um. Visitors under twelve years are not permitted . . ."

Sollers taps the black desk with three white fingers. He prefers to delegate this sort of decision to his colleagues.

"Dr Hamel is quite permissive," he concludes. "He is on duty the whole week."

Headoncollisionnightmares
at full speed relentlessly moving—boiling—jostling
dissonantobsessivegummy sticky music
live OR ELSE die
not both
no.
Not both at once.

After the meeting with Sollers, Caroline leaves the hospital without stopping by intensive care. She feels guilty because her anger prevails over every other emotion. She can't muster the strength to confront David's tortured face right now. As she heads toward the exit, the beige tiles make her nauseous and the beds in the middle of the corridor make her skin crawl.

It's a beautiful June day. A beautiful day. But she goes back home even so. Last night she called just one person, Adèle, knowing she would spontaneously take it upon herself to spread the news to friends, acquaintances, all of Quebec. "Communication"—it's in her blood. Mission accomplished: Caroline has seven voicemail messages. The only one she answers is from Alex, a close friend of David. His message suggests that he expects them to go out for a beer on Saturday afternoon—might as well free up his schedule right away.

Alex greets the news with a curse, followed by a list of practical questions: "Which hospital? Oh, that one—I thought it was an English hospital? Fairly bilingual? Well, anyway. Visiting hours? Do you need anything? No. Okay. Let me know if you do." He can't wait to hang up but doesn't dare. So she does.

Then she runs the bath and keeps her head under water for a long time. While submerged, she pictures herself in David's position. Do the voices reach him like this, scrambled, distant, like the doorbell coming to her diluted, barely audible? The ringing continues and she finally steps out of the bathtub.

She answers the door in her bathrobe. Roger Pitt is wearing a suit and tie.

The sky moves away the asphalt moves closer.
My helmet follows my glove
  my head follows my helmet
    my shoulder follows my head
     my ribs follow my shoulder
      I'm aware of falling

*   *   *

I have enough time
more than enough time to think:
  I'm

     falling

       I'm
       fall
       ing.

The foreman has just trudged up the Novaks's staircase for the second time in two days. He doesn't want to be there, but the company insisted: "It's really the decent thing to do."

He already had the scene of the accident inspected, along with the condition of the scaffolding and the work site. He nervously wonders whether the inspection report will take into account last week's downpour and the subsequent delay to the formwork. To stay within the time frame, he prioritized speedy execution. He also used a free-standing structure for the access scaffold to respond more quickly to upward development. He let the men make do with whatever was at hand, and the scaffold floors were knocked together with boards and pipes that were too narrow or too long. Several ledgers turned out to be hard to fit together. He neglected to call the safety officer following the last-minute changes. He is aware of all these factors and of Novak's predilection for aerial acrobatics. The man is a ballet dancer in work boots. The foreman winces as he recalls over and over Vidal's remark at the start of the day: "Frankly, boss, this is borderline."

Roger Pitt has prepared himself for this meeting with his employee's wife. He duly filled out the form detailing the medical care and has already sent it to whom it may concern. He is sadly familiar with *Form 7*, but this is the first time he had to forego the accident victim's co-signature. It was demoralizing. On the other hand, he did get the information about applying for compensation and plans to offer Caroline the union's assistance with any administrative procedures. Under the circumstances, he'll also have to utter words that are both costly for him and beneficial for Mrs Novak.

Words such as "disablement," "monthly indemnity payments," "annual indemnity payments."

Such as "in the event of death," "funeral expenses," "on presentation of vouchers."

"Etc."

Roger Pitt didn't just prepare himself mentally; he also gave himself a very close shave. He considered the possibility of bringing flowers but couldn't decide on an appropriate variety. This is the first time he's driven his pickup in a suit and tie, and the tightness of his pants makes it clear he has put on weight.

Bicycle
skates
diving
all my falls fall together
my helmet hits the ground
bounces
I see
parts of the scaffolding
bits of sky
and
behind my eyelids
Bertrand's blue eyes.

Caroline arranges her dressing gown as she lets the foreman in. He starts with "good day," although he doesn't know if the phrase applies to this situation, given that, to all appearances, it's not a good day. He feels the words slip out of his brain through the embarrassment hole. His clammy hands leave stains on the *Indemnity Payment File*. In the other hand he holds a plastic bag containing David's personal effects that were left on the construction site: a lunchbox, his carpenter's belt, a windbreaker. He's eager to get rid of these items and feels guilty about eating the brownie. He couldn't help it—a nervous reflex.

Caroline serves him a cup of instant coffee. Roger Pitt smoothes his tie and begins:

"Have you seen him? How is he?"

"He almost didn't make it."

Roger Pitt feels a new wave of guilt welling up.

"What exactly happened?" Caroline demands.

"What happened? Yes. Good question. What happened is that, you see, with the kind of work he was doing at the time, err, when he fell, his position was, let's say, unstable. The position was, like, he was fastening a ledger, that is to say, a beam, so, according to the guys, he was fastening a beam with both feet on the guardrail, nothing illegal, but not comfortable either. Actually, no one really saw what happened, maybe he got distracted by something, maybe not. Fact is, whenever you stand on the scaffold frame there's a risk. Eight metres or so. Yup—quite a fall."

Arms folded, Caroline tries to imagine the fall yet doesn't let the image come into focus. As for Roger, he feels his tie tightening on his Adam's apple.

"His luck wasn't all bad," he continues. "Because, you know, every team on a construction site has to include a worker who's had first-aid training, and, in this case, that worker was your husband, Mrs Novak, so we might have found ourselves with a fatality on our hands, given the cardiac arrest, but young Martin Bilodeau had just finished a training course with St. John Ambulance, and everyone was impressed by his cool-headedness. He's the youngest guy on the site, but it's the first time I've seen anyone do ventilation and heart massage in combination. You need self-confidence and, I must say, he put his heart in it, no pun intended."

Visibly interested, Caroline unfolds her arms.

"Still, it seems to have shaken him up," Roger Pitt adds. "He's been dipping into his sick leave."

"Do you think I could meet him?"

"Yeah, err, yeah, I guess, no problem, Mrs Novak, I can take you to see him myself..."

Seeing Caroline's expression, he backpedals:

"I'll leave you his address. I'll let him know you're going to get in touch, because ... Like I said, he seems shaken up."

Roger Pitt finally pauses to take a sip of lukewarm coffee. He points to the file folder, spotted with fingerprints, that he deposited on the table in front of him.

"Mrs Novak, here's the information about the payments you're entitled to as the spouse of a work-accident victim. I realize that your husband's case is open, I mean, depending on events, his status will evolve, and things may get a little complicated for you, but here ..."

He rummages in his pocket.

"... here are the particulars of a union member who's willing, in fact designated, to help you through the process, so, there you go, and be sure to contact him if need be, don't be shy."

"What I want is my husband, Mr. Pritt."

"Pitt."

"Mr Pitt. It's my husband, my son's father. Not the government's money."

"Yes, I know, Mrs Novak, clearly. It's just that the government doesn't provide husbands, whereas the money ..."

"Obviously."

The foreman nudges the folder toward Caroline, who doesn't react. He waits a little, and then decides to stand up. At the last minute he remembers the statement the company instructed him to make:

"Your husband is a good employee, Mrs. Novak. A very good employee, skilled and hardworking, and appreciated by his co-workers and his bosses. This was an unfortunate accident and we sincerely hope that he'll make a quick recovery."

Back inside his pickup, Roger Pitt, sweating profusely, realizes he felt just like that through the whole conversation: perched on the guardrail, back twisted, vision obstructed, hands pressed against a ledger that was hard to fit in. Nothing illegal, no. But not at all comfortable either.

After he leaves, Caroline finds a word on the Internet that encompasses all of them: David, herself, her in-laws, Bertrand, Alex, Martin Bilodeau, and Roger Pitt. "Trauma," from the Greek for wound, damage, defeat.

Wednesday, June 8, 2011
Day 3

Caroline ought to call her mother today. It weighs on her, but she can't see any other way of finding her sister. At lunchtime, she finally decides to dial the number, half hoping Lorraine has gone out to treat herself to seafood at her golf club's restaurant. Her love affair with Florida actually began with a well-boiled lobster served to her on a Christmas Day while Montreal froze its butt off under six feet of snow and Caroline raised a glass to the memory of her recently deceased father. Anyone who saw Lorraine going through the Nothing To Declare gate on January 5 with that air of contraband, tanned skin, gold nail polish, and spangled sandals, would have realized she'd been seduced by the States.

"I left my boots in my suitcase, you understand, to make the pleasure last as long as possible."

David almost burst out laughing but managed to keep a straight face. Through the big airport windows you could see the asphalt covered with salt and the sidewalks strewn with grey lumps. Lorraine took exception to the climate—she'd "already paid her dues"— and went about retrieving her boots directly in front of the door, exposing the contents of her bag, entirely pastel except for thirty packs of American cigarettes. The travellers did their best to manoeuvre around her with their overflowing carts. Bertrand, still in diapers, ferreted in the suitcase, looking for his Christmas present. Caroline sank into an all-too-familiar abashment. David, his hands hidden in the pockets of his heavy coat, continued to keep a straight face.

The following year her Christmas holiday trip lasted all winter. After that, Lorraine didn't even bother to buy a return ticket. She sold her house in the Ahuntsic district and bought a beach-view condo in St Augustine, who she thought was "a saint from Spanish colonial times." She never spent more than a week in Quebec each year, during the July heat wave, and constantly complained about the traffic, the potholes, the cyclists, the organic food fad, voluntary simplicity, the humidity, and the price of scampi.

Caroline dials the number. She gets the area code wrong twice and is finally met with an English voicemail message: "You have reached Lorraine Auteuil . . ." Maybe she should hang up . . . "I am unable to take your call . . ." How can she summarize the situation . . . "but if you leave your name and . . ."

"Hellooo?"

"Oh! Mom? It's me, Caroline."

"Darling! I was having a snooze, heard the phone ring . . ."

"Would you like me to call back?"

"If it's not too much trouble, call me in five, no, let's say ten minutes? I just need to fix my hair—I look a mess!"

"Okay, I'll call back."

Caroline hangs up. The conversation has hardly begun and already she feels she's being driven up the wall. If only David were there, keeping a straight face. But David is absent, and that's precisely the point of the call. To fill up the ten minutes, she empties the washing machine and folds the dry clothes. When she opens the hatch, she sees that David left a Kleenex in a pocket of his shorts. Navy blue, to boot. The white fluff has fouled the whole load; Bertrand's socks look like angora kittens. She throws them in the trash with tears in her eyes.

"Hellooo?"

"It's me, Mom."

"I was thinking, while I was doing my hair, I was thinking, how odd—Caroline calling me like this in the middle of the week, in the morning. It's not as if you call very often as it is, but in the middle of the week, in the morning, out of the blue?"

"Yes, it's been a pretty strange week, Mom."

"Oh? What's going on?"

"It's David."

"David? What's he been up to again, our handsome David?"

"He fell from a scaffold."

"He was always a daredevil."

"He's in really bad shape, Mom."

"Oh my God!"

"He's in intensive care."

"Oh my God, Caroline. Oh my..."

"It happened the day before yesterday."

"Is it serious? I mean, of course it's serious, but is he going to, I mean..."

"He's stable. They've even started to reduce the anaesthetics."

A gloomy silence sets in, until Lorraine breaks it with her voice pitched a notch too high:

"You know, I'd be glad to come give you a hand, but I've got a tournament here, golf, you're thinking, but it isn't, no,

I've taken up mini-putt, I'll spare you the details, I'm very busy right now…"

"I understand."

"Are you getting help?"

"My boss is accommodating. I've put all my sick days together."

"It'll do you good, to get away from the library a little, give you time to take care of yourself."

"Mom. By any chance… Have you heard from Marie?"

"No, she's telephone-shy, too. Try Sasha."

"Why him?"

"Because he was touring Asia through the winter. Like you, he called me to get back in touch with her. Good timing, because she'd just sent me a postcard from Bali. He may have managed to track her down."

"Do you have his number?"

"I must have it somewhere. Hold on for a second."

Caroline hears the sound of bracelet charms, plastic on metal, metal on glass, and then of notebook pages hastily flipped through.

"Ah! Here it is. Sasha. *Gorgeous* Sasha. Do you have a pencil?"

The scaffolding is jerry-built
but we've seen worse
Max: his brother-in-law bought a chainsaw, now he wants one too.

Is there or isn't there a Nazi officer with us on the platform and why would you want a chainsaw in the city?

Max fiddles with the dials on his radio. He changes stations, but it's even worse, the music sucks, day after day after day.

If only his radio would drop and smash on the pavement once and for all

that's what I'm thinking
just before the level goes flying.
I watch it.
I watch the level in free fall, I crane my neck, my foot slips.

Sasha is the director, co-founder, and head choreographer of the "eclectic dance" company Aelectia. He directs his dancers while plugged into his mobile phone. He's also Marie's last known lover; she tried to leave him not once but twice and sums up her predicament to Caroline this way: "What can I say—he moves like a god." A body like Adonis, a golden voice, the look of an angel, refined tastes: a genius of seduction. "What can I say—it's Nirvana within easy reach." The same man cheated on his tax returns, blackmailed his donors, bribed the media, fired his star dancers without giving notice, and bedded the rest of the company without batting an eyelash. "What can I say—heaven and hell under one roof."

Caroline met him only once, when Marie had gotten her tickets for the opening night of a show. He was wearing tight leather pants, and afterward David repeatedly threatened to buy himself a pair just like Sasha's. In a word, that first impression wasn't especially favourable.

One day, Marie pinched a nerve in her back trying to retrieve a spoon from behind the stove. At the chiropractor's, she began to cry and couldn't stop. The chiropractor was reassuring and told her that tensions frequently build up in one spot in the body and are released in the course of treatment. That night, Marie continued to weep as she sat in her freshly stripped rocking chair. She wept out of rage and humiliation. She suddenly perceived Sasha in the fullness of his imposture, and she hated herself for having let him into her heart, her womanhood, her Facebook account. Three months on, she closed said Facebook account, chucked her mobile phone into the Mille-Îles River, broke her lease, sold her car, and quit her job at the daycare centre. She said her thoughts amounted to one word ("yoga," which means "practice") and that her sole possession was a one-way plane ticket to Delhi.

Her sister's departure was the hardest thing Caroline had gone through in recent years. Worse than her father's death, worse than her mother's submersion in pools of Martinis. But she knows Marie. No half measures. An unflagging fascination with invisible worlds, an instinctive search for intensity. Sooner or later, with or without Sasha, Asia would have bumped into her somewhere along the way. Still. A one-way ticket. And scarcely a word of news: three postcards, one letter, eighteen months.

> *Suspended in empty space.*
> *I'm going to fall.*
> *I'm falling.*
> *Below?*
> *Nothing.*
> *Just emptiness*
> *empty   emptiness.*

The good thing about Sasha, if one must be found, is that, with his mobile plugged into his ear, he's easy to track down.

"Yes?"

"Sasha?"

"This is he."

Always that phony European accent.

"This is Caroline Auteuil, Marie's …"

"… sister. Well, well. To what do I owe this honour?"

"I need to get in touch with Marie right away. A family matter. I was told you might have seen her during your tour last winter."

"'Family matters,' 'I was told that'—so mysterious! And how do I know that Marie *wishes* for you to get in touch with her?"

The way Sasha stresses "wishes" annoys Caroline no end.

"I need her. It's urgent."

He pauses for aesthetic effect before adopting a different attitude.

"I haven't seen her."

"No? Perhaps you've talked to her?"

"No, I haven't. But I know where she was in early March. In Lhasa."

"Where?"

"Tibet. I have the name of someone who will probably be as glad to help you as he was to brush me off."

"Really?"

"You're delighted, aren't you? His name is Christian, but he's a Buddhist. Rimbault—a Rimbaud without the genius. You're calling me on your mobile, so the number on the display is yours? I'll text you a message tonight with the address."

Then Sasha hangs up.

I reach for the framework
too late:
nothing to grab on to.
How could I have been so stupid?
A pipe end rams into my ribs.
My helmet follows its arc.
I see the building across the way, a bank, upside down.
Upside down, an employee watches me, cup in hand,
mouth agape, frozen.
I shift the angle of the sun
Max leaning toward me
the asphalt

a half-erased parking stripe.
I bring my arms up around my ears, tuck into a ball, trying to
land feet first, not head first
anything but my head.

Bertrand is in a bad mood. He refuses to eat his banana, do his homework, or take a bath.

"Is Dad coming home today?"

"When's he coming home?"

"Why's he in the hospital?"

"Does he have a cold?"

"Do you think he's bored? I could lend him my remote-controlled car."

"Where is the hospital? Which bus do you take to get there?"

"Who's taking care of him? What day is he coming home? Will I be in school? Is he going to bring me a present? When?"

The evening goes by with no news from Sasha. His message arrives just before midnight and catches Caroline off guard in the child's bed with *The Jungle Book* wedged under her shoulder blade and Bertrand, all warm and a little damp, pressed against her chest.

It must be one in the afternoon in Lhasa. She decides to call immediately, being drawn to anyone who brushes Sasha off. Christian Rimbault answers after one ring.

"Hello, my name is Caroline, I'm . . ."

"Marie's sister?"

His lilting accent places him squarely in a Provençal field of lavender. It's hard to picture him in the Himalayas.

"I . . . I need to speak to Marie. Do you know where she might be?"

"I can find her. Give me a day or two. You're not doing so well, am I right?"

"Me? Yes ... No. I mean, my husband has had an accident."

"What sort of accident?"

"At work. A serious accident."

"I'll find Marie for you as soon as I can."

"Thanks."

"You're calling from Montreal?"

"Yes."

"It's the middle of the night, isn't it?"

"I know."

"You can't sleep, right?"

"Exactly."

"I understand ... Did you know they call Tibet 'the roof of the world'? From here we can keep an eye on the whole planet. I'll be thinking of you."

Caroline hangs up in a kind of trance. Talking to this perfect stranger with the sweet accent has affected her like an injection of valerian oil. All she wants is to obey him and drift off imagining that an anonymous force made of eternal, lavender-coloured snow watches over her as she sleeps.

Thursday, June 9, 2011
Day 4

Bertrand is nervously twisting a drawing he's made. His sneakers squeak on the shiny floor. Caroline would have preferred to wait until David was less disfigured, but Dr Hamel spoke in favour of this visit.

A specialized nurse intercepts them in the waiting room, where Caroline has already spent a good part of the week and whose every detail has become all too familiar to her. The drinking fountain with its slim thread of water, the chairs that scrape and those that creak, the ones where the vinyl has been slashed, the muffled phrases, the panic attacks, the beginnings of conversations. The persistent ringing of whoever wants to make their presence known or ensure they're not forgotten, the sucking sounds the airtight doors make on opening. The smell of iodine, bleach, sweat. The nonchalant coming and going of mail clerks, the regular swish of the mop. The announcements, the fluorescent lights, the waiting.

Bertrand listens to the nurse explain why his father won't be able to answer his questions or smile at him, why his face has changed. Yet she insists that Bertrand should talk to him. She maintains, paradoxically, that his visit means a lot to David. Bertrand's bewilderment gradually comes out in a frown, and Caroline feels angry at life for having thrown him so soon into such an ordeal. She's powerless to spare him this; she can't wake his father, soften the edges of reality, or smooth out the crumpled drawing in his fist.

After entering the room, Bertrand is brought up short by the strangeness of his surroundings. He steps back before going ahead, but they're soon hemmed in by the blue curtain, somewhat like the tent on their weekend camping trips. He climbs into the chair Caroline has placed near the bed.

"Mommy . . . why is his cheek all black?"

"Because he bumped it, but it'll heal."

"He's letting his beard grow?"

"For now."

"What's that there, in his mouth?"

"It's an air tube, to help him breathe."

"Why's he wearing that collar around his neck?"

"It's there to keep his head from moving."

"What's the thing in his nostril?"

"It's for his food. The tube goes right down into his stomach."

Bertrand makes a face.

"What does he eat?"

"Liquid food that they prepare for him."

"Like what? Milkshakes?"

"No, more like chemical stuff."

Bertrand fingers the tube.

"No, no. No, you mustn't touch."

"But look, Mom, it's like the Bailey's grandma Lorraine likes so much."

"How about that! You're right. But I'm sure this is healthier."

"Like broccoli."

"There you go."

"Is he sleeping?"

"Yes, the doctor is keeping him asleep for the time being, while he gets better."

Bertrand studies his father closely and then places the crushed drawing on his immobile chest. He waits for a reaction.

"Mom, he's dead."

"No, I've already explained. Look, he's breathing."

"Are you sure? I think it's the machine that's breathing."

"Dad and the machine, together."

Bertrand stands up on the tips of his toes, puts on a thoughtful face, and starts to recite:

"Our Father, in heaven, let your kingdom come, let what you want for us happen, down here as it does up there, give us our bread today, forgive our bad behaviour, and deliver us from Jonathan Louvain, for you have the Power and the Glory."

He pauses and turns toward his mother.

"Mommy, I can't say Amen."

"I understand, buddy. Me neither."

Caroline wonders where he got this prayer. His Polish grandmother is the only plausible suspect.

"Is it Babcia that taught you the Lord's Prayer?"

"Yes."

"And who exactly is Jonathan Louvain?"

"He's the kid who keeps me from being nice in school."

"Oh? How so?"

"He always makes me lose my temper."

"Some people are like that."

"But why?"

"That's just how it is. It's a shame."

They keep quiet for a while, making the respirator sound louder.

"You know you can talk to him."

"I don't feel like it."

"Why?"

"He isn't even looking at me. He looks like he's made of plastic."

"Why don't you start by touching him?"

Bertrand lets his fingertips brush against his father's skin, but he immediately pulls his hand away.

"Try again. What would he say if he thought you were afraid of him?"

"He'd say, 'Come over here so I can eat your feet.'"

"Exactly. Try again."

Bertrand puts his hand on David's wrist, where his watch has left a white stripe. He senses the warmth climbing up to his shoulder and it feels good. Encouraged by this, he clasps the sheet in both fists and, making a huge effort, he lets rip:

"Dad, I made a drawing with an ambulance and a sun and two red lights. It's cool, because the ambulance is running the red lights."

Max leans toward the street. Roger waves, Martin straddles a post and climbs down like a monkey, Vidal gets out of the pickup and slams the door shut, the others show up one at a time, passersby stop, a woman puts her hand over her mouth, another shakes as she fumbles in her purse, a man bursts out of the bank and dials 911 on his cell phone.

Martin kneels down.

Move on, Roger shouts, there's nothing to look at. Just move on.

They scatter when the ambulance pulls up.

The stretcher comes down and goes back up.

The flashing lights go on, the ambulance turns the corner, it runs all the red lights.

Friday, June 10, 2011
Day 5

Dr Sollers presses the fingertips of both hands together, moves them apart, joins them together again. His office is suffused with an overpowering musky scent. He has just explained to Caroline why David hasn't woken up even in the absence of sedatives. He took the liberty of digressing about the phenomenon that sees a third of intensive-care patients mimicking a comatose state to escape from the trauma of the situation, but then assured her that David's coma, on the contrary, is quite real. The scans, not to mention the circumstances of the accident, leave no room for doubt.

Dr Sollers does make an effort to report plenty of positive news. The edema, for instance, is rapidly shrinking. The electroencephalogram confirms the presence, albeit reduced, of electrical activity in the brain. David is much calmer and the restraints have been removed. On the Glasgow scale, which is used to measure the depth of the coma, he scores 8. It could be worse.

"8? Meaning what?" Caroline asks.

Dr Sollers's jeweller's fingers mime a pair of slightly limp quotation marks.

"Remission possible. Aggravation not ruled out."

Caroline opens her eyes wide. Either she is stupid or the statement is meaningless.

"Your husband is *perfectly fit*," Sollers continues. "It gives him a good *head start*. No pun intended."

"How much time?"

"That is always the difficult question. The majority of similar cases *resurface* in less than two weeks. After four weeks, *let's say*, it will be necessary to update the diagnosis. We are keeping him under constant *monitoring*, naturally. In the interval, some advice, Mrs Novak: speak with him. It is positive for you and positive for him. It can facilitate the *comeback*, because it draws him toward reality."

"Will he hear me?"

"We are not aware if your husband hears or not. Many comatose individuals hear. Take a chance."

Dr Sollers gives her a hasty smile. He closes the file folder. The time for the appointment is over and, truth to tell, it seems that only his bushy eyebrows have made an effort to be less distant.

"*Is there anything else?*"

Caroline hesitates. There's a question gnawing at her, yet she's not sure she wants to hear the answer.

"How will he be when he wakes up?"

"Cranial-cerebral trauma always has consequences."

"What consequences, exactly?"

"Presently, it's impossible to say."

I've stopped falling. I'm stretched out somewhere. I can't move.
And them, they're still there. They never leave.
Who?
They say aquatic things, cavernous things.

They communicate. They plot. They talk about me.

Has someone gone to fetch Bertrand from school?

That damned electricity bill must be lying around on the counter—will Caroline notice it?

They touch me and prod me. They stick things into my skin. They obviously despise me. They won't leave me alone even for a second.

I'd like to sleep. They won't let me sleep. I wait for night-time. The night doesn't come.

Neither does the day.

Back home, Caroline feels completely numb. At a loss for something to do, she falls back on surfing the Internet. "Glasgow Coma Scale," for starters:

> A standardized system for assessing the severity of a comatose state based on eye movement, verbal behaviour, and motor ability. A score of 15 indicates a normal state; 3 indicates a vegetative state.

Glasgow. Caroline has always been attracted to Scotland. She pictures wild shores with dark rocks, giants in kilts bringing England to its knees with one hand and celebrating their victory to the nostalgic sound of bagpipes. It would never have occurred to her that Scotland would bring her this scale of hope and hopelessness.

She continues to surf. Going from one site to the next, she gobbles up all manner of data: statistics, mysticism, contradictions, miracles, and fiascos. After reading that pieces of dead brain are liquefied and then disappear, absorbed by the adjacent cells, she gives up. The search ends up in this black hole, exactly where it started. Caroline shuts down the computer and lingers in front of the monitor, chewing on her one remaining fingernail.

Saturday, June 11, 2011
Day 6

There, the fog is lifting.
The hospital.
I'm in the hospital.
I fell. Then what?
I'm paralyzed. I don't feel anything. What's the matter with me?
A bubble. Silent. Insipid.
Did they come? Caroline, Bertrand, my parents? Alex? Vidal?
Will they come for me?
I have to get out of here.
Stand up and walk, David.

Karine presses her cheek against David's puffed up cheek and transfers a patch of her foundation onto it. She'd like to feel Janek's presence, his sloping shoulders, his nicotine-saturated coat, his familiar warmth. But Janek hangs back. His ice-blue eyes don't even dare to settle on his son.

The Novaks have had their share of troubles. But this one is hard to swallow.

"Dawidek, Dawidek," Karine murmurs.

Janek keeps silent and will continue to keep silent. He grew up in an apartment where the walls had ears, in a building where the neighbours moved out during the night, in a paranoid city, in a country jolted from one calamity to another, century after century. His spontaneity comes down to the art of shutting up.

It's absurd, but in the hospital room he thinks back to his honeymoon. David, the reason for their rush to marry, accompanied them as an embryo on their pilgrimage to Częstochowa. Janek sees again the famous icon being lowered slowly from the vault with a block and tackle. Karine, whose name then was Katarzyna, was counting on the Madonna's intercession to give birth to a healthy child. Janek, who believed only in Katarzyna, instead defied the dark-face Virgin to give them an open and prosperous Poland.

He felt his prayer had been answered when, in the early eighties, Solidarność, the union organization campaigning for a viable socialism, began to grow by leaps and bounds. He took an active part in the movement, to the point where he was regularly tailed by the secret police. Then the government declared martial law. In the throes of a crisis, the country shut itself off. There were tanks in the street, hundreds of arrests, armed Poles against their fellow Poles, and the Soviet army massed at the border, ready to stifle any unrest.

Like many activists, Janek was presented with an ultimatum: exile or prison. Broken-hearted, he chose what eventually became known as the "silent immigration." The family's reunification would depend on a roll of the dice; his wife, with little David, had a chance of joining him because, after the Second World War, Poland, despite its hermetically sealed borders, was eager to be rid of its citizens of German background. Katarzyna's maternal grandfather was German, but she had never tried her luck, fearing Janek would be left behind the

Iron Curtain, and Janek, convinced a free Poland was in the offing, had never insisted.

It took them eighteen long months to reunite, and they chose to settle in Canada because they dreamed of North America, in Quebec because they were Catholic, in Montreal because it was an island.

Janek sighs. He finally directs the ice floe of his gaze at his son. The dark profile stands out against the white pillow. It's the respirator's turn to sigh. All he wants now is for David to wake up. Whatever it costs, whatever it takes, at any price. He pictures himself carrying David everywhere in his arms, like a child.

An alarm goes off at the far end of the room, followed by hurried steps, the sound of someone crying. On second thought, Janek prefers to wait on the other side of the curtain.

My mother's going to touch me like she used to when I had an all-day fever.

She's going to negotiate for me in prayer, though I'm an atheist.

Always treading water amid contradictions

> *classical music and romans-fleuves*

> *contagious laughter, hand over mouth*

> *genuine pearl necklace on a Dollarama blouse*

My mother: a hibiscus flower gently opening in a glass of Canada Dry

Janek—he'll stay in his corner over there, all wound up

damp moustache

paralyzed like me

but sleepless

worried, like her

but faithless.

For weeks I've been promising to go take down his Tempo carport.

It's been over a quarter of a century since the Nowakow-skis arrived in Montreal. At first they lived on the two meals a day supplied by the Notre-Dame-de-Częstochowa parish hall, on Rue Gascon. No effort was spared to help them find a lodging. It was almost as if the Black Madonna were actually lending a hand. After taking some refresher courses, Janek re-entered the plumbing trade. He was hired almost imme-diately by a local company on the condition that he be on call Sundays, nights, and for emergencies—a condition no one else would accept.

Katarzyna did housecleaning in the wealthy Outrem-ont district. Occasionally she would come upon a piano. If she was alone she played a little, only Chopin, especially the mazurkas, having resolved to begin teaching music again as soon as her French was adequate. Right from the start she had adopted a French version of her given name that she liked very much. Janek, on the other hand, refused to change his. It was at the priest's insistence that he simplified their surname. "Nowakowski already means 'newly arrived,'" the cleric kept reminding them. "No need to overdo it."

They received what they felt was a warm, almost noncha-lant, welcome from the Québécois, as if they'd always been part of the furniture. When the Novaks spoke English to an anglophone they were assumed to be francophones; when they spoke French to a francophone they were assumed to be anglophones. In both cases, they were assumed to be locals. Even though they'd expected it, they were taken aback by the abundance of goods. Choosing a shampoo or a jar of mustard could take them forever. They gorged on bright colours like people miraculously cured of colour-blindness, turned gro-cery shopping into a family outing, squeezed the pineapples, passed the lychees around from hand to hand, marvelled at the lighting, superfluous by day, excessive at night.

They could sleep easy in their furnished and heated apartment in the Hochelaga-Maisonneuve area. Even the police looked honest, and Bell Canada couldn't have cared less about their telephone calls. The pay cheque arrived on payday, with the correct amount, the bank accepted it, no questions asked, and Karine filled the pantry to overflowing every Wednesday morning.

During the first few months they went from one surprise to another and yielded to the integration process like a plank of wood to a plane. But the post-Christmas sales marked the beginning of a time of crisis for them. On the surface, life was just fine. Everything was going smoothly; yes, smooth—that's exactly how everything was.

They found it hard to own up to their unease, let alone put a name to it. Was their adopted country too new? Too hygienic? Too easy?

To find their bearings they sought a form of historical remembrance in the facades of houses. But Montreal homes were utilitarian and without baroque ornamentation, catacombs, drawbridges, battle scars, traces of victories or defeats. Modern and comfortable, they spoke of the present and the future, but not of memory.

A host of details left the Novaks deeply disconcerted. Homeless people, for one. The uneaten fries in downtown trashcans. Unemployment levels. Variety shows. Before, thinking had represented a real danger, but they suddenly missed sharing a few risky confidences in the parks of Cracow, the many layers of meaning conveyed in a mere exchange of glances, the courage of words written by the country's best minds, who as a consequence chose exile.

They were constantly presented with messages at odds with their socialist values: "Look out for number one," "Listen to your body," and so on. They felt people orbiting lazily around each other, preoccupied with their appearance, their astrological sign, their success, their lottery ticket, their happiness. The social fabric tightened around the issue of Quebec independence, but the referendum question was yet another source of confusion for the Novaks.

Nor did the availability of consumer products bring them the relief they so desired. Instead of finagling an extra egg into their shopping bag, they bought them by the dozen at the supermarket; oddly enough, goods not acquired through struggle seemed to have less value and even less taste. Their fighting spirit was swamped by a tide of liberality and friendliness; the lack of adversity left them confronted with intractable dilemmas over shampoo and mustard and everything else.

In short, much to their astonishment, they fell prey to nostalgia, a genuine case of *tęsknota*, at once tender, strong, sweet, bitter, and sensitive.

Karine got through the crisis on the strength of her sociability and creativity. Every form of diversity interested her. She loved the cinema, get-togethers, Italian cooking courses, and volunteer work. Thus, she redefined her balance around a few friendships, an artisanal bakery, and a knitting club. Janek, meanwhile, was unable to move on. He had left his country and his country haunted him. There was nothing he didn't miss, from the rickety streetcars to the flocks of crows, not to mention the thousand uses of cabbage.

He took heart from knowing that David never went hungry. That David could grow up without looking over his shoulder or wearing his pants too short, and that he could come to know the world unfiltered by censorship. He was already fluent in French, played forward on his neighbourhood hockey team, and wanted no more sauerkraut in his lunchbox. Janek watched him turning day by day into a true little Québécois. Too bad that he himself was stuck straddling two chairs; in a way, this was as it should be. Because fundamentally, all this, the whole exile, was for David.

He kept an eye on Poland's transformation. The underground survival of Solidarność, its re-emergence, its triumph. Lech Walesa, president. The opening up of the economy, the fall of the Iron Curtain, NATO membership, admission to the European Union. Now the border was open and the country was thriving, but it was too late; if they moved back to Poland, David would not follow them.

And all this was for David.

His coma is the beginning of another, far deeper exile. If he dies there won't even be any chairs left to get caught between.

Sunday, June 12, 2011
Day 7

Dad! Dad!
I'm coming, Bertrand, wait just a minute.
Daaad!
I'm coming.
Wait.
Just a minute.

Bertrand had bad dreams last night, and, while Caroline drinks a cup of coffee for every hour of lost sleep, he keeps busy in the yard with some long-neglected toys. After filling and emptying the shovel of his plastic crane a dozen times and making a few loosely packed sand cakes, he has to face facts: this is all so boring. He comes in and plants himself at the living-room window.

Usually, he goes out with David on Sunday. They play catch or go for a bicycle ride or watch a game of baseball or God knows what—in any case, they always come back with muddy knees and full stomachs. Today, David won't be taking him anywhere. Bertrand knows this but waits for him anyway, just in case, and sucks his thumb, something he'd stopped doing until last week. Oh well, Caroline thinks as she comes over to him, braces will fix whatever harm it does.

Outside, the view is nothing special—an ordinary street in an ordinary neighbourhood. Brick fronts, grey spiral staircases fitted with non-slip treads, weatherstripped doors that make a sucking noise. Black trashcans, recycling bins. Square front yards, most of them untended, except Mrs Levasseur's, with its collection of garden gnomes. Their own place is a little different: set back from the street, a single staircase, short and straight, and a red maple taller than the house. An old house with hefty heating bills. Each year David works on it during his vacations.

"Would you like to go to Mount Royal?"

"With Maxime?"

"Why not?"

On the mountain, the two boys have fun with a kite. The red and yellow ribbons glide like silk against a perfect sky, borne along on an ideal breeze, while Caroline lays out the picnic on a beautiful, tender green lawn. There's no hint of the parched expanse hidden beneath her calm movements, nor the infinitely slow passage of minutes on this first Sunday without David. There's no way to imagine how dreary Beaver Lake appears to her, how grey and tired Montreal looks from the Belvedere. Even the sun seems defective; it takes forever to reach its zenith and just as long to go down again. She misses David. Each of her cells miss David. She'd like to talk to someone about it, but who? To David. She'd like to talk to David about how she misses David, how she worries over him.

She'd like to know if he's in pain.

If he's conscious.

If he hears when people speak to him.

If he'll come back. And when.
She'd like to know where he is, exactly.

Nowhere.
A coma. Is that it? A coma. Must be.
Why me, why now?
In my thirties, in the middle of June.
Shit.

Inexorably, the planet turns, the horizon draws closer to the sun. Maxime has to go home for supper and homework. When his father opens the door, a barbecue smell wafts over them.

"Did you have fun? Yes? Maxime, what do you say to Bertrand's mom?"

"Thanks for inviting me to play."

"You're welcome, Maxime. It was a pleasure to have you along. Eh, Bertrand?"

"Yeah, it was great. Next time we'll go with my father. He can't wait to try the kite."

"Would you like to have some hot dogs with us?" Mr Giguère asks awkwardly.

"We're vegetarians!" Bertrand protests.

"We have to get going, thanks," Caroline answers.

"Bertrand can come over to play this week after school, if that works for you. I'll bring him back home, before or after supper. We can skip the meat, too, you know."

"Tomorrow?" Bertrand exclaims.

"Soon. Thanks, Mr Giguère."

They have a chart, that's for sure, with quantifiable data
Heart rate, blood pressure, temperature, that sort of thing.
I still exist—is that in the chart somewhere?

I still think. I wait.
I exist, I persist, I have a name.
It's David.
This is absurd.
Get me out of here, someone.

Already, a corner of the sky is turning purple. Caroline and Bertrand are walking home. He hops and skips, while she fights the old Sunday blues that date back to her childhood and have now reached unbearable proportions. Luckily, this is the night Sandra has chosen to pay them an impromptu visit.

The daughter of an Argentine father and an Irish mother, Sandra is a force of nature with sea-green eyes who speaks straight from the shoulder and works indefatigably at the Botanical Gardens. She is sitting on the stairs, where she's been waiting for them with a huge dish of lasagna perched on her knees.

Caroline is so relieved by what she sees, she nearly shouts:

"Great timing, Sandra, my fridge is empty!"

"I figured as much."

During the meal Sandra has the decency not to say "I understand" even once. She urges Caroline to have a nibble, if only to be polite, and then takes it upon herself to put Bertrand to bed. He gives her the most beautiful compliment in the world—"Dad would have loved your lasagna"—and falls asleep the instant he finishes the sentence.

She finds Caroline motionless in front of the dishpan and instinctively rolls up her sleeves.

"You need Marie," she says, with a slight push to make room for herself at the sink.

"I talked to someone who can find her. Seems like a nice guy."

"Really? She's with a nice guy?"

"I know—amazing."

"Where's he going to find her? Trekking in Nepal, at an ashram in India, a cave in Tibet?"

"A hundred bucks on the cave in Tibet. He lives in Lhasa."

"She'll come back sooner or later."

"That's right—sooner or later."

Soapsuds, clink of dishes. The hot water is slow to come.

"Carol, do you remember the day your father decided to buy a hot-air balloon?"

"Poor Papa," Caroline smiles.

"Bertrand is a little like him, I find."

"A kook?"

"No, an optimist. You really should sit down."

Caroline goes to sit, but the telephone rings and she leaps up as if she's been bitten. The hospital? No. The display shows Adèle and Simone's number. They call every night, with no end of advice. She sits down again.

"You know what, Sandra?" she says after a while. "Today, for the first time, I didn't go to the hospital."

"You're feeling guilty, I bet."

"No kidding. Then again, it's always the same thing. He lies in his bed sprouting tubes everywhere and lets out a groan from time to time. When he stirs, you get the feeling he's going to wake up. Bertrand always asks the same questions and my answers are always the same and we took the bus and Metro every day last week to go make sure he was breathing, hoping his doctor would tell us there've been changes, hoping his doctor would just talk to us. We eat supper late every night, frozen food thawed at the last minute, and Bertrand's homework only got half-done. The accident was so stupid."

"Accidents are always stupid."

"Is he going to wake up, Sandra? He's the sort of guy who wakes up, right?"

"Yes."

They each quietly mull over David's sort of guy, but Caroline, feeling overwhelmed, dwells on the mental image of the fall—and all the ways it could have been avoided. She tries to concentrate on Sandra, her mop of red hair, her down-to-earth common sense, her slightly watery lasagna, her poorly rinsed dishes. Anxiety stops her from concentrating for any length of time; her mind behaves like an occupied territory.

Her private Poland. Her little world war.

Second Week

Monday.

Bertrand won't tie his shoelaces. He demands to have his apple sliced into quarters. For the fourth day in a row he wears the Italian soccer club sweater that David gave him for Christmas. He sucks his thumbs while waiting to cross the street. At school, he latches on to his mother so tightly that Mrs Monet has to step in.

Caroline goes back home but is repulsed by the too-familiar familiarity of the house. Was she right to take a leave of absence? She wanders from room to room wondering how to use her time wisely, where to go exactly, how to avoid David's things, and then she stumbles upon the book he left lying around in the living room. Nicolas Bouvier, *The Way of the World*, a travel story. She opens it at the bookmark, an old hockey ticket. It's a fine book, a very fine book, well chosen. An excellent, meaningful title. She mechanically checks the library's return date and decides, absurdly, that this is when the coma will end. Just three more days, then.

She snaps the book shut. There's only one thing that would do her good now: to go swimming. To swim until her shoulders and thighs ache, until her goggles have etched circles around her eyes. The pool is in the same community centre as the library. Once there, it takes her scarcely two lengths to decide to go meet her supervisor. Straightaway, Mrs Blouin, a smile stretched between her Day-Glo earrings, intuitively suggests that she come back to work.

Caroline then makes her way to the intensive-care unit, where Sue triumphantly announces that the brain edema has been completely resorbed and the doctor is considering— very cautiously, as with any chest injury—removing the respirator. She looks at Sue, then at David, hugging her swimming gear bag.

> My back was twisted when the level fell.
> I watched it drop.
> It broke, the fluid spilled out.
> No fluid, no bubble,
> no bubble, no level.
> It made me feel somehow dizzy, I lost my balance.
> What a fool I was, I could kick myself.

That night, after brushing her teeth with David's toothbrush and slipping into the last shirt that still smells of him, Caroline goes to bed late. She falls asleep utterly exhausted.

Loud knocking at the door. An infernal racket. She runs downstairs wondering why she went to bed wearing a ski suit. Outside, the snow is piling up by the minute. Through the door's frosted pane she sees snowflakes furiously swirling around a woollen pompom. It's David, pounding away like a madman. "Open up!" he screams, "Caroline, open up!" His voice is muffled by the steel and polyurethane door he chose himself after searching the web for countless hours. She grabs the doorknob and twists it, to no avail. She looks for the key, which is hung on a hook. The adjacent wall is covered with bunches of keys. Her fingernails sink into a swarming mass of cold metal, while David continues to rap on the windowpane. She eventually finds a key that looks like the right one, but the lock eludes her. He shouts. She hammers on the door. The doorknob breaks and falls to the floor. The key suddenly weighs a ton. In fact, it has turned into a toaster. David stops shouting. He presses his reddened hand against the window, his strong, stout fingers spread apart. She in turn places her hand on the pane. Triple glazing. The benefits of perfect insulation, in good weather or bad. "Open up, Caroline, please." The voice grows weaker. She strokes the hand through the glass, then starts banging her head against it, hard, too hard.

She wakes with a start. Real life, a real headache, her nightshirt dripping wet. A sweltering night in June.

Wednesday afternoon, Caroline waits in a corner behind the schoolyard fence where she can avoid chitchatting with other parents, who don't know "what to say under the circumstances."

Among the stream of children, she spots Bertrand as he comes down the stairway looking for her. Just ten days ago he was horsing around with his friends, checking the sky on the chance of seeing an airplane's vapour trail, or picking up the pencil case that was forever slipping out of his half-open schoolbag. Now, he carefully zips up his bag, shows no interest in airplane trails, and doesn't talk much to his friends; after school, his priority is locating his mother. Two little mice in the storm, each constantly making sure the other is okay, still standing, still speaking, walking, breathing.

"I've got a surprise for you," she announces when he joins her under the willow, where she is almost entirely curtained-off.

"Something to eat?"

"No."

"Ah."

"We're going to meet Martin Bilodeau, the boy who saved Dad's life."

"Really?"

The bus takes them along the endless Boulevard Pie-IX until they reach a low-income neighbourhood where the apartment buildings hugging the sidewalk try to outdo each other in shabbiness. Caroline rings the doorbell at the address Roger Pitt provided.

"Who is it?" a smoker's voice asks on the intercom.

"Caroline and Bertrand Novak. We're here to see Martin."

Every landing in the stairway has a different smell: curry, bleach, fried food, raspberry shower gel, overripe trashcans. They stop at pork sausages and cigarette butts.

A man opens the door, potbellied, bare-chested, beer in hand. He looks Caroline up and down appreciatively then turns his head and shouts Martin's name as if he were calling a high-spirited stallion. After a slight hesitation, he stands aside to let them in, apparently wanting to offer them something but not quite sure what. He switches off the TV and points to the plaid sofa.

Before they can sit down, Martin comes into the room. A tousled scallion of a boy, the nondescript features of a teen-ager on his way to a predictable life, levelled down just like his elementary school classes were. He doesn't know where to put his hands. After wiping them on his jeans he hooks his thumbs into his pockets.

"Mrs Novak, I, um, I'm sorry about your husband."

He leans toward Bertrand and specifies: "Yeah—about your father, that is."

"Hi Martin," Bertrand answers in awe, certain he's dealing with a super-hero. "My mother says you saved his life!"

Martin blushes and gives a limp shrug.

"I'd just taken the St. John Ambulance course at my high school."

"When you were still going to school," his father mutters from the far corner.

Martin cuts him a look of both fear and contempt. A heavy silence descends on the room, during which Mr Bilodeau takes a gulp of beer, Martin inspects his sneakers, and Caroline tucks in the label of her son's T-shirt. It's Bertrand who finally dispels the awkwardness.

"How did you do it?"

"I just did. I can't explain it. He wasn't breathing. I gave him first aid."

"Mouth-to-mouth and cardiac massage, combined," Caroline points out, directing this information mainly at Mr Bilodeau. "He made Dad breathe and massaged his heart."

"Why?"

"Because after four or five minutes without oxygen, your brain turns all mushy," Martin answers. "It takes the heart to pump blood and it takes blood to carry oxygen to the brain."

"The heart's a pump?"

"Actually, it's like an electric engine. There's a spark that starts it up, and without a spark it stops."

"How come Dad ran out of sparks?"

Certain that no worker on the construction site could answer this question, Caroline jumps in:

"The doctor said that he hurt his spleen when he fell and too much blood spilled out inside his body."

"I noticed a pipe sticking out quite a bit," Martin adds. "I guess that's what he hit."

"You saw my father fall?"

The teenager shakes his head as if to brush away the memory.

"Yeah."

"So what did you do to put the spark back?"

"I didn't put any spark back, I just pressed with my hands, to make as if his heart was working. And then I let the air from my lungs go into his mouth."

"Yuck!"

"Bertrand," Caroline interrupts.

"But yuck—it was dirty air."

"Well it wasn't new air, that's for sure, still better than nothing, though," Martin says with a laugh.

"So how were you able to do everything at the same time?"

"You're a curious one, eh? I did one thing at a time. You breathe, your heart beats, your blood circulates—it doesn't all happen at the same time."

"That's what makes it difficult," Caroline cuts in. She knows how much her son likes to get to the bottom of things and can foresee the infinite paths that the conversation can take.

"Wow."

Martin keeps rocking on his heels.

"Roger Pitt tells me you've taken some days off?"

Martin averts his head as if to duck the disapproval so plainly visible on his father's face.

"Well, at first it felt a bit weird."

"What?"

"I don't know. The guys wanted to buy me a beer. 'David owes you one, it's on us,' that sort of stuff."

"Why did you find it weird?"

"That somebody owes me one. It got me thinking."

"What about?"

"In the end I decided to go back to school."

"Excuse me?" his father blurts out, stifling a belch.

"That's right," Martin confirms as he turns toward him. "I realized that I'd learned something useful in school after all."

"About time," his father grumbles

"Which grade will you be in?" Caroline asks, hoping to lighten the atmosphere a little.

"Eleventh grade. But then I'm going to vocational school. Electrician."

"That's good!" his father chimes in. "An electrician in the family! I never thought I'd ..."

He seems to suddenly regret being shirtless. He goes to get another beer and opens the can as he hands it to his son. The foam runs down both their hands.

"We wanted to thank you, Martin," Caroline says. "We wanted to get you a present but didn't know what."

"I don't need a present."

"On David's behalf."

Martin turns so red that his pimples disappear.

"We'd be very pleased to help you become an electrician, if ever ..."

"There's no need. It's because of David that I'm going to be an electrician."

"Okay," Caroline smiles. "All I can say is thanks again."

She slings her bag over her shoulder, takes Bertrand by the hand, and steps toward the door.

"Wait," Martin stops them as he fishes in his pocket.

He pulls out a Swiss army knife. Caroline recognizes it instantly: it's the Victorinox multi-blade she gave David, her very first lover's gift, chosen with much care and wavering.

"I borrowed it the day that ..."

"Keep it."

"But this is a really good knife, it's expensive ..."

"Keep it."

Martin turns the implement over in his hand as though seeing it for the first time.

"Okay. Thank you very much."

Caroline and Bertrand negotiate the landings in reverse order—garbage, shower gel, fried food, bleach, curry—and come out again in the unwholesome air of Boulevard Pie-IX, filling their lungs with it. Bertrand thinks about the spark that makes his heart beat. Caroline thinks about how, if he'd been born in a different neighbourhood, Martin Bilodeau might have become a first-rate surgeon.

Mouth empty.
Mouth empty but not hungry.
They feed me, I hate them.
I depend on them like a baby.
I hate them because without them I would die.
They play God with my body.
I hate them because I can't move or feed myself. I hate them
because they do move and
while we're at it
I hate God because he doesn't exist.

On Thursday, Caroline is surprised to find David disconnected from the respirator and still alive. The doctor on duty, a woman with very dark rings under her eyes, repeats three times that this is excellent. She also stresses that David has avoided aspiration pneumonia, "so common among intubated patients." Another twenty-four hours and, if everything goes well, she'll authorize transferring him to intermediate care. He's made "remarkable" progress during his eleven days in intensive care. She shakes Caroline's hand as if to personally congratulate her for her husband's endurance. She doesn't linger; there was a massive pile-up this morning, and she knows that, among the injured sent to hospitals throughout the city, many are on their way to her unit.

The secretary accompanying Caroline to the door informs her in a low voice that, given "the dramatic shortage of staff," intermediate care will probably be just a quick transitional stage, the idea being to ensure David continues to breathe on his own.

"And after that?" Caroline asks.

The secretary doesn't answer. She gently touches Caroline's shoulder and then leaves her on the other side of the airtight doors, where five new families have just begun the long ordeal of waiting.

Lost.
Lost. Furious.
Something says:
It's only an experience.
An experience? My ass.

The next evening Caroline visits the intermediate-care unit with Bertrand, even though visiting hours coincide with his bedtime. Now that David has been assigned a room, he's sure to have a nightstand too, and they plan to use it to brighten up the faceless decor. She brings a carefully chosen bouquet of flowers, which cost a fortune at the florist near the main entrance; even a single faded petal would be an unbearable metaphor to her. Bertrand carries the vase, handling it as if it were a Ming dynasty treasure.

The room is full. Four beds, four pairs of feet pointing toward the ceiling.

"Mom, will Dad be coming to our year-end show?" Bertrand whispers while fidgeting with the vase.

"That's not very likely, Bertrand. Actually, no, he won't."

"But maybe he'll wake up in time? Just in time?"

"Even if he wakes up in time, he'll be a little tired and he'll want to get some rest."

"What? More rest? No, no, Mom, he's always wide awake when he gets up. You know, in the morning he jumps down the stairs saying shit, shit, shit, I'm late ..."

"Bertrand, watch your language."

"Well, that's what he says, shit, then he puts on his T-shirt with a slice of toast between his teeth. You know, it doesn't bother me if he comes to the show with his piece of toast."

"I promise to be there, at the show. I'll sit up front, in the first row."

"That's not as special—you always come."

From a corner of the room, where someone is constantly groaning, a nurse tells them: "Flowers aren't a good idea, ma'am."

"Why?"

"Hygiene. Speaking of which …"

She gives Bertrand a once-over.

"How old are you?"

"Six and three-quarters."

"They let you in at the reception desk?"

"Uhm, yes," Bertrand stammers, though there was no one at the desk and he went by unnoticed.

"He's a little young. Have him wash his hands whenever he enters or leaves the room. And get him to wear a mask, as prevention."

"Prevention of what?"

The nurse doesn't answer; she slips on a pair of surgical gloves, rips open a syringe envelope, and grasps a vial. She has no time to spell out what should be obvious. Hospitals are forever battling potentially germ-infected organic matter: saliva, breath, mucous, skin, clothes, kisses. Besides, flowers are a drain on oxygen. And who's going to tend to them when they start wilting? Who's going to change the water? Certainly not the patient. All this goes without saying.

Caroline collects the flowers; Bertrand retrieves the vase. They go out, leaving a trail of water drops behind them.

It says: accept

Accept? How? In what sense? Vegetate at home? Six feet underground?

Who's talking, anyway?

Who?
Am I crazy?

As a rule, Dr Sollers schedules his round of visits for a weekday. Yesterday, however, he attended a conference at the Convention Centre, another opportunity to raise his international profile. He's applied for a prestigious research grant and is doing the back-room work needed to secure it. Consequently, he bumps into Karine and Caroline on Saturday, both looking rather drawn, which is typical of the post-adrenaline phase.

"Ladies. Good to see you," he says in greeting, although he senses the start of an impromptu consultation, whereas he much prefers to have them by appointment. He's aware that what families want is a bridge to their loved ones and that they believe the doctor embodies that bridge. He has learned to respect the expectation but knows he can never fulfill it. He ushers the visitors into the corridor and cleverly anticipates their first question.

"I don't really have any news for you. We have just re-evaluated him. He is still not presenting signs of consciousness. He is not reacting very much to stimuli."

"What sort of stimuli?"

"Visual, tactile, auditive, olfactive ..."

"Your tests are based on his ability to react?!" Caroline protests.

"What else do we have, Mrs Novak? Do you have any suggestions?"

"I'd just like to know what's going on inside his head."

"Ah, that is something everyone would like to know, but it is not easy," Sollers says soothingly as he leans on a cart that starts to roll away.

"It seems to me, Doctor, that you're dwelling on the envelope without bothering to read the letter."

Caroline is the first to have doubts about David's mental activity and is utterly beside herself on hearing those doubts echoed in the doctor's assessment. What's more, she's confronted with a remorseless line of reasoning: if David is conscious, he's probably in agony; if not, she must accept that he's gone. In either case, there's no way out. She prefers to stay at the crossroads.

As for the doctor, he is a man of certainties and he avoids grey areas. The real limitations of science don't fit easily into his career plan, and encounters like this always leave him feeling slightly torn.

"Mrs Novak," he answers calmly, "my work consists in dealing with biochemical processes and treating pathologies. I attend to his brain, his glands, his nervous system. Not his spirit, a notion I actually find quite dubious. But if you would like to speak to a priest I can arrange it."

At the word "priest," Karine shakes off her lethargy.

"Can his condition improve, Doctor?"

Sollers smoothes out the lapels of his smock. David displays all the signs of a patient who is foundering.

"Yes," he replies nevertheless. "But beyond four weeks we enter a zone that must be described as a persistent vegetative state."

Caroline feels her irritation gaining the upper hand. She spent her sleepless nights reading up on the vegetative state, but to her it's still a hazy, elusive thing.

"And what exactly is a vegetative state, Doctor?"

"A vegetative state," Soller begins, fully aware that the phenomenon is far more complex than what the Wikipedia entry suggests, "can be defined, shall we say, in opposition to other states. The normal state, first of all, as well as the other comatose states. The worst-case scenario is brain death, but we are not there yet."

He pauses to clear his throat. In a flash, Caroline pictures his luxurious condo with a view of the river, a sprinkling of crystal-ware display cases, and an array of halogen lamps, some fitted with magic eyes so they turn on automatically when he goes by.

"In the vegetative state," the doctor continues, "the brain-stem processes vital functions such as breathing, digestion, and sleep cycles. The individual can even open his eyes. In addition, he may possibly receive information via the five senses. But all the information is collected by the cortex. This is where the individual's identity lies, where he recognizes his environment, controls his movements. Mr Novak's cortex is working at half capacity."

"So no consciousness," Caroline says ironically.

"No. No self-consciousness, no awareness of his surround-ings. In a less profound coma such as the state of minimal consciousness, the individual can follow an object with his eyes or recognize himself in a mirror. There may be moments of communication. That is not the case for your husband, Mrs Novak. When he opens his eyes, if we show him, say, a pencil, he does not see it. He presents no signs of communication or comprehension, he does not respond to instructions. He has reflexes, nothing more."

"In short, Doctor, if someone doesn't follow your pencil with his eyes he has zero consciousness. Correct?"

"Consciousness is produced by chemical processes. It depends on special conditions that are presently absent."

Sollers's patience also depends on special conditions. He steals a glance at his watch.

"A vegetative state—how long can it last?" Karine inquires. For her the debate is not about consciousness; it is about hope.

"The world record is thirty-seven years. But after twelve months it is considered permanent."

Karine puts her long hand over her mouth.

"So to speak," Sollers adds in an attempt to reassure her. "There are cases of awakening even after several years. Rare but not unheard of."

"And what's the explanation?" Caroline asks.

"There is no explanation. It is a phenomenon that happens. Cellular and molecular mechanisms begin to function again in the associative cortex. We do not know why. We only know that the brain is always active and creates new connections and occasionally repairs some of the damage. One thing is certain: the longer the coma persists, the more severe the after-effects."

The doctor would like to stop here, but he can plainly see that Caroline expects him to elaborate on the subject of after-effects. She absolutely wants to take advantage of their chance meeting.

"Motor problems, behavioural problems, cognitive problems," he resumes while openly checking his watch. "Anxiety, speech difficulties. It is very hard to predict. We are doing everything possible to maintain Mr Novak's good health, to help him come back. His fractures have healed well. His immune system is robust, even without the spleen. He has physical therapy each day to keep his muscles supple. We are doing everything we can."

"But?"

"Excuse me?"

"There's a 'but' in what you just said."

"He is brain damaged, Mrs Novak."

He opens his arms in a gesture of powerlessness and closes them amid a whiff of musk.

"If it is any comfort to you, we are not yet talking about a vegetative state."

Then he moves off. He was planning to carry out his own assessment of the patient, which he could then compare with the nursing staff's, but the tests involve painful stimuli. Spraying ice water into the ear canal, for example. Pressing a finger against the cornea, thrusting a finger down the throat, etc. The timing couldn't be worse. Mrs Novak would accuse him of wanting to rip open the envelope.

It would be easy to accept if there was a good reason, just one, to stay in limbo.
I fell. It was stupid. End of story.
And now? I want to move, I itch. There's nothing I can do.
Nothing I can do except listen to advice from beyond the grave.
Accept what, exactly? And why?

Today Mrs Monette informed Caroline that the botched homework and inattentiveness in class would not be tolerated for very long. How long? She didn't specify. In the evening, they take the bus and the Metro, cross the parking lot, and make their way toward the intermediate-care unit, all without much enthusiasm. In the room, family members are visiting two of the patients. A nurse has been buttonholed into a long, hushed conversation. But no one has come to visit David's immediate neighbour, a moaning shape with a surprising odour: a body in decline, with its fetid folds. A cold meal sits under a beige plastic dome.

"Like in a hotel," Bertrand thinks as he steps hypnotically toward the tray. His mother calls him back, but the temptation is too strong; he absolutely has to know what's on the menu. When he leans over the plate, the patient extends an arm so wrinkled that he scampers away.

"So? Today's special?"

Bertrand makes a face.

"It's the same colour as the cover."

"Okay, come see Dad instead."

Caroline leans toward David's ear. She'd like to stroke his hair, but the bandage is in the way. She'd like to put her hand on his shoulder, but the splint stops her. She recalls Dr Sollers's advice: "Speak to him."

That is incredibly hard in face of this incarnation of absence, a contradiction in terms and in fact. Speak to him—yeah, right.

"David," she begins in a declamatory tone of voice, "it's us. Caroline. Bertrand."

"Hi, Dad!"

Bertrand's attitude is so natural compared to hers that Caroline spontaneously lets him take over.

"Look, Dad, the receptionist gave me a sticker and I stuck it on my sweater. Did you know that school ends next week and after that comes summer vacation? We're putting on a neat end-of-year show—really, really neat. I'm going to be dressed up as King Arthur."

He strokes David's hand gently, affectionately.

"Are you going to wake up in time to come see me with my crown on? I made it myself with real aluminum foil ..."

"Bertrand," Caroline chides him softly.

"Anyway, Dad, next year I'll be in second grade and we're going to be working with numbers in the hundreds and Jerome's going to the Magdalen Islands for his vacations, he says he'll be swimming in the ocean all summer, he calls it the ocean and I asked him if that's like the sea and he said bigger, but what do you think, is there anything really bigger than the sea? And maybe when you wake up, we'll go on vacation us too, because I like to swim and it's been a long time since we tried our snorkels ..."

Caroline envies his innocence, and thinks that soon she'll have to tell him that they'll be spending their summer vacations in the city if David doesn't wake up, and spending them in the city if he does wake up. In spite of herself, she pictures the day when she may have to explain to him why Dad doesn't play hockey anymore, why he needs to be spoon-fed. Why he's forgotten his son's name.

An orderly enters the room and walks straight toward the rancid shape. She talks to him as if to a preschooler.

"You're not hungry, Mr Girouard? Would you like me to help you eat, Mr Girouard? Mr Girouard?"

By way of an answer, Mr Girouard groans.

"Do, you, want, to, eat? Yum, yum? Well, in that case I'm taking your tray back to the kitchen. But the cook's going to be disappointed, Mr Girouard. All those nice mashed potatoes."

She disappears with the daily special.

Bertrand has kept on eagerly chattering away the whole time. Caroline, meanwhile, has just noticed little creases forming at the corners of David's mouth, at the point where his cheeks sag. Unbearable creases. The bruises are fading but his immobility will continue to disfigure him. She steps away from the bed and goes to stand by the window, which she tries to open for a good breath of air. The window is sealed.

Outside it's raining and the drops are being driven almost horizontal by the wind. Car doors slam shut. Headlights turn on and off. Visitors come and go with reasons to hope or give up. Workers go back home, exhausted. Most are alone. Of all the imaginable landscapes, a hospital parking lot must surely rank among the dreariest, but no matter. It's a landscape. It's outside.

Accept accept accept
Fuck. Fuck. Fuck.

Caroline renewed her loan of *The Way of the World*. The entry of a new due date, as uncertain as the first one, brings her a measure of relief. A childish superstition, clearly. Instinctively sowing signs in an insane world—for the comforting illusion that among all these identical days some will do her the favour of standing out. "It's a symptom," her psychotherapist friend Simone would conclude.

Of course, David's ability to breathe unaided does give cause for cheer. But the truth is, his stable condition, by virtue of its stability, makes the hours dissolve into each other without going by any faster. Actually, they don't go by at all; the weekend arrives and not once has Caroline had the impression that the week has even begun.

When Bertrand goes to his grandparents' house on Sunday, Caroline chooses the grocery store over the hospital. Canned corn, cream cheese, chips, ketchup, Oreos—they all drop into her cart, though she has no recollection of having touched anything. She stays wholly indifferent to the fact that none of these products meet the health, freshness, and organic standards that she held up like a banner less than a month ago. At the bread counter she crashes headlong into another customer, whom she didn't see, and gets bawled out for having left her cart crosswise in the middle of the aisle.

It says:
Give up.
Give what up?
The lost world.
Why?
It keeps you from seeing what remains.
Remains? What remains?
All that remains.
Everything to be found in the void.

Karine, who wouldn't miss Sunday Mass for the world, drags Janek and Bertrand to the church on Rue Gascon. After the service, she takes the time to genuflect in her favourite chapel. A reproduction of the icon of Częstochowa had once hung there, but someone stole it. Karine often wonders how a Pole could have dared. It had to be a Pole.

She derives a good deal of inner peace from her natural piety. She addresses the Virgin Mary with formal deference, but is on familiar terms with God. She speaks to him uninhibitedly, and her words take in everyone around her. She prays for the thief, among others.

Janek patiently waits for her in a pew. He has always found churches too cavernous and sermons just deadly. Even during the pilgrimage to the hallowed site he was unaffected by the sacred image, whereas the other pilgrims, even the most skeptical, felt shivers up and down their spines. Lech Walesa himself wears a badge of the Black Madonna at all times. Does Janek suffer from a sort of faith disability? Well, he could certainly use some now. Work? He's able to work. Fitting pipes, repairing valves, purging drains—he's always dealt with any situation like a skilled, a very skilled, manual worker. But in the face of a coma, he doesn't know what to do with his hands or where to turn his eyes.

Karine finally crosses herself. Janek collects his cap and smoothes his moustache, which the last thirteen days have turned permanently white. Bertrand stays rooted before the altar, wracking his brain trying to understand how angels fly. He has a feeling Caroline will be waiting for him at home this afternoon in a sweatsuit, her hair tied up in a loose ponytail, a book turned upside down in front of her. He even saw her avoid putting the milk carton in the recycling bin so she wouldn't have to rinse it out.

It's no fun eating sandwiches for dinner. He'd like to have the courage to say: "*I'm* here, Mom." If *he* were an angel, he'd go for a spin up in heaven, just to take a break.

In the void
without legs or arms or anything—what remains?

81

It's not answering. It's turning its back on me. It's leaving. I wonder if it even came.

If it did come, what is it?

The cheese sandwiches are already on the table. Bertrand throws his bag down on the floor and runs to shut himself in his room.

"Hey, what's going on?"

"You never cook anymore!"

"It's true that ever since Dad's . . ."

"But *I'm* here, Mom!"

The remark comes down like a whip. Caroline tightens her ponytail and hikes up her sweatpants. There's no question— she has to pull herself together. For Bertrand. She must learn to live with uncertainty, to value the small things, which are just as genuine as the big ones. She has to get back the joy of tickling him, of chasing him through the bushes in the park, of hearing him work out new words. But everything tastes like dust, everything sounds flat. Even Mrs Blouin's Day-Glo handbag looks drab.

What do you call it, when everything crumbles, when everything you touch dissolves? Is there a word hollow enough to say "nothing"?

Sure, the wakeful nights, the cold bed, Caroline owns them—they come with the territory. They're clichés. But the dirty dishes, the rings in the bathtub, the loads of laundry, the overgrown lawn, the paint flaking off on the porch, the daily grind to cope with, from start to finish—isn't that what loneliness is all about?

In other words, it's mundane. Caving in would be stupid, and there's nothing heroic about surviving.

Third Week

Caroline and David met in a crematorium. She harks back to it often, maybe too often. She's afraid the story will end abruptly where it began.

David was there to repair a leaky roof. Caroline, meanwhile, was attending the funeral service for her father, who had fallen asleep at the wheel of his car. She adored her father—adored him. She just as fiercely despised her mother's high-heeled shoes, which sank into the grounds of the funeral complex. Her sister Marie wore several layers of loose-fitting clothes, and Caroline, a red dress with a thread hanging down from the hem. The thread brushed against her calf and she kept slipping her other foot out of her sandal to scratch with her toe. Why these details? She stored all these details but never even noticed David.

He, however, remembers her very well. He would always emphasize that moment, especially the red dress, but also the golden highlights in her auburn hair, her freckles, her square shoulders, her slender nose. He even went so far as to think "just my type of girl" and to deem Jean-Claude, her boyfriend back then, "inadequate, aloof, unsupportive."

As she was climbing into the limousine, she glimpsed a yellow flash in the side mirror. Was it David putting his helmet back on? Maybe. Maybe not. A non-event, in sum. An aborted beginning. Not much recyclable material, memory-wise.

Fortunately, libraries are home to self-educated people like David and librarians like Caroline, and they saw each other again at the loans desk. David recognized her immediately and said a friendly hello. She squinted, searching her memory, and, certain she didn't know him, smiled at him mockingly. He just about bolted with his books.

After that, though, he got into the habit of visiting the library every Saturday morning. They chatted for five, ten minutes, depending on the queues. She wasn't fooled. Whenever there was a long lineup she could see him waiting on the sly for a quiet moment. In the meantime, she'd taken the trouble to consult the list of books he'd borrowed so she could smooth the path of the conversation.

For months they confined themselves to these brief exchanges, with a big counter sitting between them. Even though David was an old hand at turning on the charm, he was inhibited by the memory of the inadequate boyfriend, while Caroline, despite having dumped Jean-Claude, felt stymied by her powerful attraction to David. She had never met a man like him. Not one who carried his body like the lightest piece of clothing, like something self-evident, nor one with such an engaging smile. He was comfortable in the material world, happy to take part in the game of life, and she didn't feel cut out for such a natural happiness.

One April morning, in a stroke of genius, she added a slim, brand-new volume just acquired by the library to the pile of books he was borrowing. She had already checked it out under his name and entered the return date. The book was

Première Heure, the story of an Italian mason who wakes up at first light—hence the title— to write and study before starting his day on a construction site. David found this inspiring, and began to do the same. He said that spending the early morning this way brought him closer to his truth.

Poor David. No work now, no day. Condemned to an endless dawn. What about his truth?

Velvet. Threadbare velvet. Rain showers, dust. The scent of ink, of new, bleached paper.
The binding cracks, and the floor
skin, skin, skin.
Skin like marble, like the desert.

"Will he recognize us?"

Caroline puts the question to Sandra over the phone, very early in the morning, before she heads out to water the medicinal herbs at the Botanical Gardens. Sandra leaves the question hanging.

"And us? Will we recognize him?" Caroline goes on. "I find it so hard to understand what I'm hoping for. Last week all I could think about was his survival, but now, I'm thinking, if he ever wakes up … I'm afraid to …"

"You're wondering what your life would be like with an invalid," Sandra says, filling in the blank. She prefers not to beat around the bush.

"I'm ashamed."

"Why?"

"It's terrible, isn't it?"

"No, it's not."

"Selfish, at least."

"No."

"Normal?"

"Caroline, what does normal mean? It's a wash cycle."

"So, natural. You think it's natural?"

"I think it's futile to indulge in scenarios. The past is already far behind. The future will arrive in due course. Your only option is the present."

The little bells chime one-two-three-four.
They go away, return.
Rain against the window. Laughter through the plywood.
Wet books, wet lips, skin.
Skin.

The stay in intermediate care was brief; given that David is breathing very well on his own, he's been transferred to the neurological-care unit. Caroline dives back into the maze but manages to find the third floor of the B Wing, where she's greeted by Lily, the receptionist, who sports a smiley button on her uniform and candy-pink hair that contrasts with the pale-green walls.

The semi-private room, in which the other bed is unoccupied, has tall windows that again look out on the parking lot. Car roofs gleam in the setting sun. Steam rises from the soft, shimmering asphalt. David has just arrived, along with all his attachments: bed, chart, serum, coma.

Caroline barely has the time to look around when three knocks on the door signal the entrance of a tall male nurse with straggling locks of hair and comforting shoulders, his sky-blue uniform a touch too short. Aware of how important the first contact with family is, and that Mr Novak's stay could be a long one, he takes the trouble of introducing himself:

"Steve, nursing assistant."

"I can read," Caroline shoots back, pointing to his badge.

"I figured as much," he replies without missing a beat.

He busies himself a little in the room, pretending not to be there. Based on his long experience, he believes that a discreet presence is better than a hasty departure. Caroline would rather he go away. She folds her arms, hiding her gnawed fingernails in her closed fists. The hospital atmosphere throws her off balance—its incomprehensible blend of cordiality and coldness, humanity and protocol. In addition, she finds it annoying that the nurse's name is Steve. Just as it was annoying that Sue's name is Sue. Not to mention "no-cell-phones-on-the-premises." What's even worse is his pretending not to be there. How can you not feel that you're being observed? She's about to touch her half-dead husband once again. To once again listen to his heart beating, the same heart that was there on their hikes in the Montérégie, their Sundays in bed. What an idiot this Steve is to think he can go unnoticed.

However idiotic he may be, Steve heads toward the door on his own initiative. Alone now with David, Caroline feels even more awkward. Without Bertrand's liveliness, what can she say to David? The nurse should have stayed after all; he provided her with an excuse and shouldered all the blame.

Barefoot.
One
two
three
four steps.
As beautiful as a marble object, perfect,
perfectly polished
and pale
touch me Caroline, please.
Touch me.
Give me a shape with your hands.

Caroline has managed to get the head nurse in neurology to agree to more flexible visiting hours for Bertrand. So long as they stay no more than half an hour each time, they are free to come at any time in the afternoon. School vacations have just begun, and as of the first Tuesday they show up at three o'clock sharp, on the heels of the new occupant of the adjacent bed.

Laura, a blonde, energetic, short-legged nurse on the day shift, has just informed them that David has contracted a urinary-tract infection, which the antibiotics will completely take care of, and that, "on the plus side," the neck brace will soon be gone. When she tells them there's a support group for loved ones, she hits a wall of indifference. So, alternatively, she offers to introduce them to oral hygiene techniques.

Bertrand appears delighted, although he has questions about the meaning of "hygiene" and "oral." Caroline, however, stays aloof; she's busy imagining Laura in a duplex with wall-to-wall broadloom and white plywood furniture.

"Comas are mysterious," the nurse remarks.

"It certainly looks that way," Caroline replies with a note of cynicism in her voice.

"Let me tell you what we know about the subject, Mrs Novak. 'Coma' from the Greek *kōma*, k-long o-m-a, deep sleep."

The Greeks, Caroline thinks, them again. If they hadn't created all those etymological roots, would we still get the illnesses they refer to?

"With your long years of experience, Laura, the best you can do is spell out a Greek root?"

"It's one of the great mysteries of science, Mrs Novak."

"So science admits there are mysteries?"

"At its best, yes. Does that surprise you?"

"I find it reassuring."

"Well, that's good."

"And disheartening at the same time."

"I'm sorry. Then what about massaging the pressure points—would that interest you? We do it every two hours, so if you'd like to take a turn ..."

Just then, Dr Sollers marches in accompanied by Hattie, Laura's teammate, a size-zero perched on stilts, with her jet-black hair in a bob. He greets them with a nod and comes to an abrupt halt at the foot of the other bed, a position that puts him happily in mind of a ship's helm. He flips through a colossal chart, occasionally glancing at the new patient, rattles off a series of instructions in a jargon beyond the ken of common folk, and goes out, leaving behind his musky aura.

Hattie comes to stand beside Laura. She towers over her colleague. Everyone calls them Laurel and Hardy.

"See that!" she exclaims admiringly. "He's amazing! One of the best minds in the province."

"Who? The new patient?" Caroline asks sarcastically.

"No, no, our very own Dr Sollers. Apparently he's got an IQ of 150."

"Someone should teach him to say hello."

Hattie raises a pointy shoulder.

"It's a matter of style," she laughs, playfully arranging her hair with her fingertips.

Caroline instantly imagines her kitchen with Milanese-design, canary-yellow barstools.

"Anyway," Hattie adds, "you're in good hands. What a lucky break for Mr Novak!"

Realizing her unwitting pun, she blushes to the roots of her bangs.

"Yes, he was really very lucky the ground was there to break his fall," Caroline retorts.

The two nurses beat a somewhat hasty retreat. Bertrand, his head resting on David's pillow, starts to suck his thumb. The person in the next bed sleeps on.

In the sudden calm, perhaps because of it, an especially sweet and painful memory foists itself on Caroline. Of all the precious moments of the past, this would be the one to avoid, to forget.

David had finally invited her to the Cinémathèque québé-coise, the perfect cross between a library and a cinema. He came to pick her up at work, taking advantage of the opportunity to borrow the maximum number of books. His bag was heavy, and he kept shifting it from one shoulder to the other. The street smelled of dust. It was pouring rain. Caroline had brought a badly wrinkled windbreaker, but David had nothing on but his T-shirt, which was already soaked. They ducked into a bus shelter to wait for the shower to taper off.

After two or three flashes of lightning over the Jean-Talon Metro station, Caroline summoned up all her courage. On the pretext of lending him dry clothes and having him taste the ginger tea her friend Élise had brought back from Shanghai, she invited David to her place on Rue de Lanaudière. He had hardly stepped through the door when he peeled off his T-shirt, but he didn't put on the one she held out to him. Instead, he unlaced his sneakers without taking his eyes off her, in case she decided to throw him out. She sensed he was a bit keyed up. She was quite nervous herself.

She slipped out of her sandals and stepped toward him barefoot. Scarcely four, maybe five paces, little bells jingling around her ankle. David leaned over to kiss her, cautious at first, until she clasped the nape of his neck with one hand and pulled his hair with the other, with the clean T-shirt crushed between them.

David lifted her up; she felt light in his arms. He crossed the room, throwing all the cushions down on the floor. Then he kneeled down, let go of her, looked at her for a long time, lying there, her hair spread out. He lay down near her. Already their mouths were different, familiar. The rain pattered on the roof. The neighbours came home with their grocery bags, laughing. The cushions slid. The floor creaked. Outside the rain came down harder.

Caroline would like to drive the memory back to where it came from, a place too far away, too close.

The sound, that sound,
between panic and ecstasy,
halfway between two worlds
undecidable, affecting.
Hunger.
This hunger in my skin
under my fingers.
Caroline stretches, bites me. She comes apart
collects herself
falls asleep in my arms.
Her sleep so beautiful. Her confident, untethered breath.

"Mommy, he's smiling."

"Oh?"

"Look."

A corner of David's lips has curled up a little.

"Hey, you're right. Maybe he's having a nice dream."

Bertrand strokes his father's hair.

"You're having a nice dream, eh, Dad? Is it about baseball or hockey?"

David starts to scratch the sheet.

"Go on dreaming, Dad. Enjoy. Outside it's really not a nice day, so we couldn't even play catch. I wish I was in your dream with you. Would you like that, if I came into your dream? Yes? He's smiling again, Mom. It's awesome."

Bertrand has succumbed to Laura's charm, and now he can't stop talking about oral hygiene. Caroline would have preferred to spread the visits out more and fit in a bit of ordinary life instead of sterilizing the first week of the holidays, dousing it with iodine and cluttering it up with carts. Outside, the sun is shining brightly; inside everything is a faded green. But she follows Bertrand's lead and adopts the pace that suits him best. She recalls how, when he was very small, he specialized in seeking out sharp objects and then touching them with the tip of his finger. Despite her efforts to store them out of his reach, he always managed to track down a new hazard. It was his way of taming risk, just as seeing David again and again, plunging repeatedly into the disturbing atmosphere of the hospital, is probably his way of assimilating the situation. So they are back there again on Wednesday, only to find the curtain drawn around David's bed.

"Can we come in?" Caroline asks.

"Yes, yes."

With Steve's help, a greying nurse is changing the sheets, working briskly and with remarkable efficiency, considering the sleeper's inertia.

"There's been a little accident," the male nurse says by way of apology. "Usually, the sheets are changed in the morning."

"Yeah, the orderlies take care of it ordinarily," the other nurse adds crossly.

Steve motions to her to spare the visitors their infighting. Bertrand lowers his eyes. He finds it humiliating that strangers are meddling with his father's sheets, and even more humiliating that his father is offering no resistance, not to mention the "little accident." The male nurse comes over to him, smelling of detergent. Bertrand takes a step back.

"Did you make that?"

Prominently displayed above the bed is a badly crumpled drawing, which arrived from intermediate care two days late.

"Yes."

"What's your name?"

"Bertrand."

"I'm Steve."

"It says that, right there," Bertrand shoots back, placing his finger on the badge.

Caroline lets out a laugh in spite of herself.

"Wow, unbelievable," Steve says. "Anyway, I like your drawing."

"Did you see what it is?"

"An ambulance running the red lights."

"Yeah. Cool, eh?"

Who? Everything's hazy.
People here.
Real people?
Speak. I want to speak. Impossible. I want to shout. Scream.
Roar. There's a roar rolled up in my throat, a big lump, jammed inside.

"He groaned," Caroline says, surprised.

"Yes," the grey-haired nurse concurs.

"What does it mean?"

"Nothing in particular."

"Can I write my name on his cast?" Bertrand asks.

Getting no response, he steps up to the bed.

"You're groaning, Dad? Why are you groaning?"

The nurse senses a false hope, which she is quick to head off:

"Don't you start getting all sorts of ideas. Comatose patients groan, swallow, sigh, yawn, cough. All it means is they're groaning, swallowing, sighing, yawning, and coughing."

"What's 'comatose'?"

They're here.
I know they're here.
Who, exactly?
I'm here too.

Six feet under my skin.
The nut inside the bark.
The pit in the apple.
Inert, hidden, alive.
I'm here, in the margin
repressed
rebellious
alive.

"We're going to start shaving him soon," Steve announces. "His skin has improved."

"You're going to shave my husband?"

"It's one of the things we do."

The other nurse gestures to her colleague to hurry up.

"It seems to me I should be the one to do it," Caroline insists.

"Another time, maybe?" Steve suggests as he pulls back the curtain. "When his skin's completely healed?"

"He'll wake up before then," Caroline asserts.

"Okay, Steve, we have to get going," the nurse says.

"But what's 'comatose'?" Bertrand repeats.

Seeing the nurse leave without answering, Bertrand sets about contemplating the remote control for the bed. He desperately wants to touch it. The moment his mother decides to ignore the sign forbidding visitors from using the patients's washroom, he gives in to the temptation. The mattress folds upward at knee-level, the upper half rises. This is fun. His father's bum sinks lower and lower, his torso leans forward, the nape of his neck, just released from the brace, bends. Bertrand realizes his blunder and starts frantically pushing all the buttons, just as Caroline reappears.

"Bertrand! What are you doing?"

She grabs the remote away from him.

"Do you ever think first? Oh, crap, how does this thing work? Go get Steve or the other one, you know, the grouch, go get someone, move it!"

When Bertrand comes back, shamefaced, with Steve in tow, Caroline has managed to lower the legs. The nurse resets the mattress, adjusts the pillow, and repositions David's head. She notices that he touches her husband much more confidently than she does. As he puts the remote control back on the side table he calmly asks:

"Did you get the message, Bertrand?"

Bertrand stares at the tips of his feet.

"What do you say?" Caroline asks testily.

"Thank you."

"No, did you hear Steve's question?"

"Yeah, okay, I get it. It's not a toy. Sorry, Dad."

"That's alright. The fact is, there's not a lot to do in a hospital room," Steve acknowledges as he heads toward the door.

Caroline hesitates:

"Steve, could I ask you a question?"

"Yes?"

"I was expecting you to speak English."

"I'm from the North Shore."

"Your name gave me the wrong idea."

"Ah, my name. It's because of the bionic man, Steve Austin, astronaut. My mother thought he was really cute."

"Steve Austin, astronaut," Caroline echoes in astonishment.

"Cool," Bertrand says approvingly, his cheek pressed against David's hand.

A shock. A tiny little shock.
An electric current.
Electric, but human.
Human.

Someone is touching me.
Who?
Human.

The next day, at the same time, they find themselves stand-ing once again in front of the big cement block of the hospital. Bertrand is still wearing the Italian soccer team T-shirt that Caroline barely managed to wash. In the parking lot, his ball gets away from him for the third time, and he chases after it to a gutter grate.

"To think we lugged your ball around all afternoon just so you could have it here!" Caroline says irritably, her patience coming in dribs and drabs today.

"Oh, Mom . . ."

"Why were you so set on bringing it, anyway?"

"I want to show it to Dad."

"But Bertrand . . ."

"What?"

"Nothing."

Caroline picks up the ball and wedges it under her arm.

"It needs to be inflated a little, doesn't it?" she offers by way of making up.

They arrive at the entrance of the B Wing and mount the stairs. When they arrive in the room, they freeze on the spot. David's eyes are wide open. And they're moving.

"Dad!" Bertrand exclaims.

It's in the bag, he believes. Things will be back to normal, same as before, intact. He was right to bring his new ball. David has opened his eyes especially to see it. Yet Caroline has to admit that Dr Sollers was right. David's blue eyes are as expressive as a carp's. His eyelids are heavy and about to shut. A thread of saliva trickles out between his dry lips. The skin of his cheeks sags slightly near his earlobes. It's David without David.

"Dad?" Bertrand says, full of doubt.

Caroline gently ruffles his hair.

"Sometimes people open their eyes in their sleep, did you know that, Bertrand?"

"No."

He's frustrated. The open eyes make the coma even worse—more like death than sleep.

"Would you like to help me pin the pictures up on the cork board?"

"No."

The head nurse suggested that they post family photos and surround David with familiar objects to help him stay connected to reality, to make it easier for him to resurface and facilitate his rehabilitation when the time comes. She suggested they play his favourite music, but not too loud or too long. As she was choosing the pictures, the music, and the scarf, it seemed to Caroline that the string between the real and the unknown, the past and the present, would be of more use to Bertrand and her than to David. A slender thread, at most—relics.

"So should we put on some music?"

"Will he hear it, Mom?"

"He's more likely to hear it if we put it on, right?"

"Uh-huh."

With a look of resignation, Bertrand pulls the CD out of its sleeve and inserts it in the player.

"Have you picked a song, buddy? Not 'Big Time,' all right, we're clear about that?"

"No, no. Your song, Mom."

"'Washing of the Water'?"

"Oh, I don't know. Number 15. Anyway, Dad likes all of Peter Gabriel's songs."

"Yes, but while he's resting we're staying away from 'Big Time' and 'Sledgehammer.'"

"'Don't Give Up?'"

"'Don't Give Up' is perfect."

"It'll be a change from Babcia's music. She always puts on Chopin."

"That's because Chopin is Polish."

"She knows him?"

"In a way, yes. Bertrand, do you mind if I go get some thumbtacks at the nursing station? For the pictures. I'll just be a minute."

Halfway there, Caroline is stopped short by a clamour of voices. A woman gasps, a man yells, Lily screams "Poliiiice!," a huge commotion gives way to sudden calm, which is broken by remarks about dysfunctional families and respecting visiting hours.

Bertrand finds his mother's minute rather long and decides to try something different. Following a line of reasoning that in his mind is flawless, he's reached the conclusion that the ball will persuade David to use his eyes correctly. He positions himself in a corner, slowly takes aim, just the way his father showed him, and throws the ball, which then bounces off a bedrail. The metallic clang gives him the shivers, but the considerable rebound lets him catch the ball on the fly. He instantly throws it again. This time the ball hits the motionless joints of David's hand, loses its momentum, and rolls across the floor. As Bertrand bends down to collect it, a surge of rage rushes to his brain. He doesn't even notice that his father's eyes have already closed again. He hurls the ball one last time with all his strength. The projectile just barely misses the feet of the man in the other bed, who, fortunately, appears to be made of cardboard. It strikes the Formica cabinet and ends up wedged between David's shoulder and the pole for his drip-feed. Out of the blue, the cardboard neighbour starts moaning.

"BERTRAND NOVAK!" Caroline yells. "I'm going to confiscate your ball, just you wait!"

She witnessed the last throw through the glass door. Bertrand, hugging the ball against his navel, gives her a defiant look.

"What's going on here?"

They wheel around.

"Well, what on earth is going on?" the greying nurse demands, with fists on hips.

"Nothing out of the ordinary," Caroline is quick to reply.

"In that case, lower your voices."

"Sorry."

"This isn't an amusement park."

"We've noticed," Caroline says sarcastically, sweeping her hand around the strictly functional decor.

"What do you expect?" the nurse says, already on edge in the wake of the dysfunctional family episode. "If you're looking for an HD screen, an ergonomic armchair, Old Masters on the wall, and satin sheets, I know just the place."

"But . . ." Caroline stammers, having had no intention of launching a debate about health care.

"In the States," the nurse goes on, "you'll find everything you want, and then some. The Resurrection, while you're at it! But it'll cost you an arm and a leg, Mrs Novak, your house, your retirement fund, your family jewels."

"Yes, I know, I know," Caroline says, defending herself halfheartedly, while a frightened Bertrand drops the ball and clutches her thigh with both arms.

"People forget how things were before. They take everything for granted. The decor may be bland, but the health care is free. Universal. FREE!"

Visibly relieved by her rant, the nurse adjusts the collar of her blouse. Honestly! She's had her fill of cutbacks and insults. Whether at work or at home, the gratification she gets has never been in line with the effort she puts in.

Despite being traumatized, Caroline chalks up the nurse's outburst to compassion fatigue. Simone, her psychotherapist friend, is forever complaining about this herself. When you're constantly rubbing shoulders with human suffering, you naturally end up wearing yourself down. Better change the subject.

"What's your name?" she inquires, since the woman's ample bust has been left without a badge.

"You can call me Nurse Pronovost."

"*Nurse* Pronovost?"

"You find that old-fashioned? Too bad. It's Nurse Pronovost or Madame Minister."

On that note, Nurse Pronovost attends to the man in the neighbouring bed. Given Bertrand's look of terror, Caroline decides to go home.

Since the beginning of the week, apart from the daily hospital visits, they've seen a children's show at Place des Arts, another at the Grande Bibliothèque, and still another at Complexe Desjardins. They rode along the bicycle path all the way to the Lachine Canal and went swimming three times in the local swimming pool. Not to mention the exhausting day at La Ronde amusement park, including endless waiting in line before every ride and the mandatory break to throw up. Caroline feels she won't be able to keep this up for very long. She's afraid of overdosing. Day camp can't start soon enough.

But Bertrand refuses to spend even a single day without seeing David, and Caroline relents. At least he very clearly voices his needs, she tells herself. And, besides, the visits can't all be as trying as the last one.

She's wrong. The moment they step into the room they're assaulted by a nasty smell, the reek of poorly maintained public washrooms. And this time it's futile to blame the other patient—he's gone. The source of the smell is easily identified:

none other than her child's father. Without saying a word, she takes Bertrand by the hand, hails the first orderly she comes across, and retreats to the lounge to wait until the matter has been dealt with.

Bertrand looks so upset, she allows him a can of Pringles from the vending machine. In the lounge, with his mouth full, he repeats in disbelief: "Diapers, Mom! Dad wears diapers? For real?" His whole conception of the universe has been thrown into doubt. And Caroline's logical, logistical, technical, hygienic arguments don't even begin to reassure him. Meanwhile, Mr Jouvert is wheeled into the lounge. It's time for the TV quiz show that was his favourite before the car accident. At a fever pitch of excitement, he jumps in ahead of the contestants with utterly surreal answers.

Caroline lets a good quarter of an hour elapse before going back to the room, now scented with an artificial fragrance that would be perfect for Bingo Night.

"Hi, Dad. You, er, smell nice. It's me, Bertrand. Can you make a little room for me in your hand? Why's your hand so stiff? Should I maybe bring you a tennis ball, eh? To practise keeping your hand open?"

"Bertrand…"

"Okay, no tennis ball, Dad. Maybe a hockey puck?"

He gives Caroline a pleading look as he pummels the inside of David's rigid fingers with his small fist.

The obstetrician.
Her pink blouse, yellow hair,
white clogs.
The sounds in this room
in the adjacent rooms and the sounds outside,
Caroline's
groans.
The baby's wailing.

The scissors, in my hand. The cord, resistant, tough. Inside it, dark, rich blood.

I cut.

He has a nose like a shirt button.

Puffy eyes, curled lips, wrinkled face, red and purple. He grimaces in slow motion.

I never held anything so fragile or lifted anything so light.

He's here, now, Bertrand,

he's touching me. Where? He's here. Is he speaking, too?

He withdraws his hand and puts it back, struggling. I feel his struggle.

Bertrand gives a sudden, radiant smile.

Intrigued, Caroline asks: "Are you okay?"

"Guess what."

"What?"

"He likes it when we talk to him."

"He likes it?"

"A lot."

"How do you know?"

"He told me so."

"He spoke to you?"

"Well, no, but it's just as if he did. He told me in my head."

"Ah, in your head."

"Or maybe in my heart. In my heart, he even said, 'Thanks for coming to talk to me.' I said, 'You're welcome,' with my mouth."

"Yes, I heard."

His downy skin, his sturdy body, his still-chubby hands.

Sorry, Bertrand.

Caroline clenches her teeth. Now Bertrand is hearing voices in his heart. Hello, Joan of Arc. She is unsure what annoys her most, Bertrand's illusion or her own inability to hope for a presence. She looks at the diver's watch with its two chronometers.

"Time to go."

"Already?"

"Come on."

On the overcrowded bus she nibbles away at her nails. She doesn't want a summer obliterated by that seasonless room, the big sky confined to four pastel walls, the heat magnified by the concrete. Bertrand still wears the halo of his state of grace. He tells himself that of all his activities, those that include David, however nauseating, are still the most wonderful. The others, flooded with sunshine, laughter, and games, are already slipping through the net, and their only purpose is to help pass the time between visits.

"You look angry, Mom."

"Me? Why, no."

"You always look angry these days."

Home, supper, bath. Insomnia.

The end of the rope is getting dangerously close.

July

Day camp has finally started, and Bertrand comes home every afternoon, properly tanned, exhausted, and scraped, with mosquito bites as big as dimes and "lots of stories to tell Dad." Caroline, determined to space out the visits, has him tell the stories to Maxime instead, or even Mrs Levasseur, the neighbour who collects gnomes and whose endless supply of date squares manages to distract Bertrand.

In any case, if Nurse Pronovost is to be believed, there will be time enough for the visits. She says they've begun to implement "long-term strategies," including a tracheotomy. Apparently, swallowing at the right moment is a complex task that requires skills in which David is increasingly lacking. He's in danger of choking on his saliva. Caroline saw the incision in his throat and heard the gurgling of the tube. She puts off confronting Bertrand with this.

"Tomorrow," she nevertheless just promised him, since he was so insistent. Tonight, like every night, he is slow to fall asleep. She lies down beside him. The half-open curtain moves in the warm breeze, muffled sounds rise from the street: cars stopping at the corner and driving off again, people talking on a porch, a dove cooing, a bicycle bell. The air smells of summer, a blend of overheated asphalt, ice cream, green leaves, and chlorine. Bertrand rubs his feet together, Caroline gently strokes his back, slightly lowers the sheet with its rocket motif. She knows his breathing, the way it slips down a notch when he relaxes, and she waits.

No sooner has he started to go limp than the sound of someone hammering on the door makes them both jump. Caroline, half-asleep herself, wonders if this is another nightmare. But the banging resumes.

"I'll be right back."

"I want to come with you."

"No, stay in bed. I'll come right back."

"I want to go down with you."

"No."

"Mom…"

"Okay, but put your slippers on."

At the door, all Caroline can make out is a slice of twilight. But she opens it even so and instantly finds herself imprisoned in familiar arms, redolent of patchouli.

"Aunt Marie!"

Bertrand hops up and down beside them. His crushed slippers drop away.

"And Sandra! Sandra! Sandra!"

Sandra ushers everyone to the living room without loosening the embrace of the two tearful sisters.

"Aunt Marie, did you bring me a present from your trip?"

Marie tears herself away from Caroline and tries to lift up Bertrand.

"Oh my lord, Bertrand, you've grown way too much for me to pick you up! Let's have a look. A giant! What in the world have you been eating? What's the recipe? I brought a present for a little boy, but you're too big now. Too bad, I'll have to give it to the Salvation Army."

"No!" Bertrand implores her.

Marie leans down to whisper a secret that he appears to find completely to his liking.

"Well, I have to get going," Sandra announces.

"Stay a while," Caroline insists.

"No, no, I've done my job. I drove your Marie here from the airport, and now I'm going to bed."

Sandra waves and jumps into her old car through the passenger door.

"Why's she doing that?" Bertrand asks in amazement as he watches her twist and bend her way to the steering wheel.

"The other door is jammed," Marie explains.

Caroline clasps her sister by the shoulders and looks her up and down. Her thick, dark curls, brown eyes speckled with gold nuggets, fair skin, loose clothes. No one else can mix so many prints without looking like a clown.

"How long are you staying for?"

"Carol! I've just arrived, and already you're thinking about when I'm leaving?"

"I missed you."

"Me too."

"We didn't hear much from you, eh?"

"So you're going to start by scolding me?"

"Sorry. I meant to say thank you. Thank you for coming."

Tonight, in the living room, they pick up the thread of their never-ending confidences. Caroline would have a good deal to say about David's situation, the cortex, the neocortex, antibiotics for the urinary-tract infection, but these are things she has already discussed with others. What she saved for Marie was her own emotional situation. But now the time has come, and she falters. She talks about being in a fog, groping, doubting, worrying. She talks about how violent her love for Bertrand can be and the mystery that David has become, with his unfathomable present and uncertain future.

Marie, seated on a cushion in lotus position, twists a lock of her hair around her finger. So many others would just be waiting for the first chance to voice their opinion, but she listens, quite simply; her way of being present has already lifted a huge weight from Caroline's shoulders.

"You've come in the nick of time, Marie."

"That's good, Carol. That's good. What about the in-laws? How are they taking it?"

"They're doing the best they can. Karine is as sweet as ever. She calls me every week offering to help. We had lunch once or twice. Funny, it would never have occurred to us to do lunch, before. Whereas with Janek, things are more difficult. The big freeze."

"I suppose they spend all their time at the hospital?"

"No, it's odd. I think Janek has put a cap on the number of visits. I get the impression it makes him uncomfortable."

"What about Mom? Have you called her? What did she say?"

"She had news of her own."

"Ah?"

"She's taken up mini-putt."

"You don't say."

"Yes."

Marie unties her scarf. A wave of heat washes over her each time the topic of their mother comes up. She changes the subject.

"And your friends? Sandra? Adèle? Simone? Élise?"

"Sandra's the only one who's come to the hospital. She left almost immediately, saying she was sorry. Hospital-phobia."

"At least she made an effort. What about the others?"

"Meh. The occasional phone call. It's as if I'm speaking a foreign language with them. And poorly, to boot."

"Are there support groups at the hospital?"

"Apparently, yes. But, you know, me and groups …"

"I know. What about the library—does it help? Or not?"

"It makes the time go by. They say time heals all wounds."

"So, basically, the help you've had is on the surface."

"It's still help. Nothing to spit at."

"It's not enough."

"At least it keeps me in touch, yes, with the surface. I've been living through everything at such a distance. Remember when we used to make telephones with tin cans and a string?"

"You're in sort of a coma yourself."

The accuracy of Marie's comment leaves Caroline stunned.

She looks at her sister intently. Marie has changed. The assertive features, the calm gestures, the fine lines at the corners of her eyes. An attractive, even magnetic transparency.

"And yet, I'm trying to resurface. I'm trying really hard."

"Why?"

"Well, to be part of real life."

"But who says real life is on the surface? Maybe, while you're struggling to keep afloat, another part of you is trying to reunite with David?"

"… Maybe."

"Do you talk to him?"

Caroline sidesteps the question.

"Bertrand claims David hears him. But the truth is, Marie, behind his face, there's nothing."

"I doubt that. Did you know that some traditions recognize up to twenty different levels of consciousness?"

"Twenty?"

"Some say four, some seven, and for others it's fifty. There are serious grounds for doubting that consciousness even resides in the brain."

"You should talk to Dr Sollers."

"Why?"

"In his view, consciousness is entirely the result of chemical processes."

Marie's disapproving gesture makes her yak-horn bracelets clink together.

"Typical. He trusts what he can measure. And that rules out the invisible."

"Anyway, he's apparently a leading authority and he's of the opinion that David has no awareness of himself or the outside world."

"Maybe of the outside world. But of himself?"

"What do we know, Marie?"

"Nothing, I guess, but we can still broaden our outlook, evolve a little."

Caroline fidgets in her armchair.

"Are you telling me I should take David's accident as an opportunity for personal growth?"

"I hate that expression. You know I'm not a fan of ego-building."

"Well, what then?" Caroline asks testily.

"More like a chance to explore. Ordinary reality has a hidden side, Caroline. Once you've glimpsed it you find it hard to accept the common view of things. Take it as an initiation."

"That's a pretty vague concept. It's condescending and it annoys me. I think I'll go to bed now."

"Caroline . . ."

"I'll get your bed ready, and you can settle in."

Caroline sets about opening the sofa. The springs resist and rasp. She keeps at it.

"Carol. It's okay, I can manage."

"I'll shut the door. That way you won't be disturbed. You can perform all your Buddhist, Hindu, Sufi rituals. Make yourself at home."

From a chest, she produces a pillow and sheets and throws them on the wafer-thin mattress.

"But there's one thing that *is* clear," she adds before leaving the room. "A stick of incense is not going to change my life."

Totally adrift
the wreck unmoored
except maybe
Bertrand.
The others? Where are the others?
Come back, Bertrand
come back, touch me, take me back
please.

Marie is still asleep. Jet lag will likely keep her pinned to her wafer until noon. Not to mention the change in altitude, in every sense of the word. Caroline broods over last night's conversation while tiptoeing around the house. Her head is buzzing. Her sister's passions have always made her mind whirl. Whales in the Saguenay fjord, trekking, dart tournaments, Ozzy Osbourne, bio-dynamic farming, body art, contemporary dance, Sasha. She should have kept her guard up and cut short any turn towards metaphysics. But it was a delicate moment, meeting again after the long absence, and the abyss where she just spent the last three weeks.

One way or another, Marie's arrival is a turning point. It's possible, for instance, to set the table for three again. And she has to make room for her sister, which means storing the absent one's belongings. Caroline sets to work on a typically Davidian pile that's been shunted to one end of the kitchen counter: socks with holes, the sports section of *La Presse*, a loose CD, newspaper clippings, a subscription form for a science journal. A bolt slips out of the paper and rolls under a chair. The blank form momentarily paralyzes Caroline:

should she renew the subscription? She drops it in the trash-can.

In the hallway, overloaded hooks still hold winter's remnants. Whatever belongs to David she stuffs into their bedroom closet, apart from a red scarf she's especially fond of. Then she moves on to the shoes, which he would wear until the soles fell off. The only exception are his skates. He pampers them so much that he keeps them hanging all summer long next to the windbreakers and sunhats, just for the pleasure of catching a glimpse of them. As she dreamily runs her hand along a flawless blade, Caroline catches a whiff of patchouli.

"I apologize for last night," Marie says, kissing her on the cheek.

Her tangled locks hide half her face and she's wearing an oversized T-shirt with a Sanskrit mantra that's been worn away.

"No need to apologize."

"I went a bit overboard."

"That's okay. It's just that I'm having a hard time seeing the positives of the situation, Marie, understand? I can't go on living with my head in the clouds—there's no choice. I'm the one who keeps things on course. There's nobody else. And, let me tell you, everyday life outweighs exploring levels of consciousness. Packing lunches, getting a bus pass, sewing buttons on, laundry, parent-teacher meetings, gas and electricity bills...Want some orange juice?"

"I'll get it. In the fridge?"

Marie heads toward the kitchen without waiting for an answer, and Caroline follows her like the little lapdog that she's basically always been.

"I can fix supper tonight, if you want?" Marie offers, with her head tucked inside the refrigerator. "And no veggie pâté, I promise. Or do the groceries? Or the vacuuming? Give me part of your everyday world and I'll do what I can."

"There's cereal in the cabinet," Caroline answers. "I want to ask you…"

"What?"

"Christian Rimbault in Lhasa?"

"Christian Rimbault? He's way ahead of us, that's all I can tell you. You eat Cheerios? They're nothing but sugar, you know…"

Caroline rolls her eyes.

"Christian, Christian," Marie sings quietly while serving herself a big bowlful of Cheerios. "You so much as come near him, and you're caught in a web of tranquility."

"Caught in a web of tranquility…"

"Yes, that's the effect he has. Caught as in 'caught in a snow-storm' or 'caught in a traffic jam' or 'caught off guard.'"

"I can attest that it works even by long-distance phone call."

"Really?"

"I slept like a log after I talked to him. My best night. How many levels of consciousness did he visit before turning into valerian oil?"

"No idea," Marie concedes as she sniffs the milk carton.

"And he's able to function? I mean, in the material world?"

"Totally. He's a trekking guide. His mind is clear, bright, and unclouded."

"Sounds like an ad for the Tibetan sky."

"Yup. In fact, the altitude and the pure air apparently puts travellers into an altered, even exalted state. But as you go higher, if you climb too quickly, things can deteriorate. Breathlessness, lack of sleep, dizzy spells. You can even end up with a sort of brain edema…"

"No kidding?" Caroline asks in astonishment.

The possible resemblance between David's accident and mountain sickness is comforting somehow.

"Yes, a coma, I'm not kidding," Marie says as she takes a

second helping of cereal. "You have to take the time to adapt at every stage."

"And the people who live there?"

"Tibetans—apparently—have a genetic feature that enhances oxygenation of the blood. Their hemoglobin works in a different way."

"Oh? Is there a gene for enlightenment, while we're at it?"

"Enlightenment is possible anywhere. Even below sea level."

"And you, do you believe that?"

"I've seen phenomena this year that can't be explained, Caroline."

"And you feel different? You look different. Happier."

"Peaceful, yes. But the real difference is that I firmly believe in transformation. I mean, radical transformation."

"Radical. Right. By the way, you just ate three bowlfuls of Cheerios."

"You see? Another inexplicable phenomenon."

"Seriously, you're referring to the transformation of what, exactly?"

"The transformation of our little selves into something bigger."

Caroline, last night's irritation welling up in her again, violently wrings out the dish sponge.

"Take Dr Sollers, for example," Marie continues, determined to hold her attention.

"What about Dr Sollers?"

"He pledges his research tools to the five senses. Take David, in the opposite corner."

"What about David?

"Right now, David sees nothing. When you touch him, he may not feel anything. When you speak to him, he may hear you. Then again, maybe not. But has he stopped existing, even so? He must be experiencing something, no? Scientists are constantly finding new forms of life at the bottom of the ocean, new insect species in the jungle. Did they exist before we found a way discover them? Yes. I'm sure it's the same for David."

"So now, Marie, you've become an expert on comatose states?"

"All I'm saying is, if he's still alive it's probably because there's something he has to do here. Not necessarily with us, but at least among us. Bertrand feels his presence, doesn't he?"

Caroline wipes a soapy hand across her forehead.

"Bertrand also believes his stuffed tiger might pounce on him during the night."

"But what if he actually sensed David? It's worth being open to the idea, at least as a hypothesis."

"Maybe…"

"A loving hypothesis."

"Maybe."

The sponge is lying at the bottom of the sink.

They come and then go away again—who? Nebulous. Pieces of humanity, fibres, yes, promises
hands
within them a vast, uncontainable world
a density
a colour a flavour a fragrance
fluid, shifting
each time unique
more and more recognizable.

Thanks to Marie, the days can finally be told apart. Accordingly, Caroline decides on a regular, well-spaced schedule for visits to the hospital. Monday and Wednesday after school, go in through the B Wing, climb the stairs to keep in shape, a dash of antiseptic soap, a half-hour of monologues that invite the very legitimate question of whether they narrow the gap or widen it. The tubes gurgle like a swampy, pond-bottom melody, which Bertrand listens to with a frown. Detour to the vending machine for a bit of compensation, then back down the stairs. *Preventing Infections*, bus, meal, bath, stories, hugs. Sometimes, Caroline drops by alone on Friday night. On the weekend, they go together with Karine and Janek's shadow. Should it drag on, they've agreed to alternately visit David every other weekend.

Caroline often sees the same faces on the floor, though the only people she knows by name are the nurses who look after David. On the day shift, Laurel and Hardy, politely reserved, in the British tradition. On the evening shift, the team of Steve and Nurse Pronovost, as efficient as they are unalike. Steve works only Monday through Wednesday. On the other nights Nurse Pronovost sulks; she's not fond of her co-worker Solange, too apathetic for her liking, and prefers to handle David's case, her "Sleeping Beauty," alone.

Truth to tell, the staff seems more familiar than David himself, whose body is dwindling. He's lost the physique of the man his supervisor so appreciated. His muscles, built up by dint of hammering, made to lift studs and endure impossible contortions, have given way to limp arms and withered legs. His forehead is as smooth as a child's and his face has grown chubby through lack of exercise. The pale stripe of his watch across his wrist has completely disappeared.

Particles gathered under their fingers
under their fingers
I assemble myself
and they
obstinately
resemble each other.

Their anger is a sting
their sadness, a wave
their indifference, molten lead
their pity, a mud puddle.
The rare gem is compassion.
When it leans close to me speaks to me, it permeates every-
where casts a wide net nearly cures.
I recognize them.
I know who gives me up for dead
who hopes for my waking
I wait for them.
At times I wish they would leave
often I'd like them to stay.

Marie the psychic has succeeded in penetrating the mystery of Bertrand's insomnia—he wants "to sleep without sinking into a deep sleep." Caroline, busy making sandwiches for the day camp, recognizes Laura's definition of a coma. She's so dumfounded she slaps her forehead, lets a slice of bread drop on the floor.

"You're telling yourself you're a bad mother," Marie observes as she picks up the slice, which of course fell butter-side down.

"How do you know that?"

"It's obvious."

"That I'm a bad mother?"

"No, that you spend all day finding fault with yourself."

"True."

"You're doing all you can, Caroline. Life is hard by definition. Bertrand is learning sooner, and all at once, what others learn later on."

"I could do a better job of helping him learn."

"You're already helping him so much."

"How?"

Marie stops grating the cheese.

"He's learning that a person can be terribly sad and still go on loving her little boy with all her heart."

Doubt like quicksand
I hear a rosary always the same
in a loop.
Caroline confused troubled troubling brings nothing else
what a pity. A pity for her and for me and for us.
Doubt: all that's left of my wife,
now.
Now that professionals wash my balls, massage my legs
handle me like a piece of Tupperware.

The city is sweltering. The heat is a dirty heat saturated with exhaust fumes and the noise of lawn mowers. Even the dandelions bend their heads. Day camp ended with a very amateur show. On Caroline's work days, Marie takes the liberty of bringing Bertrand to the hospital whenever she feels like it. Lily, at the reception desk, is absorbed by her Facebook account and pretends not to see them walk by. Her tasks include screening undesirables, whom she refers to as "spams." Marie's step is too light, her charm too genuine for her to fall into that category. As for Bertrand, he's Bertrand, and the whole floor has a soft spot for him.

At David's bedside, Marie and Bertrand have worked out a method of talking to him that spares them the drawbacks of a monologue. They sit facing each other across the bed, and Bertrand gets things rolling:

"Hi, Dad, it's me, I've come to see you with Aunt Marie. It's nice out today. You know, I've got another loose tooth, and I think it's going to fall out soon. Would you like me to bring it to you when it comes out? If the tooth fairy lets me I'll bring it to you, I promise, but maybe you'll wake up before then, who knows, eh, Aunt Marie?"

Marie jumps in as soon as Bertrand's sentence reaches its natural end point.

"The tooth fairy is likely to go bankrupt these days..."

The moment she starts speaking, Bertrand raises his hand as if in school and rocks from side to side, eager for his turn to come again.

"Know what, Dad? Jerome has gone to the Magdalen Islands for the holidays, but we're staying in the city, staying with you, and that's okay because the swimming pool is open now at Parc du Pélican and Aunt Marie will take me there every afternoon..."

Marie signals to him to ease up.

"Well, maybe not every afternoon, but as often as possible anyway, and sometimes Mom will come with us and we'll let her do her laps, her long laps, you know how Mom likes to do laps, and soon I'll go with her in the grown-up lanes."

"It's true, David, Bertrand's swimming is steadily improving. It's hot, so we stay at the pool for a long time, and afterward we play in the park."

A warm bridge, above me, beautiful bright orange.
It's good. Reassuring. Very dense.
The bridge absorbs them, merges them, merges us, together
and then it lets me go
motionless
powerless
deaf and mute.

Whenever they speak to him, David eventually groans and feebly scratches the sheet with a fingernail. Marie notices his nails are too long; she'll let one of the orderlies know. Bertrand, however, likes the scratching sound. He regards it as a way of saying hello.

"I know you can hear me, Dad, I'm sure of it. Are you cold? Your sheet isn't right, see, your toes are barefoot."

Marie glances at his toes. Again, the nails—honestly...

"It's so warm today," she says.

"Warm and sunny. Maybe, Dad, we can take you outside one day..."

"Hmmm..."

Marie learned from Nurse Pronovost that the only patients who get shifted to a sitting position are those whose cerebral functions can be significantly improved through exercise, which she seriously doubts is the case for David. She added, "by the way," that none of the staff have any time to waste, and concluded with a rant about free health care.

"And Dad, I could even push your wheelchair. Aunt Marie, would he like a walk in the hospital parking lot?"

"Talk to him directly, Bertrand."

"Yes Aunt Marie, you're right. Dad, Aunt Marie is right. She's staying with us now, you know, she sleeps on the living-room couch and makes supper so Mom can get some rest, she tells Mom to go soak in the bath twice a day, she even bought her an inflatable pillow for the bathtub, would you like one, too? In the bath, Mom puts her head underwater and imagines she's you. She thinks maybe you hear us like that, like your head is under the water, is that how you hear us, Dad? Eh? Last night, Mom got out of the bath and her fingers were crinkled like an old lady's and Aunt Marie made us an omelette..."

"A bit runny."

"A bit runny, and toast..."

"Burnt."

"Burnt, and a cake..."

"It was flat."

"A bit flat, that's true, Dad, but even so, Mom stayed in her bath a long long time and then she smelled nice nice nice and she was in a good mood. I'd like you to talk to me sometimes, Dad, just a little. Are there words in your coma? Aunt Marie, is he going to talk some day?"

"I have no idea, Bertrand. Actually, he may be talking to you in his own way. Let's be quiet for a while, eh, and try to hear him in our heads."

"In our hearts."

"That's it, in our hearts."

They fall silent. Bertrand, both hands resting on David's forearm, looks increasingly joyful.

"Well?" Marie whispers.

"He's happy when we talk to him."

"And you're happy too, eh Bertrand?"

"Yes. Very."

Bertrand his heart on his sleeve
comes to get me at all costs
draws me to the surface.
I want to move a finger, a foot, my eyes under my eyelids, the
voice in my throat, for him.
To budge for him. To talk.
Nothing.
Traces of traces of traces
of the blackout.
It leaves me drained, disappointed.

"Aunt Marie, where is Dad?"

"What do you mean?"

"Is he here or somewhere else?"

"It's hard to explain ..."

"Try."

Marie looks for a suitable metaphor as she twists a lock of hair around her forefinger, then untwists it, then twists it again.

"Imagine a house with many floors, Bertrand. And even several basements. We live on the ground floor and we meet and talk. There are people who visit different floors of their house and other people who always stay on the same one. And your father, well, he's on a special floor."

"Maybe we can go there, too?"

"Unfortunately, it's such a special floor, and he's the only one who knows how to get there. But we can still talk to him, and he can still answer, in his special way, in our hearts."

"Is my heart like a kind of elevator?"

"Exactly."

Bertrand thinks for a moment.

"Did you know that Dziadzio learned Russian in school when he was little?"

"Really?"

"Babcia too."

"I see. And soon you'll be learning English."

"Yes. Then I'll be able to speak to English people."

"That's right. And you'll be able to understand them."

He gives it some more thought.

"Aunt Marie, you think there's another language we could speak to him so he really truly understands us?"

"I'm pretty sure of it, Bertrand. It's just that . . . that we can only guess what that language is."

"I'm going to work very hard on it, Aunt Marie. I'm good with riddles."

While Marie and Bertrand are experimenting, Caroline is having lemon-ginger tea in the cafeteria. This morning she again renewed her loan of *The Way of the World*, which she takes along everywhere but never opens. The title is enough for her. Her chin resting in the palm of her hand, she scans the room in much the same way you'd look at an aquarium.

Employees, dressed in blue, green, or white according to their jobs, thread their way through the tables, greet each other, chat, and move on, their manner casual and unaffected. The visitors, meanwhile, all have a case in tow. Cancer, fracture, heart attack, embolism, birth. It's evident in their posture, their shoulders, their faces. Some cry openly, others are radiant; many seem absorbed by the effort of not letting anything show. Like a big tent of chance, the cafeteria houses fragments of stories with nothing and everything in common. The food is bland, human life is precarious, complex, miraculous.

Caroline catches sight of Steve and Laura sliding their trays along the serving counter, interrupting their conversation just long enough to choose their meals. At the cash, Steve pays for Laura, who, after examining every dish, settled on a pre-wrapped muffin. He kisses her on the cheek and looks on wistfully as she heads toward the exit with the muffin tucked inside her pocket. Perhaps they live in the same house. In that case, no wall-to-wall carpet. A dog, maybe? Maybe a cat. Venetian blinds. A Bodum coffee-maker.

Steve picks up his tray and approaches Caroline with a look that asks if he can join her. He sits down and starts to toy with his mashed potatoes with a dreamy expression enhanced by his long eyelashes.

"She's pregnant," he finally announces, in spite of his compulsive discretion.

"Laura?"

"Yes. I ought to keep it to myself, but the whole floor already knows about it."

"Happily pregnant?"

"Very. Some issues with eating, but otherwise everything's fine."

"It's the first?"

"Yes."

"Fantastic."

Steve acquiesces as he chews on his potatoes. His black hair keeps falling over his forehead.

"And you?"

"Me?"

"Are you happy too?"

He realizes the mistake and laughs. As an old friend who's been treated dozens of times to a detailed account of the artificial insemination procedure, yes, he's delighted.

"I'm happy for them."

"Ah. And do you have kids?"

"No."

She thinks she sees his green eyes darken. "You're projecting," Simone would tell her.

"Mashed potatoes and meat pie, eh?" Caroline says to dispel a silence she finds awkward.

"I know. Carbohydrate heaven."

"You won't need any more slow carbs today."

"Or for the rest of the week. Still, it's 'vegetarian meat pie.' The staff has been pressing to have more vegetarian dishes. So we got the meat pie, the hot dogs, and the burgers."

"They also serve healthy salads, don't they?"

"They leave me hungry."

The conversation peters out again. While Caroline tries in vain to find something to say, Steve shovels down the rest of his meal and pushes his plate aside.

"Where's Bertrand?"

"Upstairs with my sister. They're practising a new method for speaking to David. They call it 'continuous conversation.' They go back and forth talking without taking a break."

"Excellent."

"Bertrand makes a big deal out of the tiniest thing. A moan, the hint of a movement. I'm a bit worried."

"Who's to say he's wrong?"

"Who's to say he's right?"

"I noticed your husband is calmer when Bertrand is with him."

Caroline arches her eyebrows in bemusement.

"He's often restless, especially at night. But never when Bertrand is around."

Caroline pretends to drink—her cup is empty. Steve senses that she's wracked with doubt.

"In terms of communication, I've witnessed some astounding cases," he ventures.

"Really?"

"One in particular—a mother with her ten-year-old son. I was in the pediatric ward at the time. Everyone insisted on talking to him as if he were awake, very loud, very logical, repeating his given name, the date, and all that. But his mother mimicked his moaning, the rhythm of his breathing. Softly, in his ear. For a long time."

"And?"

"And one day he simply woke up and talked to her. All of a sudden, just like that. Then he slipped back into his coma, but whenever she was there, he spoke to her. We figured out he was having some sort of dream, a sea voyage, and he would tell her about where he'd landed."

"Incredible. But was it an actual coma?"

"Vegetative state, according to the neurologist. Even now, he still believes the boy's mother made the whole thing up."

"Did he eventually wake up, the boy?"

"He got an MA in anthropology from the Université de Montréal."

Steve lifts the leather bracelet hiding his watch face.

"My shift starts in two minutes. It's your husband's turn to eat now."

"His healthy salad."

"More like his meat pie. I'll say hello to Bertrand while I'm at it."

"You're working late?"

"Midnight."

Despite having signalled his departure, he stays put, fidgeting with the leather bracelet.

"Do you ..." Caroline hesitates. "Do you find it depressing, the hospital environment?"

"No, why?"

She peers at the bottom of her cup to avoid looking at him, his thoughtful gestures, his friendly, complex gaze. There's something suspicious about him, she finds, this Steve Austin, astronaut. He's hiding something. When he finally does stand up, she surprises herself as she blurts out:

"Would you mind if we called each other by our first names?"

"Not at all."

He goes out, forgetting his tray.

He comes often
to take away my hunger.
Sausages, fatty soup
hard-boiled eggs
bread made with shortening.
He is handsome, very handsome, swathed in true, sincere
humanity,
but there's also a dark night
around him
all around a private chaos, dead seaweed, drownings
that upset me, sadden my soup
scramble the compassion, so rare, so precious.

Marie comes away from the nonstop bedside conversations as radiant as from her endless meditations. The very opposite of her days in the handicraft store where she's found a part-time job, and from which she brings back inordinate quantities of pipe cleaners and baize cuttings. According to her, David's presence is steadily becoming more intense. She loves to see Bertrand's face light up on the inside, and to sense that something tangible has managed to pass between them.

Caroline, too busy digesting David's absence, does not want to hear about his presence. She feels such a large part of herself has been severed that she has the urge at times to change her name. She'd take an androgynous name, while she's at it, given that her woman's body has been left lying fallow, given also that she now mows the lawn, changes the faucet filters, and purges the pipes. Charlie would do the trick. But Charlie who? Novak? No, Auteuil.

Even so, she does notice Marie and Bertrand's enthusiasm. They enter the hospital arm in arm with a conspiratorial air, like accomplices in a hold-up. On one hand, Caroline is delighted by this. Whenever Bertrand is with his aunt he soaks up optimism, and optimism is something you can never have too much of. It's as if they've both inherited the positivity gene of her father, the man who bought a hot-air balloon.

On the other hand, Caroline wishes she were the one helping Bertrand communicate with his father, the one giving him reasons to believe in a bright future. Not the one hiding in the broom closet waiting for the hurricane to blow over and for the electricity to come back on. And not the one, either, who feels left out by their enthusiasm, although they'd like nothing better than to include her.

"You act as if you're afraid of David, Carol," Marie volunteers one evening while serving her a bowl of the "wholesome homemade yogurt" she insists on making despite the lumps. "Come with us. Give it a try, you'll see."

"I'm afraid of talking into a bottomless well."

"But what do you have to lose? If you talk into a well, the well doesn't care. If you talk to David, you help him live."

"I find that hard to believe."

"But he's alive, Caroline. The fact is his heart is beating, he's breathing. Think about his life instead of his death, damn it."

"I'm afraid to believe in his life only to have him die on me."

"That's up to him, one way or the other. Anyway, you can never lose when you believe in life."

Caroline shakes her head. The conversation is floundering, and the lumps disgust her.

"You sound like a book."

"What sort of book?"

"I don't know. The Khalil Gibran sort. A book of aphorisms."

"Does that irritate you?"

"Yes."

Marie collects the hardly touched bowl. Sometimes she worries David won't hold on long enough for Caroline to make peace with him, with herself, with the universe. She sighs loudly:

"No one is a prophet in their own land."

August

Soon it will be Bertrand's birthday. Seven years, the age of reason, although, in his case, reason was called on months ahead of time. Sandra realized this at her own expense when she offered him a book about the human body. After turning the pages one at a time, systematically lifting the flaps to reveal the small intestine and the Eustachian tube, perusing the illustrations, and being read the description of the body as an "extraordinary machine" and of the brain as a "super-powerful computer," he declared:

"It's not like they say, Sandra."

"How's that?"

"Because if Dad was just a robot, now that he's broken they would have thrown him in the trash can."

"Err…"

"What's the human body used for, Sandra, eh? Not to be a robot, I'm sure of that, I've thought it over."

"I see."

He turns the pages scornfully. She folds her arms.

"The good news, Bertrand, is that I kept the receipt. Don't bend the flaps too much, okay? We'll exchange it for something else."

The age of reason, then.

The little party held for him in the hospital room is interrupted by Nurse Pronovost, who's come to massage David's pressure points on the pretext that the family surely couldn't be bothered to do it today.

Bertrand goes through his other party, at home with friends, like a sleepwalker. The gift he wants more than anything, no one can give him, something made painfully clear by the greeting card that arrives from Florida a week late: *Have a wonderful day on your birthday. May all your wishes come true.* Since the text is already printed, Lorraine's personal contribution is confined to the grease stains on the pale blue envelope—Cuban sandwich, according to Marie.

The loans desk floats like a small island in the middle of the open space, among the tables and rows of books. A few readers are permanently ensconced in the square armchairs, among them, Mrs Langevin, famous throughout the Montreal library network for once declaring that her favourite Québécois author was Agatha Christie.

Having just spent her morning at the helm, Caroline feels as if she's climbing out of a submarine. Her supervisor, following an intense Eckhart Tolle phase, recently became infatuated with a Belgian writer, Dieter Verkest, a "veritable prophet for our times." She tasked Caroline with finding all his books that have been translated into French, from his latest bestseller to his most obscure chapbook, put out by a publisher in Liège, who, as it happens, subsequently went bankrupt. Perched on her stool, Caroline gives herself a one-minute break, letting her eyes drift over the tinted-glass walls to the park, where a young mother has just had a fistful of sand thrown in her face.

She jumps when the corner of a book grazes her elbow. She mechanically takes in the title: *Première heure* by Erri de Luca.

Her heart sinks into her boots. She goes pale. But this is the loans desk, and she makes a super-human effort to attend to the borrower. Early forties, good-looking, pearl-grey shirt under an elegant suit, salt-and-pepper temples.

"*Première heure,*" is all she manages to say in a reedy voice.

The man says, "Yes," and smiles. Caroline finds that the smile does not become him. Not as much, say, as the shirt. She opens the book to the page with the checkout card, already old, and lingers over the very first line: April 16, 2001. The card number is David's, the damaged borrower.

Times have changed since then; everything is digital now. But the red laser beam quivers ineffectually over the salt-and-pepper user's card. Caroline is shaking too much to read the bar code. For the date, at least, there's the stamp. But where to put it? The tears fog up her eyes and she struggles to fight them back. The card is as blurry as a windshield with the wipers off. She raises her reddened eyes. The man looks surprised. He wants to say something but holds back.

She shuts the book and slides it toward him. He reaches out the perfect half-moons of his fingernails, pockets *Première heure*, and heads toward the exit. The front panels of his expensive jacket spread like wings over his nicely pleated pants. Caroline concentrates. Don't cry. Not here. Not now, after all the weeks of self-control that earned her compliments from Mrs Blouin. It would be unacceptable. She lowers her eyelids and breathes deeply, a mindfulness exercise Marie suggested. It works. She feels calmer. She can come back, slowly open her eyes. To her bewilderment, the incarnation of elegance has re-materialized in front of the circulation desk.

"Miss …"

"Did you forget something?"

"Well, actually, yes. Something I always forget when I come here."

"You come here often?"

"Every week."

She gathers from his tone of voice that he's disappointed she hasn't noticed him before.

"Ah. That's good."

"Yes. Hmmm. Would you be free one of these days to go for a coffee, by any chance?"

Caroline suppresses a retch. No, no, no. No dates, no guy in a grey suit having an Americano at some snooty café. No, I'm not free. I'm married. Can't you see I'm married? Can't you see my husband-ache? Doesn't it show?

And David, too, with his ideas about not exchanging rings. He refused to wear one because of the construction work. Apparently, a ring can cost you a finger if it gets caught in the sawbench. And since he wasn't going to wear one himself, he didn't want Caroline to wear one either.

"Imagine if I take you out and people think I'm carrying on with another man's wife. Imagine, Caroline. If I put my arm around your waist, if I kiss you, and people see your ring and assume we're having an affair. No. No ring. I want to be able to kiss you in the street with no second thoughts. I'll give you an ankle bracelet, okay? A really beautiful ankle bracelet, forever."

She will not be showing this man the bracelet that David kneeled down to slip around her ankle on their wedding day; he looks at her in puzzlement, his tie slightly askew, just enough to lend him a human touch. Whatever is stuck in her throat is so painful that she can't allow herself to respond with words. She shakes her head.

He purses his lips a little. Such a handsome man. Probably not used to being turned down. Still, a woman this confused does not bode well. He marches away.

It's because they touch me that I still exist.
They fill my nothingness
they invent a New World for me
with their hands their hands their hands
yet all I want
is to get out of here.

"What's this Caroline? You secretly remarried today?"
Marie points to the ring on her third finger.
"I married my husband."
"Meaning what?"
"I wanted the fact that I'm taken to be visible."
"Someone came on to you, right?"
"Someone invited me for a coffee."
"A coffee would do you good, no?"
"Oh, Marie. No."
"And where did you buy it, your ring?"
"Canadian Tire. In the plumbing department."
"I see. Platinum or white gold?"
"Stainless steel."
"Durable."
"Exactly."

A waxed floor.
There, in front of me, at my feet, the actual ground. It appears,
it disappears.
Ceramic? Linoleum?
Earth, sand?
Ground to walk on to leave.
To leave.

The pellucid August light makes the grass and trees, the staircase handrails, and the windows gleam. Marie has sacrificed the International Reggae Festival to go to the Laurentian Mountains with Sandra. She wants to enjoy the beautiful red leaves already adorning their crests. She even promised Bertrand to catch one as it fell, which she says brings good luck. But her secret goal is to leave Caroline to manage on her own at David's bedside. The time has come to leave them alone one on one.

She sets out on Thursday, the very day Mrs Blouin, after much dithering, has chosen to pass on to Caroline the reference for a radio interview with Dieter Verkest, an interview she "considers relevant" but "in no way wishes to impose." Mrs Blouin absolutely dreads negative labels. Her position as head of a team of city employees demands that she consistently maintain a secular stance, and Eckhart Tolle already aroused suspicions about her. She deplores that spirituality is so easily taken for bigotry and that mysticism should be regarded as a mental illness, but she keeps her opinions to herself.

During the coffee break, Mrs Blouin ferrets in her bag for a Post-it with a web link written on it. Caroline sees her ten fingernails glowing in the dim interior of the huge handbag and is surprised to learn that fluorescent nail polish exists. She's sceptical about the Post-it, but to please her supervisor she listens to the interview that night.

"I bring neither solace, nor certitude," Dieter Verkest declares with a strong Flemish accent. "I am a researcher. Due to the subject of my research, I am attracted to individuals who find themselves on the fringe of consciousness. The dying, for example. Or ordinary people who have extreme experiences that cannot be explained and that, more often than not, they dare not discuss."

Gildas Robitaille, a veteran radio host, adopts a pseudo-erudite and slightly aggressive attitude. He is lacking in inexplicable experiences and the research subject eludes him. However, he has skimmed the writer's books and quotes them profusely. Dieter Verkest decides to respond to him on a personal level.

"Everything starts with a mundane, or at least widespread, experience. Like me, you've no doubt felt that your life, often frustrating in its particulars, unintelligible in its overall pattern, illogical in its messages, and transient besides, could not be the be-all and end-all. You've been in love, I suppose?"

"Err..."

"Of course. Things appeared easy and grandiose, didn't they? You were cheerful, inspired by everything, even the daily newscast. The drafts in the Metro seemed poetic to you, you noticed heart-shaped pieces of chewing gum on the sidewalk. Correct?"

Gildas Robitaille clears his throat.

"Yes. Life blessed you with an extraordinary destiny, the veil hiding the divine within you had been lifted. I've been through it myself, naturally. Like me, you felt determined, prepared to do anything, and you needed just one thing: the presence of the other. That's all. And then the great expansion began to recede, no matter what you did. Renew your vows, resurrect your shared plans, dim the lights, open a better bottle, opt for lace, have heart-to-heart conversations—nothing could halt the atrophy. Am I right?"

"Well, that is,..."

"Romance shrinks in the wash, it's a fact. Obviously, you could always choose the lukewarm comfort of everyday joys, great and small. Or you could simply end the relationship and strike out toward new adventures. Whatever the end of your story was—which, by the way, doesn't interest me at all—you experienced that expansion and contraction. Your love bore you along for a while and then it wore out. I know. I know exactly how it feels when one's destiny shrinks. When our deepest certainties strike us as gross mistakes. I'm not to blame if we are blind. And deaf."

"To get back to the specific area of your research, Dieter Verkest…"

"Yes. What interests me, ultimately, is understanding what happened when you felt you were more than yourself. The fact that it took place through meeting another person is secondary. Some people report meeting their God in the same circumstances. What interests me is the true nature of what possessed you. You see, I'm not sure we fall in love with a person; I believe we fall in love with love. I'm not sure we meet God; I believe we open ourselves up to the true nature of existence. I think of lovers as transmission channels. We tend to confuse the messenger with the message. We take others for what they let flow through them, and in the end no one is equal to such a role. Right from the start, and involuntarily, the other was a usurper. When the usurpation becomes apparent, the magnifying glass opportunely brings all the shortcomings into focus. The beard shavings in the sink, the morning breath, the snoring, the burnt bread, the glass too many, the verbal tics, the mother-in-law."

Dieter Verkest's demonstration rises in a crescendo that peaks at "mother-in-law." A contemporary prophet? Yes, possibly. In other words, an anachronism. Gildas Robitaille is about to speak, but Verkest doesn't break stride.

"The truth, in my humble opinion, is that we are made of love and that love is everywhere. Everywhere. It yearns to occupy every dimension. It steals its way onto every possible road, if need be by borrowing the faces and personalities that come within its reach. It presents itself, always pure, even in the most vulgar iterations of earthly attraction, like 'be mine,' 'how can I live without you,' 'I want you.'" Why? Why must it take those roads? Why doesn't love present itself as it is, without asses and breasts, without love letters and bouquets of roses? Why?"

"Well..."

"You'll never guess."

"Dieter Verkest, can you enlighten us in seventy seconds? We're running out of time, unfortunately."

"I'd like to propose two answers, which are in fact my working hypotheses. First, we are too lazy to reach the outer limits of our consciousness, the region where, freed from our mental jabber, love approaches its purest emanation. Second, we are too weak to look love in the face. You and I, we would be pulverized. For now, our lives are echoes convinced that they are voices. We need to get rid of our petty selves, escape the illusion of identity. At this point in time, there may be a handful of super-evolved individuals on earth who have accomplished that feat. Needless to say, they are not our political leaders. There you have it, Mr...?"

"Robitaille."

"Right. Remember your greatest love. Can you accept the fact that the tremendous energy that filled you then simply ceased to exist? I'm sure it's impossible. I'm sure there is a way of experiencing it directly. I asked life a question and life propelled me into this research. Since then, I squat hospital rooms because there the chatter stops and many people have nothing more to lose. I squat hospital rooms because I believe there are bridges to the light and that each of us has an incommensurable hidden potential. A potential made unthinkable by causality and choked off by egocentrism."

"Thank you, Dieter Verkest."

Cut. A honeyed female voice: "You have been listening to Dieter Verkest in conversation with Gildas Robitaille about his latest book, *Seeing The Invisible*, launched in September by Le Havre Publishers."

Caroline immediately replays the interview. She wants to hear a sentence again but can't remember which. Toward the end. This one: "We are too weak to look love in the face."

She notes it down on Mrs Blouin's Day-Glo yellow Post-it and sticks it inside the kitchen cabinet, where she puts the cups, because she opens it often.

The Saint Lawrence licks the rusted ships in the Old Port
and leaves the city.
It runs along suburbs villages
gets a taste for salt at Les Éboulements
swallows the Mingan Archipelago
flows into the Atlantic.
I want to leave too.

After listening to Dieter Verkest, Caroline can no longer go on speaking without speaking, touching without touching, or shunning the unknown through narrowmindedness.

She contemplates the needle marks on David's atrophied arm, which scar as soon as a new vein takes charge of the glucose intake. The resealed holes leave behind shadows, a sort of dotted-line calendar. This week the head nurse opted for gastrostomy feeding with a Malecot catheter, inserted directly into the stomach, another long-term solution. The ousted nasal-gastric tube has left a slight irritation on the wings of his nose.

On the opposite side of the bed, Bertrand throws himself wholeheartedly into the continuous conversation:

"...and then Jonathan Louvain pushed me and I fell down and that's why I have a scratch on my forehead and the counsellor said it could've been worse, it's just a scratch and she put on peroxide and merc...mercu..."

"Mercurochrome."

"That's it. I'd like it better if Jonathan went to another camp, but Mom says you can't always choose. Do you know I can read what it says on the cereal box? Just on the French side. Mom, is it the same letters in English?"

"Yes, it's the same alphabet. And ... David? Bertrand reads the back of the cereal box, but that's not all, he eats what's inside, he's growing so fast ..."

"We even bought a new pair of sneakers and Mom says I hope you don't outgrow them before Christmas."

Caroline strokes the motionless arm, but all her attention is focused on Bertrand as his hand forces its way into his father's. He enjoys the impression that the stiff muscles are clasping him tenderly, and he modulates his voice, as if he were going to meet David somewhere very far away. Marie is right: something does register beyond the boy's face. Like an ecological lightbulb slowly, slowly starting to glow.

Does Bertrand owe his happiness to the depth of his imagination? Or does he really pick up on a presence? Caroline's doubts have started leaking. What will she find there, beyond? At least she finally understands how this game works: If you don't bet, you lose all your chips.

This is it.

The fluorescent lights on the floor, the squeaking carts—get out of this place. Outside, the warm night, the crowded, polluted parking lot—get out, get out, I head east, like the river, polluted too. Everything's dirty.

Head east for a long time, till Rue d'Iberville. Then north, toward home.

The street streams past. Maybe the street is what's moving the street is what brings

bits of houses, sidewalk slabs and cracks, utility poles and wires.

The red maple, its rough trunk trembling leaves
the garbage collectors have been by, trashcan lid left lying on
the ground
the porch is peeling little mouths opening in the paint.
Our door. Triple glazed. I'm scared.
I'm scared, it's too familiar. Too strange. I'm scared the door-
knob could come off in my hand.
I'm scared of seeing our bed. Caroline.
Bertrand's cheek all warm under the rockets of his sheets.

The nights without Marie are difficult. Caroline's reacquaintance with insomnia is so easy she doesn't even try to sleep tonight. She reads until very late and then putters around the house in her slippers. Just before dawn, when the lack of sleep sheds its tragic hues, she finally drifts off on the couch with folded arms, cold feet, and her neck at an angle that invites a crick.

She dreams that David comes into the living room. He's stark naked, and the gleam of the streetlamps filtered through the curtains highlights his sturdy build. Young, strong, whole, at the masculine midpoint of his life, the peak of his abilities, every muscle knotted to the next, every cell exactly where it should be, he moves easily, sure of his position in space. As she watches him step closer, Caroline is paralyzed with recognition. She gasps for joy and breathes in relief.

Familiar, necessary David. His approach lasts forever. Each time his foot leaves the ground it seems as though his whole body is taking the time to reconstitute itself, to recover its density, its substance.

He's very close now, his toes just a few millimetres from hers. He goes no further. He smiles sadly, tenderly. All his intelligence is gathered in his sparkling eyes, he seems to know a lot, to know too much, to know more than he can share. She reaches out her hand.

He vanishes.

She wakes with a start, hand stretched out, body shivering, and a pistachio texture in her throat that makes her cough.

She calls to him in a low voice. It was so real, so very very close. In the drabness of her living room she starts to sob. Her life force dissolves, gone to waste in the mirage of a resurrection.

In the morning she subjects herself to a scalding shower and swallows a double espresso before waking Bertrand, who, for his part, appears to be in a particularly good mood. Between two gulps of orange juice he declares:

"You know, Mom, last night was special. Dad came to lie down in my bed and he hugged me for a long long time. It made me feel good."

She lets the glass of milk overflow. What's going on? The boundaries of reality have moved. The markers are being erased. Common sense is slipping away. She wipes up the mess without a word.

The trek in my calves my knees my thighs, the weight of a backpack
the weight the resistance, so good—the air, on my skin: the cold bites my cheeks, the wind from the river pulls off my scarf
this isn't Montreal anymore
but I know this snow too, granular blond brittle.
Bundled-up people greet each other. They don't see me.
Two men shake hands through me.
To the left, a dark, narrow street. Its name? The letters grow distorted
they spell words that I don't want.
The cold invades my coat. My soles are buried in snow.
I've been here before
beyond the streetcar tracks.
Here—but where?

Here, on the three-sided city square named, I know,
Rynek Podgórski

"Who evaluated him this morning?"

"It was Laura, I think."

"Laura always rounds things up. 'Stairway to heaven,' her Glasgow scale."

"What score would you give him?"

"He's sinking, Steve, it's obvious. Don't kid yourself. He's going down and he'll continue to go down, believe me, I speak from experience."

"He shows all kinds of signs of life. Look at the way he wrinkles his nose. He's concentrating on an image, clearly."

"Oh, come on."

"Look how he curls his lips, Lucille, his eye movements. He sees something, I'm telling you."

"How about concentrating on his catheter instead, okay?"

The old ghetto,
The one where twenty thousand Jews were crammed together
with fear and hunger
the one with the coal-black sky
waiting room of the camps.
Auschwitz-Birkenau and its forty-eight satellites.
Plaszów, right inside the city.
My father took me here, to the ghetto. To remember.
It seemed as though he was ashamed.
My father and the scars of his people. A Slavic soul.
My mother and the between-season light. A Bohemian soul.
My parents, the two faces of their city. Kraków and Kraków.

The catheter has been inserted. Now that the great vicious cycle of urinary-tract infections has been set in motion, it will need to be closely monitored. You can never overdo hygiene in that vital zone. Steve puts the diaper back on and the gown, so threadbare that the hospital logo has completely disappeared. He arranges the soft pillow and pulls up the stiff sheet.

On Rynek Podgórski, a church with a frosting of snow. All red brick. So beautiful.

No matter how much I knock—nothing. Just wood.

This city is dead.

It's snowing on my hair. I have to persevere, I'm going somewhere.

Somewhere over there, beyond the steeply sloped park.

Gnarled trees breathing I see them breathe.

Huge mansions gnawed by naked ivy. Ghosts are watching me through the window. What are they saying? Their lips are moving.

Night is on its way. The opaque, rose-coloured sky announces more snow, still more snow. I can't stand the moving lips anymore

I realize where I'm going. The cold is inside, outside

everywhere

the gates of Cmentarz Podgórski are shaped like black suns.

"So, we're done here, big fella?"

"I'm going to stay another minute."

"The feeding tube is installed, Steve. We can leave him."

"I'll be along right away."

"But Mrs Dubuc hasn't stopped ringing for help."

"Go on ahead, I'll be right there."

Thousands of graves of beds snowed under. Frozen bouquets, amber votive candles. The snowflakes get into my boots melt on the nape of my neck.

Silence.

No engines no horns no conversations—the whole city muzzled the light comes from the snow and the souls underneath.

Part of a branch breaks under my foot. I'm barefoot.

What am I doing barefoot?
My perfect footprints, white on white, ten toes.
There's a gravestone with no snow at all. Just one. Polished
marble straight new. No flowers, no votives
a wooden angel riven with cracks
this is the thing I must touch.
The passage is narrow
the wind lashes me claws me but I get closer I'm there
this is the one. The marble sticks to my fingers, I read:
Dawid Nowakowski.
My grandfather.
UR. Kraków 2-4-1975 — ZM. Montreal 28-3-2012
I don't understand.
The wind latches onto my calves, moves up the length of my
legs.
I don't understand.

"Are you coming, Steve? I need help lifting the Dubuc woman. She weighs a ton."

"He's crying."

"Come help me with the whale instead of getting sentimental. It's almost midnight and we're not going to leave it for Brigitte, she's all alone."

"It's a shame we don't have more time for them."

"Hey, good Samaritan, we're already saddled with twice as much work as nurses in the States."

Fingers stuck to the marble I spit on them blow on them. The
skin tears.
Now?
Go back the other way. Leave the dead city.
Leave the memory of that country
walk far enough long enough south south south. Never mind
the snow

the bare feet.
Push the gate its black sun
the effort wears me out.

Marie has come back from her long weekend with two leaves, purportedly caught in mid-flight, one for Bertrand and the other for David. Bertrand examines them suspiciously; he spent two whole hours in the park trying to catch one just released from a tree. Neither he, nor Caroline, nor Maxime, nor Mr Giguère succeeded. The leaves change directions at the slightest puff of air, and when you're about to lay hold of them they swerve and flutter away. The truth is, Marie carefully selected them on a footpath and isn't ashamed of her white lie. Whatever it takes for Bertrand to keep enjoying the magic of the world a little.

She goes to the hospital that same evening to pin the leaf up on the cork board before it falls apart. Steve hails her on his way to another room to let her know, quickly and quietly, that he'd like to propose more intensive efforts to communicate with David.

Unlike Dr Sollers, he and Laura regard the coma—no matter how deep—as a trance-like or dream-like state that comes in response to a profound need. They think it's possible that patients go through crucial experiences while appearing completely passive: they also believe that close friends and relations can contribute in their own way to these invisible events.

They've done a lot of reading on the subject, but don't often talk about it. The head nurse, aligned with the hospital administration, applies a set of readily measurable objectives; comfort care is already a luxury without the additional question of whether or not it disturbs the patient's hallucinations. But to Steve and Laura, David seems an ideal subject. Marie's investigative spirit and Bertrand's natural talent are major assets. And Caroline's resistance may just be waiting for the chance to collapse.

Marie goes back to the house all excited. Not bothering to knock, she walks into the bathroom, where her sister, barely visible under the jasmine-scented foam, has dozed off.

"Steve told me something about David's feet."

"Huh?"

"Yes, he apparently moves his toes from time to time."

"Quite a scoop."

"Oh, Carol. It seems these movements, his moaning, and so on, tell us about what's going on his mind."

Caroline sits up and punches her inflatable pillow into position.

"Why did he tell you this and not us? Why now and not earlier?"

"He told me because I was there. And now because he waited until he felt you'd be interested."

"I'm interested."

"Okay."

"So what else did Steve have to say?"

"That the next time you go to the hospital on a Monday, Tuesday, or Wednesday, you should go find him so he can show you a few things."

"What sorts of things?"

"No idea. He said 'some things.' He said Bertrand will love it."

"Right. Tomorrow, then."

Steve pulls back the sheet and uncovers David's feet, two scraggy things, parched and peeling, with broken toenails and reddened heels.

"We do the best we can," he says apologetically. "There's a pedicure service but you have to pay extra…"

"Had I known," Caroline answers. "I don't care about paying extra."

"Sometimes the information doesn't get out. Put in a request with Lily; she'll schedule a treatment. Okay, shall we begin? We've only got a quarter of an hour."

Both Bertrand and Caroline gather that the quarter of an hour coincides with Nurse Pronovost's coffee break, as she doesn't approve of the more intensive efforts to communicate with Sleeping Beauty. They're tempted to tease Steve but hold back, since he has already launched into his explanation with an almost touching earnestness.

The fact that David often moves his toes could mean he's trying to move his feet or even that he imagines he's walking. By offering some resistance to his movement, they can help him rediscover where his foot is and how to control it. In other words, they can facilitate a kind of contact between intention and action, between his brain and his limbs, and stimulate new neuron connections.

Steve touches David's foot with the palm of his hand.

"Push my hand with your right foot, David, feel my hand against your foot, push my hand."

The longest minutes in the history of Quebec go by unavailingly.

"Obviously, it takes time and patience. But the slightest voluntary movement is a huge victory."

"Frankly, so far..." Caroline grumbles.

"His right foot, that's not even his good foot," Bertrand jumps in. "Dad always kicks the ball with his left foot."

"Really? His drive leg is the left one?"

"Well, I don't know about driving, but that's his strong side."

"But he's right-handed," Caroline objects.

"That's irrelevant," Steve says. "I'll bet Bertrand is right. Let's try again, David, I'm touching your left foot, I'm pushing your left foot. Can you push too? Push, David, push my hand."

More endless minutes. Nurse Pronovost has probably finished her Weight Watchers bar.

"Bertrand, take my place," Steve suggests. "Caroline, talk to him up close. Tell him which foot to push. You need to give him specific instructions."

Bertrand rushes to the other end of the bed. He's no sooner taken up his position than he shouts:

"He's already moving! He's pushing with his toes! Yay, Dad! Yay, yay, yay for pushing my left hand with your right foot—no, my right hand with your left foot, oh, whatever—yay!"

Caroline thinks he's imagining it. Steve suggests they switch roles, in the hope that David will actually move a toe, even if it's by chance, even if it's the right foot.

"Ha!" she says after a little while. "What I feel is his *intention* to move."

"What's that? You've got *hisintention*, Dad? Yay, Dad, yay! That's fantastic."

Bertrand then starts a kind of incantation, his mouth right up against David's ear.

"Dad, Mom's got her hand on your left foot, your good foot, push against her hand, push, Dad, push a little, Mom's hand is on your left foot, show Mom you can push, show her Dad, it'll do her good, push Dad, now, push…"

"Oh my God!" Caroline moans. "He's moving, it's true, he's moving!"

Before Nurse Pronovost bursts in, David moves his left foot two more times and his right foot very slightly. What's more, his neck stretches toward Bertrand while he talks to him.

"He just hit 10 on the Glasgow scale," Steve concludes.

"The Richter scale," Caroline says to correct him.

The ground is shaking. The sky is heavy, humid, lowering. Someone's crying. A muffled noise gets closer, louder and louder, deafen-

ing. A dark mass sweeps in. A train. The big, windowless cars brush past me, stinking of shit, fear, and death. Freight cars, more-freight-cars-freight-cars-freight-cars-shit-death-fear-shit-death-fear.

The train whistles, steams away, finally.

Leave this city, absolutely. South, absolutely.

Was I right to leave?

A little bell. Every chime like a hole in the density of the clouds like an unhoped-for hope.

Outside the sky is heavy, humid, lowering. Bertrand, triumphant, fidgets impatiently for the entire bus ride, rings the bell three times when they reach their stop, runs all the way home, leaps up the stairs, and almost breaks down the front door. Marie comes to open it wiping her hands on an oil-stained apron.

"Aunt Marie! Aunt Marie! You'll never guess what we did today at the hospital!"

"Steve's tricks?"

"Yesss! And you know what? Dad moved his feet!"

"What?"

"Yes, we told him to push on our hands and he pushed."

"That's amazing, Bertrand, fabulous! Come in, sweetie. Come in."

Caroline catches up with them on the porch, dragging her feet and looking drawn.

"Oh my! Your mom looks tired. Should we send her for a hot bath?"

"Can I watch TV in the meantime?"

"You can start by setting the table."

"What's for supper?"

"Lentil soup."

Disappointed, Bertrand drops his school bag in the middle of the hallway and heads toward the kitchen. Marie helps him a little and then goes to see her sister in the bathroom.

"May I?" she asks as she sits down on the radiator.

"You'll burn your bum!"

"This isn't a convent. A little pleasure once in a while…"

Caroline rolls her eyes.

"What's going on, Carol?"

"No idea."

"Shouldn't it give you some hope that David is present?"

"He moves his feet, Marie. What I need are words. I need him to tell me where he is, if he plans on coming back, if he's in pain, most of all."

"And what if, by moving his feet, he's telling you he's there? What if that was the gist of his message?"

"If he has a message then he's conscious. If he's conscious and suffering, then he's aware of suffering. What am I supposed to do with that? He's totally in hell!"

"Take a deep breath, Carol. Everyone's doing what they can. Think about Bertrand's face when he touches him."

"Yes. It's weird."

"Do you think that if Bertrand expected words, complete sentences, articulate speech, he would glow like that?"

"No."

"Adjust your expectations. Clear up your emotions. It's up to us to adapt to David's language. And, hey, while you're at it, you ought to move all the images you've stored up of him out of the way."

"Meaning what?"

"We perceive everything with images. There are even people who experience *themselves* as images. Sasha, for instance."

Marie stands up and rubs her behind.

"This radiator does burn after all."

"Funny you should notice when Sasha's name comes up."

"Hey, that's true. Fever!" Marie exclaims, Peggy Lee-style.

Caroline finally laughs.

"Pathetic," Marie admits. "I've got another example: Lily."

"Lily, the Facebook-obsessed receptionist?"

"Exactly. She created a page with flattering photos and posts about her day. She visits the pages of friends who do the same thing. Their images communicate with each other."

"What's your point, Marie?"

"Her friendships are in a coma. No voice, no hands, no stammering or embarrassment or odours. In a word, no body. It's very hygienic. When people tell me they do it 'to stay in touch'—honestly!"

"You could create a blog on the subject."

"Is that cynicism or irony?"

"Fatigue."

Marie shrugs it off.

"Remember what you said about David before the accident? One day he's a jerk, another day he's great, you trust him, you have doubts about him. One day he's the ideal father, the next he stuffs Bertrand with cookies, his Sunday soccer game annoys you, his Friday beer even more, his co-workers' tasteless jokes, the list goes on and on. Remember when he went out for a beer with one of his exes?"

"Hmm."

"What else?"

"He did a lousy job of rinsing the dishes."

"And did he snore, by any chance?"

"He snored."

"What else?"

"He left the toilet seat up."

"A classic."

"He left his socks lying around right next to the laundry hamper."

"You have to see him for what he is," Marie concludes.

"A guy."

"Precisely. A good guy, but a guy all the same. Not some angel from heaven. Except that now he leaves us with just one image, always the same, utterly unsettling image. An image we can tame provided we develop our finer resources."

Caroline sinks down in the bubble bath.

"Marie, do you take me for a Tibetan lama? I'm just an ordinary girl, in an ordinary house, with a growing boy, and a comatose husband."

"You don't need to be a Tibetan lama to be a Tibetan lama."

"Meaning what?"

"Everyone's always on the brink of something bigger. You just need to let yourself tip over."

Vacant lot.
Frozen mud
anonymous
    rusted objects
    left behind in piles
tender objects too
    broken picture frames
    mirrors jewellery
    a child's hand-knitted jacket
    a remote-controlled car zigzagging like a headless chicken.
Everything is dead; I am alive.
I have to stay standing.

Laura takes over from Steve and proposes working on the "root of the movement." Accordingly, she asks Bertrand to imagine that he'd like to turn his head but can't, and then to identify where the motion would start if it did start. In the process, Bertrand nearly twists his neck around.

"In the shoulder!"

"Now, really pretend that your head refuses to budge."

He stiffens like a toy soldier and Caroline is the one who gently turns his head, holding him by the cheeks.

"That's what we want to do for your father."

"We want to help him stretch?"

"Exactly."

She shows them how to skim their hands over David's body on the lookout for tensions, efforts, beginnings. They find a tremor around the biceps.

"What do you think he'd like to do?" the nurse asks.

"He wants to put his arms around me," Bertrand says.

"He wants to open them," Caroline suggests instead.

A tunnel. Cement walls full of structural flaws, covered with graffiti.

Unhealthy heat. The cement gives off smoke
the walls close in.

My coat makes a grating noise
my backpack rips
I'm choking.

More graffiti, still more, ugly, very ugly. Formed then deformed.
The walls almost touch at the far end—a funnel.

Rats rub against my ankles pieces of metal block the way the walls scrape my joints crush my shoulders.

I'm thirsty dehydrated compressed. It's far, it's heavy, it never ends.

I'm so thirsty.

Caroline opens David's arm, but he resists, bends his head back on the pillow, grimaces, twitches. Despite her best intentions, she has no success. No big deal, Laura assures her. He may need some rest, that's all. His limbs are especially stiff today because the physiotherapist just took three days off; they'll have to give him a muscle relaxant. And the grimaces don't mean anything since he has no control over his face. With one exception, however: if he swallows twice in a row, as he often does during the most invasive treatments, Laura interprets this as a sign of discomfort. Today he's not swallowing; he's panting.

She suggests instead that they help Bertrand fold his father's arms. This time, he goes slack, and once his arms are properly folded he lets out a huge sigh.

"Very, very good," Laura smiles. "We just helped him do something."

She doesn't linger, being already behind in her tasks. Holding hands, Caroline and Bertrand gaze at David. He looks calm now, even though his eyes continue to move under his eyelids. Caroline would simply like to stay there and come to terms with his disconcerting image, but Bertrand finds inactivity hard to bear. He starts hopping, goes twice around the room, comes back to massage a frown between his father's eyebrows, kisses his eyelids.

"Should we refresh his mouth, Mom?"

Without waiting for an answer, he slips a pink swab between the parted lips to moisten the gums. David eagerly bites down; Bertrand sees this as thirst, and Caroline as thanks.

A beautiful warm rainshower.
The walls the graffiti the backpack are gone the landscape is wide open
and me neutral as a pebble in a brook
new
earthy furrows, straight, aligned
as far as the horizon
everything is in order:
the rain in my hair
on my tongue
and, ahead
one field after the other after field after the other.

September

Since David's fall, Janek has been mired in guilt. He blames himself for having insisted on his son becoming an engineer; in reaction against this, David became a construction worker. Yes, he reacted and found himself climbing up scaffolding. With his talent, he could have done anything—medicine, law—but ended up in vocational school and plunging head first to the pavement.

Worse, and more profoundly, Janek blames himself for having named David after his own father. Is it possible he passed on a tragic destiny? The destiny typical of the generation born between the two world wars, a period when the fairies cautiously avoided cradles. Whenever he thinks back to that time, Janek shakes his head to drive out the past. But the past latches on. The cumbersome baggage followed him to this continent full of promise, to the furnished apartment in the Hochelaga-Maisonneuve district.

Dr Sollers indicated that a patient's chances of waking from a vegetative state "diminish *drastically*" beyond the three-month threshold. Three months already. All those thresholds crossed one after the other. Janek keeps hearing the doctor's husky voice, keeps reviewing his father's life.

The German occupation, in particular. In particular, the day when Dawid Nowakowski saved a Jewish child from being transferred to the Podgórze ghetto. It wasn't Janek's fault that his father acted spontaneously, out of loathing for the Nazis and abhorrence of anti-Semitism. Nor was it his fault that his father had a wine cellar where he could hide the boy, nor that he had the boy jump over a monastery wall one night in the middle of curfew, risking the firing squad, along with his whole family and the neighbours on their landing. Yet he knew, Dawid Nowakowski knew that such executions were repeatedly carried out as a warning.

Janek sees it all as if he had been there. The long trek southward, the roads teeming with refugees, then through the woods, across the fields, midstream in a river, never stopping until they reached the mountains. When Dawid arrived in Zakopane, the Polish resistance was organizing itself as an underground army; he joined immediately and, together with thousands of others, was kept in reserve in expectation of the Cracow insurrection that would never materialize. He dreamed of seeing action, of revenge, of memorable battles. But his role was confined to helping couriers find lodgings on their way to London, where the Polish government-in-exile was based. The messengers laid over in Zakopane and crossed the border by way of the mountain peaks. Thus, when the war ended, Dawid's hands were perfectly clean, he was full up on rich soups and hardboiled eggs, he had the ruddy cheeks of a mountain dweller. It wasn't until later that things turned sour.

But Janek can't be held responsible for the Russian takeover, or for the haste with which the new authorities sent the soldiers off to the gulag. No.

The horrific episode of the arrest torments him no end. His father hung from the ceiling by his wrists, methodically disfigured by rifle-butt blows, the brutal struggle between his strength of character and the physical pain. Afterwards, a broken heap on the floor of his cell, he could no longer feel his body; what he felt was the great satisfaction of not having betrayed anyone. Janek's father must have told him this story at least a hundred times; he considered it almost a privilege.

Janek nibbles his moustache and lights a cigarette, but with every puff of nicotine, the harrowing story rushes in. A train hurtling toward Siberia. Dawid side by side with two Nazi officers, their faces swollen like his. Yesterday's sworn enemies now brothers in adversity. For three years they would share the same bowl, the same hut open to blasts of wind, the same gruelling toil, the same bitter cold, the same blinding white horizon; they would be detritus left to the care of a slow, cruel erosion. On the worst nights Dawid would sleep welded to their bodies, no longer Nazi bodies, but flesh still able to give off heat.

When he was set free, there was almost nothing left of him. A bunch of bones, a decrepit youth. A character worn down by terror and hunger. In sum, a nearly unsinkable man.

Karine catches her husband nibbling at his moustache. She knows from experience that he's thinking of Poland.

"Janek?"

"*To wszystko moja wina.*"

"No, it's not your fault."

"Katarzyna…"

"Stop, Janek. Stop it immediately. Put on your jacket. We're going to church."

The current seizes the grasses on the riverbank, combs them like long hair. The light paints curves and arrows and is doused in eddies. Everywhere tall lilies in bloom. I'm diving in.

The sunbeams make way for me as I pass through.
Here, everything is cool, everything is true, the river bears me away,
the river bears me away.

Today Caroline is thinking, it's back: the same old same old.

What a relief. A workday, spaghetti for supper, Bertrand's not-too-crumpled homework, and some herbal tea before bedtime. What's more, she serenely brought *The Way of the World* back to the library. The belt of anxiety is slackening, the burden growing lighter. The thought cycle has skipped the bothersome spinning phase. In short, a perfectly Thursday Thursday, a prodigious normality.

But it's on precisely this Thursday that Marie chooses to broach the unbroachable subject that she regularly mulls over: Lorraine.

"I suppose you've spoken to her recently, Carol?"

"I called her once to find out how to get in touch with you."

"Has she called you back since then?"

"No."

"Well, she might have offered to help you out."

"I have trouble putting up with her for more than twenty-four hours, so, you know, her help…"

"How did you cope when she came for the holidays?"

"David gave me a lot of moral support. You should see his killer imitation of her. He made me laugh. He took away my sense of incompetence and imperfection."

"I know exactly what you mean."

"Not at all. No matter what you do, Mom thinks you're perfect. She's always gushed about you. 'Marie this,' 'Marie that.'"

"Did it ever occur to you that it sucks to be gushed about by someone you despise? You think I'd have studied international law if it had been up to me? All I wanted was for her to stop taking an interest in what I was doing."

"Really?"

"Really. And my boyfriends, Carol, honestly. Igor, Willy, *Gorgeous* Sasha . . . Nothing but self-destruction."

"She adores Sasha. '*Beautiful* Sasha.'"

"I really messed up."

"But you despise her, Marie? You, the lama?"

"I worked on that during my trip. Let's just say I've chilled out."

All the same, Marie suddenly feels very warm; she pauses to remove her blouse and starts to fidget with her bra strap.

"Does she know I'm here?"

"No. Not because of me, anyway."

"She's no doubt expecting me to call her."

"Are you planning to call her?"

"I should, shouldn't I?"

"Pfft."

Snap of the bra strap.

"We have to find a way of forgiving her, Carol. It's her loss. What'll she be left with in the end? A mini-putt trophy? I'll go see her. It's been years. Yup, we have to. St Augustine, here I come."

"She'll think you need money."

"Amazing insight."

"You need money?"

"I always manage."

"Tell me, if you ever do."

"Can you advance me the plane ticket?"

Hollow. Hollow.
The sludge under my fingernails.
I'm moving farther away.

Moving farther away and at the same time getting closer
with an end run
with the brightness of the reverse.

The next day, as if the prospect of her leaving wasn't enough, Marie announces an imminent disaster: Simone is organizing a girls' night out.

"Oh, no."

"Oh, yes."

Everyone has saved the date for next Friday, the restaurant table is already booked. Caroline assesses what's left of her nails.

"I'm not free."

"My eye. You're isolating yourself."

It's true. She's isolating herself, clearly. As a result, she feels alone. As of the middle of June, seeing that she wasn't bothering to answer the phone, her friends preferred to wait for her call, which never came. So not a peep from anyone, except some mysterious empty messages in her voicemail. Now Caroline lives in an uncluttered world. The unobtrusive company of a novel, the hospital, laps in the swimming pool. Bertrand's laughter, intact. Any small talk puts her in mind of a deflated hot-air balloon. Email is even worse.

On the fateful night, Karine and Janek come to babysit their grandson with an enormous Tupperware bowl full of *kapusniak*. At the sight of the plastic container crammed with large pieces of cabbage, Bertrand scurries away. At the same time, Sandra shows up in her old car and opens the rear passenger door for her friends.

After a torturous hunt for a parking spot in the Plateau district, they check the address five times and, in disbelief, step through the door of a nondescript ground-floor eatery. The bistro puts on the air of an exclusive club. Two months ago, Caroline would have found the place intriguing. Tonight it makes her nauseous. Enormous wrought-iron chandeliers thrust out from walls covered with oxidized copper sheeting, and in the candlelight every object sprouts ghostly shadows. On the ceiling, bald heads are on display in a mirror gone black. The low, grating sound of a cello fills the room, counterpointed by the clatter of dishes.

"There's a concept lurking here somewhere," Sandra whispers, her khaki shorts and tie-dye T-shirt markedly out of place.

Already waiting, ensconced in leather chairs whose backs tower over them, are Simone, Adèle, and Élise. Despite coming on bicycles, they too had to ride around the block to find a place to park. Élise's frizzy hair has retained the approximate shape of the helmet lying in front of her between the knife and fork. Simone holds Adèle's hand in hers; ever since they jointly redefined their sexual orientation, they've been inseparable. Sandra, bisexual herself, finds them altogether tiresome.

Caroline does her best to smile. After all, they've come to make her happy. She's not happy, but it's their intention that counts. Marie puts her arm around Caroline's waist in a gesture of solidarity. As they approach the table, the others stand up.

The new leather chairs receive their behinds with emphatic squeaks. Sandra swears. The shorts—honestly.

The waitress, a stunning young black woman dressed from head to toe in black, arrives at full speed, her dazzling teeth gleaming like a moon in the murky atmosphere. They all order gin and tonics but her pencil stays suspended.

"Hendrick's or Bombay Sapphire?"

"Beefeater," Sandra declares rebelliously. "Double, with 7-Up."

The pencil continues to hover. Adèle takes charge of the situation.

"Hendrick's for everyone, on me. With cucumber slices."

"Of course," the waitress notes.

The menu, printed in a gothic font, is nearly unreadable in the flickering light, but luckily the list is short. Three starters, three main courses, three desserts. One "omnivorous" choice, one vegetarian, and one vegan. Simone leans tenderly toward Adèle, offering to share a yellow-beet tapenade as an appetizer.

"I'll go for the scrambled eggs," Sandra announces.

"Scrambled eggs?" Élise asks in surprise as she brings her menu dangerously close to the candle. "Where?"

With a somewhat grubby fingernail, Sandra points to the "Nest of pan-fried quail with pink pepper buttermilk, a hint of fennel, flakes of wild parsley, and a touch of raspberry vinegar aged in cedar casks."

"Rustic," she says appreciatively. "Just my style."

With the orders out of the way, a hazy emptiness sets in. Things can go in one of two directions: either the conversation resumes where the girls left off (Élise's boss, a possible case of sexual harassment) or they jump right into the thorny subject of the coma, which does have to be broached given that Caroline has been incommunicado for weeks. Élise decides.

"How are you, Caroline? You seem to have lost weight."

"It's true," Adèle adds, "She's lost weight."

"Tell us how you are," Élise insists. "We haven't seen you in ages."

"If you want to see Caroline, you must take the trouble to go over there," Sandra says, speaking from personal experience.

She resents the others for having confined themselves to a few phone calls in June. But Marie gives her a swift kick with her Doc Martens under the table. If the girls start dropping by unannounced, Caroline will go crazy.

Élise, with her big, innocent angel eyes, is still waiting for an answer.

"I thought about you, Caroline, a lot, actually. But I was afraid to bother you. So?"

"I'm okay."

"Oh, come on!" Adèle blurts out. "Are you going to make us beg for more?"

As if to illustrate what she means, the yellow-beet tapenade arrives; it's the size of a quarter. Simone, whom they can thank for choosing this bistro, is unfazed and, sticking to the plan, cuts it in half.

"You each get a little turd—how nice!" Sandra remarks.

"Spare us your PMS," Adèle shoots back.

"Let's hear what Caroline has to say instead," Simone chimes in with a note of appeasement in her voice.

Whenever the atmosphere grows tense, Simone always speaks in an appeasing tone of voice, but this time her efforts are thwarted by the cello's dissonance.

"They removed his cast this week."

"Which cast?"

"He broke his arm when he fell."

"It's healed now?" Élise asks, as ingenuous as ever.

"Yes, completely healed. What else can I tell you? They've just cut his hair."

"Who did?"

"The hospital hairdresser. For next to nothing."

Silence, again, broken by Simone, whose voice can hardly be heard over the soundtrack.

"Do you speak to him?"

"…"

"The main thing is convergence."

"Meaning what?"

Marie gives her sister a sideways glance. She knows Caroline is going to clam up. Her reaching out to David is too new to be brought into a restaurant conversation.

"Well, simply put," Simone continues, "it's the fact that your intention, your heart, and your words all convey the same message. Telling him things that are real, speaking with the conviction that he hears you."

The clamshell is almost shut, but Simone persists.

"What about you? What exactly have you been feeling through all this?"

Caroline despises the mania for "feelings," but makes an effort all the same.

"I'm mainly worried about Bertrand."

"Clearly, Bertrand, in terms of lived experience…" Simone begins.

Caroline sighs. She can't stand the "lived experience" thing!

"Personally, I think Bertrand is fantastic," Marie interrupts.

"How so?" Élise asks.

"He's energetic, curious, bursting with wellness. He feels David's presence very strongly."

"Compensation. Perfectly natural," Simone concludes. "And you, Caroline, how do you see him? The last time we spoke he'd just destroyed a thousand-year-old bonsai and speared a carp in the Botanical Gardens."

"Yes, it's true he regressed, at first," Caroline mutters while fiddling with her raw linen napkin.

"But he's making progress now," Marie cuts in. "You should see all the things he does on his own at home. He's really growing up."

"Hmmm," goes Adèle.

The over-adaptation of the submissive, adapted child always comes at a price in the long run. Her own transactional analysis process has shown her this in a thousand different ways.

"He shouldn't be the one to act as man of the house," she says. "The over-adaptation of the submissive adapt…"

"Maybe he needs some male figures," Élise interjects.

"I really did try to find him some," Caroline says in her own defence, "but it's hard. David's friends made themselves scarce right from the start. Mr Giguère is the only…"

"Which brings us straight to the question," Simone cuts in.

Her tone is completely transformed. Not at all appeasing now. Public demonstration, taking it to the street, front and centre.

"What question?" Adèle inquires ingenuously.

"Where Are The Men?"

No one dares respond.

"Where Are The Men?" Simone repeats to make sure the feelings behind her question are plain to see, although all anyone can see are the hard feelings.

Another awkward moment sets in and is made even worse by the arrival of the main course. Sandra examines her plate in bewilderment. Minimalist composition, unusual colours—edible or not? Caroline pulls her out of her musings with a few bitter words:

"In any case, I know where mine is."

At this, she gets up to go to the ladies' room, where she takes time to concoct an excuse. When she comes back, telephone in hand, the quail's nest has turned pale blue.

"My mother-in-law just called. Bertrand is sick. I think I'd better go home."

"I'll go with you," Sandra offers, painfully wrenching her thighs off the leather seat.

Deep, deep, my head underwater. Weightless, shapeless. Jumbled sounds, the symphonies.

It's soft, it's warm. Rolling in the sludge, curling up. I'm a baby mammal.

The hospital, on second thought, has become the place that best coincides with the truth of the present. The cinema, restaurants, cafés, shops have all been demoted. Like a dog that, when there's nowhere else to go, adopts a corner of the kennel and fills it with its scent, the Novaks have settled into this vast, reinforced concrete building. Caroline could find her way to David's room with her eyes closed. She knows how many steps it takes, the sound they make on the brown tiles, the snap of surgical gloves, the smell of disinfectant blended with those given off by suffering bodies and the staff kitchenette, Lily's candy-pink hair, the greeting of the nice Cameroonian clerk that Hattie makes eyes at and the eagerness with which he clears the corridor of trollies. She can rattle off from memory the vending machine codes: Kit Kat A3, Pringles F4, dried fruit D7. She's familiar with the door's muffled sound, its heaviness, the coldness of its handle, and every detail of the room, where the other patients are all that broadens the palette of events: hydrocephalus, tumour, stroke. Comas, by and large, are rare. She knows in advance which position she'll find David in; legs stretched out, feet turned in toward each other, fingers pointed toward the palm, wrist toward the forearm, forearm toward the heart. A slow return to the fetal position, the undeniable sign of a severely damaged nervous system.

She also knows she'll get nothing out of her appointment with Dr Sollers today, yet she feels she must absolutely try her luck. Inside the large office, her nostrils are assaulted by a new blast of musk. She finally locates the source of the aroma: a small vase holding a bunch of little scented sticks. The mere sight of them makes her cough.

He gallantly offers her a chair, gallantly waits as she takes her seat, and then sits down himself in his black leather armchair, clasping his hands.

"You wished to speak to me, Mrs Novak."

"Yes, Doctor, thanks for seeing me."

"You're concerned about the new urinary-tract infection?"

"Err, no, not really."

"You're right. Everything is under control. So why have you requested an appointment?"

"We've had a number of communication sessions with my husband, and I'm convinced that he's conscious."

"Ah."

"He swallows when he's ill at ease, frowns when he sees images, turns his head toward my son whenever he talks to him. He even grunts. He scratches the sheets. In other words, he responds to us."

Sollers shakes his head: another family wrestling with the mystery of the vegetative state.

"Mrs Novak, I've examined your husband, we've run all the tests. No kinesthetic or vocal response, no voluntary eye movement, no..."

"Have you noticed that your list is negative, Doctor?"

"*I beg your pardon?*"

"It's a list of things that are missing. Things that are missing are invisible, so I have trouble seeing what they prove."

"Now, Mrs Novak, are you going to have me read the *Critique of Pure Reason*?"

"I'm only suggesting a more open-minded approach, Doctor."

He leans against the back of his armchair, which creaks voluptuously. Caroline spits it out:

"A nurse told me about a research programme using magnetic resonance imagery."

"Who?"

"Laura."

"Laura who?"

"Laura on the third floor, the B Wing, Dr Sollers. Your unit."

"She is referring to research where *vegetative subjects* are put through mental activities that are clearly visible with a scanner, correct? To verify that they are thinking? that they can comprehend a question? 'To say yes, imagine that you are playing tennis. To say no, imagine you are moving around your house,' correct?"

"Exactly. I was wondering if it would be possible to propose my husband as a subject."

The doctor wags his head, his mouth twisted into the "pfft" position, his eyebrows welded together.

"It would be necessary to transport him to Ontario," he objects.

"That would only be a problem if you expect him to drive there himself."

"Mrs Novak, you know as well as I that the *experiment* is *conclusive* if the subject manages to hear the orders, to conjure up memories, to imagine an action, to comprehend a question. Moreover, only if he is awake during the scan."

"So?"

"So, if ever the results are negative, what will be your conclusion? That your husband is not conscious? Or that he was sleeping? Or that his auditory faculties are *defective?* Or that he has lost the capacity to imagine a tennis match?"

Dr Sollers leans over his intertwined fingers.

"Will that put your soul at ease, Mrs Novak, or will you just come back to *square one*, right where you are now, *as we speak*, asking yourself if Mr Novak is conscious or not?"

Caroline is dazed and at a loss for an answer. In any case, he doesn't allow her enough time.

"The real question is why do you want this. For whom? For you or for him?"

"I want to know if he's suffering, Dr Sollers. That is the real question."

Again, the inescapable sense of déjà-vu. It's a question Dr Sollers has pondered ad nauseam. As a scientist, his approach is strictly empirical. When it comes to the families, the main thing is to lighten their burden. His ready-made answer has the added advantage of reassuring himself, too:

"As I said before, Mrs Novak, all indications are that your husband is not suffering."

"You mean, 'there's no proof that he's suffering.'"

"I mean that, within the limits of what can be known, you have no reason to worry."

"It's the word 'limits' that I find problematic."

The doctor gently presses his fingertips together.

"It must be accepted, Mrs Novak, we have no choice."

She lowers her head. He gives a little cough. She instinctively turns toward the scented sticks.

The meeting is over.

Out of the water, on the shore: flatland as far as the eye can see
long grasses, pebbles, crevices. Total, windblown solitude without loneliness.
Exile without nostalgia.
An indefinite space, like the remnants of a space, like a phantom limb.
No more past no more future, nothing but the open, vibrant plain of here and now
without friction
on the shore.

Afterward, Caroline drops by David's room and finds several people gathered around the adjacent bed. The head resting on the pillow is typically adolescent: lips too fleshy for the narrow jaw, the shadow of a moustache, a few patches of acne. His mother looks at him with her hands clasped. It's probably been years since she stopped touching him. Holding his hand as he crossed the street, combing him, quickly wiping his face with a washcloth before school. Still, it's a body she made inside her own. When her eyes suddenly meet Caroline's, they're completely blank. This is obviously not the best time to massage David's pressure points or help him walk, swim, skate, jog, or whatever it is he does down there in his somewhere.

True to their routine, Caroline comes back with Bertrand the following Monday. They give David a kiss and then step over to the neighbour's bed. The boy's mouth is half-open and his skull is wrapped in bandages. There's a long diagonal cut that starts at his ear and runs across his cheek.

"Oh, Bertrand!" Caroline exclaims as she looks at the chart. "His name is Martin Bilodeau!"

"It's Martin Bilodeau?"

"Another Martin Bilodeau."

"There's two Martin Bilodeaus?"

"Maybe more than two."

"Why are there different people with the same name?"

"It happens. Coincidence. It's called a namesake."

"Do they know each other?"

"Not likely."

"Will we tell Martin Bilodeau we met another Martin Bilodeau?"

"Err, no."

"Why?"

"Well, what are we going to tell him exactly? That we found his namesake half-dead?"

Caroline bites her tongue, but it's too late.

"He's half-dead?" Bertrand whines.

"No, no, he's in a deep sleep."

"Like Dad."

"That's it."

"Not like me when I go to bed at night."

"No, not at all. Another kind of sleep. You wake up in the morning?"

"Yes."

"You can get up and walk and brush your teeth?"

"Yes."

"You can…"

"It's okay, Mom, I remember. Not at all the same kind of sleep."

In the meantime, Martin Bilodeau's mother arrives, greets them quietly, and installs herself at her son's bedside. Lowering her head, she takes his hand, says a few words to him, looks him over. Newly cut grey hair, dark-coloured clothing made of fine fabric, freshwater-pearl necklace—Caroline imagines she's a lawyer or a judge and knows instinctively that she has a wing chair near a large window and a pair of half-moon reading glasses. She suddenly finds fault with her own loose braid, the cracked cork of her sandals, her seriously wrinkled turquoise blouse. What's more, it's high time she shaved her legs, not to mention her underarms. Despite all the body hair, the lady gives her a friendly smile.

Caroline suggests to Bertrand that he go watch the TV in the family room; he doesn't need to be asked twice. As soon as he's gone, the lady calmly introduces herself: Monique Seurat. She assumed her maiden name again after her separation. Timidly at first and then more and more confidently, Caroline asks the questions she remembers needing answers to so badly during those first days. Recounting the accident, for instance, over and over. Driving it like a nail into her familiar reality. Do you manage to sleep? Did you take time off from work? No. Monique Seurat has neither slept nor taken a leave of absence.

"What's your line of work?"

"Social psychology. Early childhood assistance. I look after autistic children who've been placed in treatment centres."

"And does being a psychologist help—to cope now?"

"Not really, no."

Caroline remembers. Actually, nothing helps. Nothing at all.

"Martin was supposed to leave on a fishing trip with his friends next weekend..."

"He likes fishing?"

"I know—surprising for a boy his age. He got it from his grandfather. The gene skipped a generation."

The rain starts drumming against the window. Monique toys with the pearls of her necklace. She thinks back to Martin as a child, perched on a rock beside his grandfather, mesmerized by the sun's reflection on the river and the little circular waves around his line. She recalls the folds in the knees of his overalls and the sparkling scales of the trout. "When the fish bites," his grandfather said, "underwater life speaks to life on dry land using Morse code. The fishing line is the only chance we have of knowing what it says." After unhooking the trout he would throw it back in the water.

"Have you met Dr Sollers?" Caroline inquires.

Monique, roused from her daydream, shakes her beautiful grey head.

"*Oh yes. He is hopeful.*"

"Did he give you a sticker?" Bertrand asks as he steps through the doorway.

"Hey, why aren't you in the lounge?"

"Mr Jouvert wanted to watch *Planet Earth*. I want a kids' show."

"*Planet Earth* is for kids too. What was it about?"

"Caterpillars."

"What's your name?" Mrs Seurat asks warmly.

"Bertrand, I'm seven years old now. Do you know what my father eats in his coma?"

"No. What does he eat?"

"Healthy food. I asked Nurse Pronovost and she explained that it's better than what we eat because it's made especially for him. For example . . ."

"Bertrand . . ." Caroline cuts in, wanting at all costs to avoid invading Mrs Seurat's delicate space.

But the educational psychologist gestures to him to go on, and Bertrand does so eagerly.

"For example, if he's constipated, you know, if his poop is slow to come, they give him fibre. Dietary fibre, like what's in oat flakes, except that Dad's . . ."

"Okay, big fella," Caroline breaks in, knowing all too well that, given a willing listener, he could talk all evening. "Speaking of nutrition, would you mind taking some change from my purse and buying us some Pringles?"

"You mean it? Pringles?"

"Yes."

"Cool!"

He dashes away.

"Sorry. You were saying, Dr Sollers?"

"He told me about the Glasgow scale. . ."

It's been quite some time since Caroline lost interest in the Glasgow scale. Steve and Laura openly reject it because it classes so many cases of minimal consciousness in the vegetative category. Even Nurse Pronovost bluntly asserts: "It's not like reading the Tarot, eh? It's just the sum of the observable symptoms of a situation that at any moment can evolve in one direction or the other."

"Eleven, a good sign, apparently," Monique continues.

"A very good sign."

"And your husband? I don't wish to pry, of course. . . Has he been here very long?"

"Three and a half months."

"It must seem like centuries to you…"

"Hmm. I'm going to get a cup of tea. Would you like something?"

"No, thank you."

Caroline leaves Mrs Seurat in her moulded plastic chair. She wouldn't want to be in her shoes. So much has changed over the last three and a half months. Centuries, actually. The early and the high Middle Ages.

The Renaissance, too.

October

Each time they visit the hospital, Bertrand demands to hear the story of Martin Bilodeau's accident, and Caroline, who doesn't know much, elaborates as best she can. Martin fell off his bicycle. He was going fast on a busy street, he wanted to avoid a pothole, was grazed by a car, and hit a pole.

"What kind of car? What kind of pole? How fast was Martin going? Very fast? Fast as a motorcycle? Which busy street? A street we know? Who dumped a pot there?"

Caroline explains: "Martin fell off his bicycle, he was going fast on a busy street, he wanted to avoid a pothole, was grazed by a car and hit a pole. A pothole is a hole in the pavement." That's all she knows.

Bertrand stares at Martin in devout contemplation. He's unable to reconcile the image of this older boy with the hospital bed or that of the bicycle with danger. So anything can happen. Anything, any time. A pole, for no reason, can throw itself into your path.

"Mom, how fast was Martin going? Very fast? Fast as a motorcycle?"

Caroline opens her mouth, says nothing, takes a deep breath. Steve, who is busy spraying the end of David's tube to fluidify his secretions, finally decides to help out.

"Honestly, Bertrand, have you noticed the bandages? The cut? Have you noticed the coma?"

"Well ... yes."

"Do you think Martin was wearing a helmet?"

"I don't know."

"No."

"No?"

"Also, he was going downhill the wrong way on a one-way street."

Bertrand opens his eyes wide. Martin Bilodeau has just become responsible for his own misfortune. Caroline lets out a sigh of relief, which, to her regret, is plainly audible. But her delight is short-lived.

"My father—he had his helmet on."

Steve's vaporizer misses the tube.

"His helmet fell down beside him," he says.

"That's his fault?"

"No, it was an accident."

A sort of ecstasy,
Of absolute freedom.
The dry earth, like velvet.

Martin Bilodeau has been sleeping for a week and Bertrand's fascination persists. Caroline has poked her head inside the nightstand in a vain attempt to find the Peter Gabriel CD when she hears him shout:

"He's talking!"

She bangs her head.

"He's talking! He's talking!"

"Who??"

"Martin Bilodeau!"

The teenager's eyes are open, somewhat glassy, but unmistakably turned toward them. His pasty mouth repeatedly says "thirsty." Caroline takes his hand. He turns toward her slightly and moves his mouth like a fish out of water.

"Bertrand, go fetch Nurse Pronovost. Quick. Run!"

He charges out of the room and comes back with Nurse Pronovost and a colleague. Solange. She takes notes while Nurse Pronovost leans over Martin and wags her index finger to verify that his eyes are following it. She speaks to him as if he were deaf:

"WHAT'S YOUR NAME? TELL ME YOUR NAME."

"The rainbow," Martin answers, shakily reaching his hand out toward the foot of the bed.

"WHAT CITY ARE WE IN?" Nurse Pronovost perseveres, raising her voice even more.

"The colours," Martin insists, as though wanting at all costs to share his hallucination.

Solange tentatively slips in something about delirium transition. But Nurse Pronovost is unrelenting:

"WHO IS OUR PRIME MINISTER?"

"It's beautiful," Martin says, shutting his eyes the better to see.

Nurse Pronovost dictates additional observations to Solange. She also sneaks a glance in Caroline and Bertrand's direction and, with a brusque gesture, prompts her colleague to draw the curtain.

A slight lull ensues. Caroline wraps her arms around her son's shoulders, and they stay rooted before the curtain as though waiting for the show to begin. It's odd, both are thinking, that they can look at Martin with all his injuries, but aren't allowed to watch him wake up. Enveloped in numbness, they feel nothing at first. As if from far away, they hear the nursing staff attending to the patient.

And then it wells up.

First, Caroline starts to quiver. Something clutches at her stomach. Something like: David, for shit's sake, wake up. She wants to rip up his sheets, to scratch him, to slap him. Bertrand, gripped by the same undercurrent but without the gates and sluices, begins howling. He throws himself down flat on the floor and pounds it with his fists.

Nurse Pronovost pokes her grey head through an opening in the curtain.

"Mrs Novak! Rein in your son or get out!"

Caroline kneels down beside Bertrand. She tries to speak into his ear, but his howling drowns out everything else. Instead, she coaxes him into her lap. His face is all red, smeared with tears, snot, and saliva. She wipes him clean with her sleeve, kisses him, rocks him.

"Come, dear, we'll take a taxi. If we're lucky it'll be a yellow cab."

He stays inert and heavy; she helps him to his feet. She pins his lunchbox and schoolbag under one arm and, with the other, guides him firmly toward the exit.

At the main entrance, there are five or six taxis waiting, all as black as hearses. They dive into the first one. Bertrand sniffles, clenching his fists.

"You said he was sleeping like Dad."

"Yes."

"It wasn't *exactly* like Dad."

"No."

"You lied."

"It's the same kind of sleep, Bertrand. But everyone wakes up their own way."

"I want Dad to wake up."

"I know. Me too."

"Dad's half-dead, isn't he? That's it, eh, Mom?

The driver glances at them in the rear-view mirror. She manages to keep her composure, which she knows she'll pay for later with a bad headache.

"Right now, Bertrand, Dad's alive."

She lets several days go by before returning to the hospital. She wants above all to avoid Nurse Pronovost's shift. In fact, she'd like to avoid the unit, period. When they go back, if anyone has the nerve to criticize her over Bertrand's tantrum, she'll lodge a complaint with the head nurse. She pictures herself a number of times venting her rage in the back of the nursing station. But what exactly would she complain about? The fact that David is foundering? Complain to whom, and why? As for Nurse Pronovost, she rules uncontested; her seniority, efficiency, and sound decisions have forged an unassailable reputation.

Instead of going to the hospital that week, they invite Maxime over for dinner, they go for a stroll in the Old Port, they visit a municipal arts centre, they try the Chinese food at the delicatessen, they build an enormous garage with the Meccano set. They wait for Marie to come back.

On Friday, at the end of the school day, Mrs Falcon, the grade 2 teacher, calls out to Caroline from the top of the main staircase. She learned about Bertrand's situation in the first week of September yet didn't bother to meet his mother in person. But today's events have brought things to a head. The crowd of parents and children retreats like the sea in the wake of her strident voice. Caroline climbs back up the stairs, leaving Bertrand to wait for her in the schoolyard.

Mrs Falcon withdraws into the shadow of the entranceway. She should have arranged an appointment in her office but there wasn't time. She also promised herself to ask after the patient, but in the heat of the moment her preamble eludes her.

"Your son's behaviour was quite aggressive this week," she declares point-blank.

"Aggressive? How so?" Caroline asks in surprise and quite aggressively, too.

"Agitated. I won't dwell on his rushed homework and his tendency to chatter in class. He fought with one of his classmates during recess. I docked him three stars."

"What stars?"

"His merit stars. Our reward system."

"Ah."

"Next time, Mrs Novak, it'll end up in the principal's office."

Poor Bertrand. Caroline turns around and sees him waiting for her at the bottom of the stairs, with his bag sitting on the ground between his feet. The schoolyard has emptied out, and he looks like a fledgling fallen from its nest.

She cooks him his favourite meal that night: pizza from the freezer. She waits for him to bring up the subject himself, knowing from experience that this is the only way to get anything out of him.

"Mrs Falcon wanted to talk to you, Mom?" he finally asks with his mouth full.

"Yes. What do you think it was about?"

"Um, my stars."

"Among other things. Can you explain how you lost them?"

"First I'll tell you how I earned them, okay?"

She grants him this small indulgence.

"To start with, I did a perfect dictation, zero mistakes."

"Bravo."

"Next, I helped clean up the confetti after the Fall celebration."

"Excellent."

"And I went to get a bag of salted peanuts for Mrs Falcon."

"Excuse me."

"I was the only one to raise their hand when she asked if anyone knew how to use a vending machine."

"I see."

Mrs Monette didn't exactly soar like an eagle, but Mrs Falcon, despite her name, flew very close to the dirt.

"By any chance, did you fight with someone today?"

Bertrand's nose drops down to his slice of pizza.

"Yes."

"With your fists?"

"Yes, Mom."

"Do you know what I think?"

"Yes, Mom."

He turns this over in his mind.

"Dad thinks the same thing too, eh?"

"That's for sure. What made you lose your temper like that, Bertrand?"

"He called me a sissy."

"Who?"

"Jonathan."

"Jonathan Louvain?"

"No, Jonathan Bilodeau."

Caroline drops her fork. Bertrand slowly looks up—he has his father's eyes—and meets her gaze. And like his father, he already knows how to make the best of his beautifully arched eyebrows. In addition, he comically puckers his lips in hopes of lightening the atmosphere. David would have done exactly the same thing. Caroline feels incapable of scolding him. Even so, out of a sense of parental integrity, she leaves the table to consult their old phonebook.

"There are at least two hundred and eighty-five Bilodeaus on the Island of Montreal," she announces as she struggles to put the directory back in the overloaded sideboard.

"Why are you telling me that, Mom?"

"Keep your fists to yourself, Bertrand. It never solves anything."

"Okay."

"You're going to apologize to him."

"I already have."

"And what did he say?"

"'You're still a sissy.'"

"And then?"

"What?"

"What did you answer?"

He shrugs.

"Nothing. I went away. We never play together anyway."

Caroline sits back down to her pizza, which tastes of wet cardboard. She watches Bertrand carefully place his crusts on the edge of his plate. If only she could find something to soothe him. One, two, a thousand stars. The moon—why not?

"What would you like to do this weekend, Bertrand?"

"I miss Dad."

"You want us to go to the hospital?"

"Yes, I'd like that."

Bertrand has probably lost his stars at the hospital, too. As Caroline climbs the stairs in the B Wing, she wonders if his special permission for afternoon visits will be maintained; her fears are apparently confirmed when Lily stops them at the reception desk.

"Can I have a word with you?" she asks without averting her eyes from her computer screen.

"If it's about the last time . . ." Caroline says threateningly.

"Yes, it's about last time," Lily begins, clicking on the mouse.

Caroline interrupts her and points at Bertrand.

"He has controlled himself for the last four months. Do you know what that means? He's just seven years old! DO YOU KNOW WHAT THAT MEANS?"

Lily turns red, the colour clashes with her pink hair. She lifts up her considerable bulk and steps around the counter, stammering half in English:

"*Calm down*, Mrs Novak. You must understand, the staff got together, *our team had a nice talk*. Come with me for a minute…"

She leaves the reception desk unattended and ushers Caroline into a small room decorated with a large papier-mâché sun and furnished with three plain chairs and two mismatched, rather soft sofas.

"*The Sunshine Room*," she explains, on seeing Caroline's surprise. You haven't been here?"

"No."

"Always open to the families."

She points out, one at a time, the water dispenser, the stack of plastic cups, and the jumbo box of Kleenex. She then instructs Caroline to sit down and, out of nowhere, produces a sticker intended for Bertrand, a symbolic gesture, a peace pipe, which he examines disdainfully at arm's length.

"Mrs Novak, our team had a nice talk…"

"Yes, you just said so."

"*Well*. We discussed the situation."

"You've found a solution to the situation? Because if you have, I'd really like to know…"

"You want a glass of water, Mrs Novak? No? Listen to me. *Please*."

At Lily's sudden firmness, Bertrand clasps Caroline's hand. He can't bear it when people are impatient with her.

"We understand this is *tough*," Lily continues. "A prolonged coma—it's always very *tough*. We thought a private room would be good."

"A private room? You mean in a private clinic?"

"No, no. Here, on the floor. We have three private rooms. We give priority to patients who need to be isolated or …"

The receptionist pauses to glance at Bertrand.

"... patients who are, let's say, at the end of their life. One's just been freed up. We could offer it to your husband, if you wish ... We decided that you qualify under humanitarian reasons, so ..."

"Humanitarian reasons? So...?"

"So there'll be no cost to you."

"Ah?"

Caroline accepts, at once grateful and surprised to be counted among the humanitarian reasons. Lily smiles with all her gapped teeth.

"I'll arrange everything. *A room of one's own*, like they say. You'll see, Mrs Novak, it'll be better like this."

Another room another bed
blue walls.
And blue uniform
leaning over me
blue the compassion
black the drowned one, algae
the lake-bottom fruit.
She sways
splendid body long golden hair
magic comb
phosphorescent eyes.
She suffers, he suffers too. She shivers, he feeds me.
Around us, the great windy plains
and overhead
the sky all white with plenitude.

Taken hostage by his nightmare, Steve turns over so abruptly that the blankets slip to the floor.

A thin layer of ice covers the dark water, an almost invisible film that will break and disperse at the slightest impact.

The purple sky in the twilight. The canoe scrapes against pebbles as it moves away from the shore. The ice breaks up underneath it. The paddle weighs a ton. The loon sings out. First Nations people say that a lake is as deep as its tallest mountain. This one is deep, very deep, too deep. Steve paddles out to the middle. He doesn't want to go there but goes all the same. Once there, he stops. The first stone hits the bottom of the canoe and starts to float. The other stones resurface one by one. They float and sparkle among the cracks in the ice. Steve doesn't want to see what follows, but he stays there. First, the bubbles. Huge bubbles. Next, the mouth. The gaping mouth and the hair. He doesn't want to see her. He can't.

He wakes up screaming, bathed in sweat.

Will he have the same dream every year? He gets up, pours himself a glass of water, takes one gulp, and splashes the rest on his face. He waits for dawn at the window.

The next day, Halloween, Bertrand throws a tantrum because Caroline refuses to let him wear a skeleton costume into the hospital. He doesn't understand what she means by "inappropriate." She has to drag him by the hand, while Laura, preceded by her round belly, guides them down a corridor where they have never set foot.

The nurse opens the door onto a nicely proportioned room with freshly painted blue walls, an armchair in the corner, a TV, and a large window looking out on the perennial parking lot. The drawing of the ambulance running all the red lights has pride of place above the bed, and a box on the nightstand bears the logo of Montreal's most acclaimed chocolatier.

"It's from Monique Seurat, you know, the mother of ..."

"Yes. Martin Bilodeau's mother."

"Can I open it, Mom?"

"Of course. Offer some to Laura, too."

The nurse fights back the urge to retch. Her nausea has come back and there are viscid aspects of her work that weigh heavily on her. She hangs on; it's only a matter of minutes before the evening shift takes over.

"No, they're for you. I'll let you get acquainted with the place. Call if you need anything. The alarm button is next to the bed, as usual. And Lily is at her desk."

"As usual."

She very gently shuts the door.

"Wow," Bertrand remarks as he scans the room.

"Wow is right."

"Dad, have you seen your beautiful room? I'm going to fill it with drawings. I'm going to make a great big bunch of drawings, so they'll have to buy a new wall."

"Bertrand, come look in the bathroom."

"What's in the bathroom?"

"A bath, actually."

"A real bath?"

"Yup."

"Can I take my bath in Dad's bathtub?"

"Err . . ."

"Say yes, say yes!"

Bertrand literally jumps for joy. Caroline doesn't have the heart to deny him this innocent pleasure. With her back turned to the sign forbidding the use of facilities reserved for patients, she pulls out a bottle of shampoo from her swimming bag. As she negotiates the temperature with the antique faucets, Bertrand pours the entire contents of the bottle into the tub and quickly loses control of the suds. He flings his clothes in every direction and blissfully dives in.

"Your shampoo smells so amazing!"

Caroline sniffs loudly as she leans down and daubs her whole face with suds to make him laugh. At this, he launches a shark attack. They don't hear the knocking and are startled when Steve appears, holding a plastic bowl. Bad omen. His unwelcome teammate can't be very far behind.

"Sorry, I knocked but..."

With his husky voice, baggy eyes, and troubled forehead, he cuts a sorry figure.

"I came to tell you to make yourself at home. Looks like you got a head start. I'll come by later."

"No, no, it's all right, there's no problem," Caroline says, giving Bertrand a kiss. "Have fun, big fella, I'm going to see Dad. I'll close the door so you'll stay warm."

She joins Steve near the bed, where he's fidgeting with the bowl.

"I'm really sorry for what happened the other day, really," Steve says.

"It was hard for Bertrand—Martin waking up."

"Just for Bertrand?"

She stares at the tips of her boots.

"It's typical in a case like that," Steve goes on. "I can't believe that Lucille ..."

"Lucille?"

"Nurse Pronovost."

He shakes his head and runs his fingers through his hair in disappointment.

"I shouldn't criticize my colleagues. Is the room okay? It was Dr Sollers's idea."

"I think it'll make a big difference."

"I also had another idea."

"Oh?"

"I was thinking. Remember, in the beginning, you wanted to shave your husband? We do it twice a week."

He proffers the razor, which she eyes like something from outer space. Ditto for the shaving cream and brush.

Emotions come and go—mirages, vapours.

Caroline covers David's cheeks with foam, raises his chin to lather his throat, and starts to realize just how tricky this will be: the slack face, the heavy head. As she shaves his right side, she feels the rough resistance of the stubble against the blade, hears its sandy susurration full of memories. She forgets about Steve until he suggests going against the grain of the beard. At this point, things get complicated: the patient doesn't twist his mouth as required. The gap between his nostrils and upper lip is a problem, the one between the lower lip and the chin, a veritable chasm. Hey, maybe he should keep the moustache.

She must have been thinking out loud, because the nurse asks in surprise:

"The moustache? Has he ever worn a moustache?"

"No. No. No way."

"So what would he say?"

"*Over my dead body.*"

She chuckles and rests her wet hand on David's temple.

"*Over my dead body,*" she repeats as she plants a kiss on his forehead.

Then she notices Steve, who doesn't find this at all amusing.

"Are you okay?"

He shrugs.

"You seem … Hmm, let's say, not okay."

He turns his head toward the window. Caroline concludes that he's part of the large demographic who take care of others but can't accept being taken care of.

"Today is a once-a-year day. Things will be better tomorrow."

"It's your birthday? How old are you?" Bertrand asks excitedly as he bursts out of the bathroom in a robe of suds.

"No, I don't think it's his birthday," Caroline says. "Just a special day."

"Special how?"

"Each year on the same day I turn into a werewolf."

Bertrand gapes at him.

"It's just a joke. Not very funny."

Bertrand puckers his lips.

"I think you're inappropriate."

Quite unexpectedly, Steve explodes with laughter, thus relieving Caroline of a weight she was wholly unaware of.

Mirages, vapours
yet higher up
the same big tranquil sky for each one of us
you just need to raise your eyes.

In the new room, Karine has taken the initiative of bringing a second cork board and covering it with old family photos, in the belief that David needs his roots more than ever. Janek tried to remove the wedding picture of his own parents, to no avail. Each time he steps into the room, the portrait hits him like a harpoon because of the striking resemblance between the two Dawids. He never noticed it before the accident. Ever since, however, David has metamorphosed into his grandfather. This may be due to the way skin stretches over his cartilage, whose contours are hollowing out. Or because his lack of expression lets one's imagination dance freely over his features. It hardly matters. It hurts him. Janek was far too young to see his father decline, wither, disappear. Why must Bertrand endure the same torment?

And then there's the name. Over and over he asks himself: Why did he revive that name? To fill a bottomless hole? To tempt fate?

The truth is, Janek knows precious little about his father. All Dawid ever talked about was the war and Siberia. There the story broke off and it was better not to insist. His mother, however, could be counted on to keep replaying the episodes that meant the most to her. Anna, the first love of a man who thought he'd already seen everything, mythologized their meeting on a crowded train. Back then she could boast about being the secretary to an official from the Arts and Culture department. Young and pretty, she fulfilled her role in the great five-year plan and never left home without her Party membership card.

Dawid, on the contrary, looked much older than he was, with his gnarled hands and furrowed brow. Half his teeth had stayed in the gulag and his lungs were consumed by asthma. But he never looked over his shoulder or lowered his voice at the approach of a stranger. Having suffered too much, lost too much to be afraid, he lived in an indomitable body and kept his head high and hatless. Anna loved his worn face. She loved his rough skin, the prominent veins in his forearms, and his singular gaze: a fire, a well, a fire in a well.

He rented a room in a house full of books in Kazimierz. The war had swallowed up his student years and he compensated by educating himself. In front of his lone window, he piled up works, none of which, strangely enough, were by Lenin, Stalin, or Marx. The first time Anna went there, he offered her some tea and the only chair, which stood against the sink. She preferred to sit on the bed.

What came next, Janek doesn't need to be told—he was there. He remembers Cracow, its pink theatres, its red bricks, and its dissimilar steeples. His father, a small cog in the vast communist machinery, worked in the steel mills of Nowa Huta, a model district. Days of toil and patience were followed by days of toil and patience. Inflation and censorship, propagandist culture, endless lineups for empty bakeries and persistently brown clothes. Yet Dawid climbed the ranks of the closed world of the factory. He found a kind of balance in his family life and a kind of truth in his sons' lives.

The balance was precarious. A minor event was enough to upset it. When the authorities orchestrated another wave of anti-Semitism, his file bobbed up again on the desks of the secret police. Former soldiers of the resistance were kept under constant surveillance; like dustpans, their files picked up whatever one comrade said, thought, suspected about another, or what their performance at the factory might indicate. Of Dawid it was said that he'd aided Jews during the Second World War. That in so doing he had put his compatriots at risk. That he had been seen at the mill in easy conversation with Rafał Abramowicz, who kept the sabbath and was under investigation himself. And while we're on the subject, was Dawid a Zionist? Why the name Dawid, for one thing?

One evening at mealtime, two men came and snatched him away from his pierogis. Janek remembers exactly what happened. After his mother forced him to clean his plate, he vomited everything up; his father came home two days later, with a pressing need for vodka. On orders issued in high places he was demoted to the position of conveyor-belt supervisor. The belt did all the work. As for Anna, she was transferred from the cultural delegation to transportation management and relegated to the role of typist for another secretary. She resented Dawid for this. She resented him for his silence, for his past, for the Third Reich, and for the People's Republic of Poland. Whenever he was around, she made a point of slamming the cupboard doors.

The need for vodka took up more and more space in Dawid's life. Only at work was he sober. He spent the rest of his time at the kitchen table. In the wallpaper's yellow stains he saw the terrified face of the young Jewish boy who had fled the ghetto. Yes, that was where all his troubles had begun. Coal-black eyes, spider hands. He stared at his glass to see something else, and the alcohol conjured up capitalist countries: jeans, Coca-Cola, coffee, pork chops, chewing gum. American cars and gas to fill them up. A steady supply of toilet paper.

His life had basically been a series of prisons: the war, the gulag, the steel mill, the Communist bloc. He didn't even believe in his sons' future anymore. Damned; they too were damned, having landed on the wrong side of the Iron Curtain. Among all the possible illusions, there remained just God and vodka.

God had never supported him. Whereas the vodka . . . Finally, a prison where the prisoner takes leave of himself.

It was 1968. Outside, the masses were on the march. On the far side of his poorly sealed window, comrades protested against the impossible price increases, demanded a measure of free expression, still hoped for a viable form of socialism. Dawid Nowakowski was drunk and solidly welded to his kitchen table. He would not take part in this slice of history. History had cheated him quite enough.

Janek remembers. He was twelve years old. The alcohol, in tandem with asthma, soon carried off his father, and with that loss Janek lost his sense of self-worth. When he later threw himself into the perils of activism, it was to pass the famous character test of soldiers under torture. When he took the risk of exile, it was to give his father a country retrospectively; he thought of him each time he started his Honda Civic. When he baptized a brand new Dawid Nowakowski, it was to grant him a posthumous redemption, to symbolically wrest him from the talons of destiny.

November

From the bottom of the ditch
a vibration rises, obsessive
insistent.
A note, a melody. Tender, sad, sweet tęsknota.
My mother sings in Polish, her hands in the dishwater.
She sings in Polish to get through the dishes faster, to get
through the evening faster, to get through life faster, and with her
back turned she believes no one hears her.

Ten after five. Not like Karine, who's always rigorously punctual. Caroline checks the answering machine yet finds nothing but another of those empty messages from an anonymous caller. She looks out the living-room window. Has her mother-in-law possibly forgotten to turn her clock back? No. There she is turning the corner and then making six attempts to parallel park in a space large enough for two Land Rovers.

Everything she does is marked by the same hesitation. She invariably gets honked at when the light turns green, she takes an inordinate amount of time to slice her vegetables, her French is riddled with pauses in the middle of words, she never comes inside without first wearing down the welcome mat. The one thing that gives her confidence is her piano. This is where she truly exists—in her music.

While Caroline prepares some Assam tea, Bertrand talks at breakneck speed about the ENORMOUS Lego airplane that Dziadzio gave him, along with a promise to take him to Poland one day in an airplane, a REAL one.

"Great. Let me know a little ahead of time and I'll help you pack your bag."

"No, it won't be without you, Mom."

"If I'm invited, I'll go too."

"And Dad?"

"Oh, Bertrand."

"All right, I get it. Can I go play with my Lego set now?"

"Yes, of course, buddy. I can't wait to see your plane ready for takeoff."

Once alone, they share some minor news, after which Karine tilts her head while holding her cup in both hands, a sure sign that a burning question is coming.

"I wanted to ask you . . . Bertrand, does he often draw disturbing pictures?"

"No. Nothing out of the ordinary, I think, for a child his age. Why?"

"He filled an entire pad while he was staying with us."

"And what exactly did he draw?"

"The rusalka."

"The what?"

"The rusalka. You don't know about her?"

"No."

"And here I was thinking he'd heard the story from David."

"So who is this rusalka?"

"She's the spirit of a drowned woman who comes to entice men down to the bottom of a lake."

"Ah. Not quite the kind of story that David tells, err, used to tell."

"Will tell."

"We'll see. Anyway, not the kind of story meant for Bertrand."

"I was surprised too, I must say. David was really traumatized as a child whenever Janek spoke about her. Very poor judgment, actually."

"And how do you know Bertrand was drawing the rusalka? Maybe he was simply drawing a witch."

"No, no. He put in all the details. Golden hair, soaking wet, phosphorescent green eyes, drawn with a marker, no less! And the fruit plate she uses to lure children into her dance and even the comb she keeps to protect herself..."

"Protect against what?"

"The comb keeps her hair from drying."

"What happens if it dries?"

"If it dries she dies."

"But isn't she already dead?"

"Apparently you can die a number of times. In two of the pictures, he drew David approaching the lake. Oh, dear God!"

Karine doesn't want to cry and buries her face in her hands. For a moment, this is all Caroline can see: her long fingers pressing back the unwanted tears, the gold-plated ring. How do you comfort such a discreet woman? She ventures to brush her fingers against her mother-in-law's blouse. Karine instantly collects herself and pulls a tissue from her sleeve.

"This must seem like folklore to you," she says.

"It is folklore, isn't it?"

"Yes, but folklore—how can I put it—is always more than folklore. You know, Janek and I, we married in haste. I was eighteen, he was nineteen. David arrived almost immediately. I'm sure he eventually put two plus two together. Or minus two. Anyway, he did the math."

"You know, these days most people don't care…"

"I know. But those were different times for me, for us. A different culture. I think David knows that he was a family secret."

Karine wipes away a streak of mascara with a corner of her tissue.

"And the rusalka—what does she have to do with all this?" Caroline asks disconcertedly.

"The girls, in the lake. What do you think is the reason they drown themselves?"

"Ah. The scandal."

"Precisely."

Karine makes an effort to swallow the cold tea. Caroline has more questions.

"But where did Bertrand get those images? From his grand-father?"

"No. I spoke to Janek yesterday morning. He swore he'd never mentioned the rusalka to him. He even crossed himself as he leafed through the pad."

"Oh, come on, it's just a bit of colouring. This is all over-blown."

"It's not just some colouring, Caroline. It's our whole past resurfacing. Janek feels guilty."

"What about, exactly?"

"The rusalka is so dangerous during the first week of June that swimming is forbidden. She makes the willow branches dance and she never stops singing."

Caroline doesn't react. The first week of June! David's fall. A child of sin. The song of the willows, the sign of the cross.

"How would you like to meet for lunch on Thursday around noon?" Karine suggests, suddenly regaining her composure.

She takes a bottle of transparent nail polish out of her purse.

196

"Is that to keep me from biting my nails?"

"I tried it with Bertrand over the weekend, and he didn't suck his thumb even once."

Caroline turns the bottle between her fingers, examines it against the light, liking the gleam of the varnish inside. Karine shuts her bag, stands up, and kisses her. As she goes past the living room, she congratulates Bertrand on his airplane assembly but suggests he put the wheels under the fuselage rather than the wings. Bertrand wants to know if the plane can float, but the front door opens and then closes again. The small heels click on the wooden porch, which should have been repainted before the winter.

Undergrowth of tender leaves.

A fine, disappointing rain, the green fragrance of ferns.

They lit a fire.

She has beautiful arched eyebrows, a very fair complexion. He has a square face, good shoulders, overlarge shoes. He gazes at her hungrily. She pretends not to notice.

The forest, the fire, the twilight. She has never been alone with a boy. At least, not on the damp ground or beneath the foliage. She has never lied to her parents.

This is the first time.

But he is a boy, and he wants to see her naked in the glow of the fire. He wants to act like the mosquitoes, unembarrassed and direct. He wants to lie down on her, to cover her with his weight, he wants to feel her grip him inside her, he urgently, obsessively wants to empty himself. He wants. It's vital. Now.

The sun descends. The fire wanes and they let it die. First, the crickets, then the owl.

He kisses her on the mouth. It's at once warm and cool.

She begins to tremble.

He trembles too.

Karine drives off with an unintended squeal of tires and goes the wrong way up 6ᵉ Avenue. Her thoughts carry her back to before David's birth. Her baby boy, her epiphany. The damp undergrowth re-emerges in great detail, teenage Janek, his timid kindness, their hidden betrothal.

She came from a good family, as bourgeois as can be in a communist country. Whenever her future career as a pianist was at stake, her parents always found a way to attract the best teachers. They most certainly would not have wanted a son-in-law from Nowa Huta. So she and Janek would meet secretly, until the day he took her on a long bus ride, beyond the zoo.

They kept on walking despite the looming rain shower. There was something in the air, something mysterious. An intimacy as dense as the woods, as rich as the black soil. She wanted just one thing: to nestle her head against Janek's shoulder, to smell his scent, to feel his warmth, to rest against him. Janek never let go of her hand, clutching it with a kind of fearful hope.

He undressed her clumsily, starting with her blouse. He was perplexed by the buttonholes, mystified by the brassiere. He groped around for the hooks to the point where she finally undid them herself. He spread his jacket on the ground for her. He lifted her skirt.

His movements, his altered state of mind, his jagged breathing took her by surprise. In her body she felt almost nothing. Pressure, pushing, clods of earth under the small of her back, a hard root under her ribs, the folds in the jacket.

She kept her eyes open; his were shut. He poured into her with a moan, which she greeted by hesitantly stroking his cheek. Apologizing, he placed her blouse over her chest and slipped his arm under her neck. When she finally nestled against his shoulder, the hot sperm slid out of her, staining her skirt.

He smelled of fire and undergrowth and sweat. This is the smell she still recalls. Fire, undergrowth, sweat. A supreme moment of ferns and crickets.

That joy—
she believes it's her romance
whereas it's me.
It's me, the prodigious energy injected drop by drop into a body yet to come.
Despite the cold
despite the impending rain, and even if
in some way
I'm going to spoil their youth
they lend me their bodies.
They stay in each other's arms, beneath the clouds. In a few minutes they'll wake up drenched, they'll just barely catch the bus. In a few weeks their angry parents will buy discounted rings.
Tonight, though,
I am invisible and ideal
I am filled with their happiness
I swim in the void where the light selects a form
where the only constant is change.

In the end, Bertrand did catch one of those well-known viruses despite all the antiseptic-soap bottles standing guard. High fever, red blotches, swollen tonsils, vomiting. Caroline never worried about his flus, taking for granted his instinctive ability to get better. This time, however, he looks dangerously pale and terribly weak. She takes time off to stay with him, listen to him breathe, reassemble the Legos that were laid out to dry on the window ledge after the plane sank.

Six days elapse and, with some misgivings, she decides to visit the hospital. If she were infected she'd probably know it by now. And besides, she never catches anything, not even the little colds that let you stay in bed once in a while. As a precaution, she could always don one of those paper masks that give Bertrand the giggles.

When she arrives at the neurology unit, visiting hours are nearly over. Lily is about to close the reception desk but lets Caroline in, as she considers her almost part of the furniture. David's eyes are wide open. His beautiful blue irises are like a stagnant marsh.

"Hi, David. It's me. I've come alone tonight."

Her voice is nearly inaudible under the rustle of the mask.

"I know you're there, David."

She puts on Bach's cello concertos and wipes his chin with a tissue.

"I would so like to know if you can hear me."

The cannula gurgles. Without Bertrand, everything is harder.

"I'll stay with you like this, I won't speak, David, okay? We'll get some rest together."

The minutes go by slowly. A wheelchair squeaks in the hallway, a door closes, a door opens, an orderly looks for another orderly, a cart rolls by. Someone talks, gives a short laugh, pauses. Nurse Pronovost berates a mail clerk.

David moves his lips, which makes his lack of speech even more conspicuous. It suddenly occurs to Caroline that she hasn't seen him naked since the accident. She didn't dare when Bertrand was present or when the staff was liable to show up. And he may be too heavy for her to be able to undress him.

The idea swiftly takes root.

To see David's skin. To touch it.

Why not?

She draws the sheet away from his protruding knees, his stiff calves, his feet turned in toward each other. She folds back the hospital gown, exposing the shrunken thighs that make his knees look so knobby. She runs her fingertips over a rib and comes across the bulging scar from the splenectomy. He swallows. She disregards this. She returns to the thighs, contemplates the slip-on diaper. Her husband's penis is no doubt asleep just like him, sheltered in its cocoon, harnessed with an unsightly catheter.

David, whose slightest touch or conspiratorial glance could arouse her. Who knows her by heart and instructed her so tenderly in the art of letting go. David, who knew exactly how to hold her, not too firmly or too lightly, even in his sleep. All these months Caroline has been in a profound state of numbness, where the very idea of desire seems as distant as the Milky Way. The woman yearning for a man's warmth—she doesn't know if she can find her again. If she ever again will plunge into that altered state, into the violent sweetness of a messy bed.

> *Something warm moves over my stomach. A huge buffalo is leaning over me, licking me with its big, rough tongue.*
> *Behind it, a massive mountain chain streaked with amber and sulphur yellow*
> *purple patches where trees still grow*
> *blue patches higher up, under the eternal snows.*
> *A challenge that can't be refused.*
> *I will climb. As high as possible. Once the buffalo has left.*
> *For the moment*
> *its burning breath*
> *its noisy breathing*
> *its horns reassure me, who knows why.*

Three sharp knocks on the door.

Caroline straightens up, mask around her neck, cheeks aflame. Steve's arrival right in the middle of her musing on desire embarrasses her no end.

"Ah, Caroline? Everything okay?"

"Yes."

"What were the two of you doing? Am I disturbing you?"

She is paralyzed.

"I can come back later."

She frowns.

"Should I come back later?"

She shakes her head.

"Bertrand has the flu."

This is all she can think of saying.

"You came anyway? It's better to stay home if you're carrying a virus."

Caroline replaces her mask.

"Sorry, Steve, for doing my best to make sure you catch it too."

"I'm inoculated. Is Bertrand very sick?"

"Last week was hard, but yesterday he put up a fuss to get some Smarties."

"He'll get through it."

Steve scratches his forearm. Caroline adjusts the elastic of her mask five times.

"I wanted to see David naked," she finally admits.

"Naked?"

"Naked."

"He's pretty heavy. Need some help?" he asks, as if the request was perfectly natural. "Here, put these on."

He hands her a pair of gloves that are as sterile as they are disconcerting.

"Grab him by the shoulder, okay? On three, we turn him on his side. One, two... That's it."

Caroline follows Steve's instructions somewhat awkwardly, and, as if by magic, David lies naked before her. Under the harsh fluorescent light his complexion makes no sense. She reaches her hand out toward the fuzz that radiates like a sun around his navel, but stops midway out of inhibition.

"I'll leave you alone," Steve says. "Ten minutes."

He slips out of the room. Caroline feels like taking off the gloves but resists the temptation. If she infected David, she wouldn't be able to forgive herself. With both hands flat against his stomach, she strokes him against the grain of his body hair. She feels the pulse throbbing in her fingertips. She ranges over his chest and then over his entire body, not missing a single centimetre of precious skin. His warmth is undiminished, but his familiar scent has disappeared under the powders and creams. She massages him a little, finding him by turns sturdy and vulnerable.

This intimacy, almost an infraction, leaves her shaken. Over the years, she maintained the illusion that David's body belonged to her a little. David himself did nothing to dispel the mirage. This is no longer the case. David's body has retreated along with him into the mystery of his deep sleep. Without the tacit consent that used to be there, Caroline isn't entitled to it anymore. Caressing him, she to some extent finds him again but loses him even more.

Caroline.
Maybe she's drawing a map of the heavens
a new constellation.
Her hand hesitates and envelops me, her hand is deeply
touched.
She detaches a piece of the sky from her drawing
and rolls it to me as a gift.
At one end is a flame.
She tells me she wants to live. I say me too.

Steve, absurdly stationed in the corridor two steps away from the room, is thinking. A long time ago, he taped a quotation inside his locker: "You only say a proper goodbye to what you have experienced to the fullest."

The statement sustains him, but it bugs him too. He wants to heal. He isn't healing. Did he experience to the fullest what he had to experience? He believes so. Firmly, absolutely. And yet, the goodbye falls short. When he changes clothes after his shift, the quote often provokes a heartfelt "bullshit." Out of a sort of anguished perseverance, he keeps sticking on more tape so that the words have practically been laminated onto the metal.

The idea of proper goodbyes is precisely what Caroline is putting into practice now. Her husband isn't dead, but he will never be the same again. She knows it. She's working on her bereavement. Defiant at first, wrapped up in her anger, barricaded inside her doubts, she became receptive, then involved, even intuitive. In a sense, Steve has learned a lot from her. Maybe he could pass the quotation on to her, a noble way to get rid of it. But he'd have to give her the whole locker along with it.

Ten minutes go by. He knocks and enters with an almost admiring smile. Together, they get David dressed again, and his curled-up hands go back to their niche, close to his heart.

"Thank you, Steve. Very much. But if Nurse Pronovost were to find you wasting your time..."

"I'm inoculated against that too. Listen, Caroline..." he adds in a low voice, drawing her far away from the bed. "You're going to find this a little weird, but usually, when we undress him, he blushes."

"...Excuse me?"

"He blushes. Erythema. It's a common reaction to embarrassment."

"Not tonight."

"That's right."

"Are you saying he recognized me?"

"That's your call. Say hi to Bertrand for me."

Right then the door swings open and hits him on the forehead.

"I was looking for you, big guy. Mrs Guérin rang forty times and it's time for Mr Lévesque's meds."

"I'm coming."

"Yes, indeed."

There's sarcasm in Nurse Pronovost's voice. She lets her co-worker out and then stands in the doorway for a moment, giving Caroline a long, inscrutable look.

Karine has heard about a new café near the Jean-Talon Market and suggests that she and Caroline meet there for lunch on Thursday, a rendezvous that was put off for two weeks because of Bertrand's flu. They choose a table near the window. Outside, people are strolling, smoking, jogging, kissing, leaving the indoor market holding large bags with celery leaves sticking out. Some brave cyclists carve furrows into the melting snow. Karine glances appreciatively at her daughter-in-law's nails; she has stopped biting them and is getting used to the nail polish. Karine is gloating. She believes that the smallest victories bring the greatest satisfaction. But she also has a major victory to report. Once they've ordered their warm goat-cheese salads, she starts in with an air of mystery:

"You know, the rusalka…"

"Oh, no, not the rusalka!"

"Wait, wait! Bertrand was a huge help."

"How so?"

"His rusalka put an end to Janek's skepticism."

"Really?"

"Listen to this. After the business with the drawings, he stopped coming with me to the hospital. I could clearly see that he was ruminating under his moustache. Then one night, before falling asleep, he told me he'd mulled over the matter and could find just one explanation: Bertrand's images came from David. He believes that, in his coma, David communicates with

Bertrand. He even believes David tried to communicate with him *through* Bertrand.

Caroline's jaw drops.

"I haven't felt so near the hand of God since the Pope's visit to Cracow," Karine says emotionally.

Caroline is unmoved.

"There was nothing left of our Poland," her mother-in-law goes on, wiping a tear from the corner of her eye. "A handful of poets and playwrights, our church spires. Our religion was a form of resistance."

Caroline makes a mental note to find her some water-proof mascara. While she manages to take an interest in the Buddha, described by Marie as "an extreme example of our human potential," she refuses to accept Karine's God and his supreme omnipotence. Her mother-in-law, on the other hand, never goes to the hospital without dropping into the non-denominational chapel. She socializes with the spiritual care provider and has even invited her to dinner. David repeatedly said there was no way to understand them, but that they deserved respect. Karine and her baroque faith, her cotton handkerchiefs. Janek and his silence, his icy gaze. They could visit his parents on Sundays, eat borscht, invite them on vacations along the lower St Lawrence, but that was all.

"Well, anyway," Karine continues, arching her lovely eyebrows, "Janek the convert is beside himself. He feels guilty."

"Again? Guilty for what, this time?" Caroline asks, having noticed how, since the beginning of the coma, every member of the family has found a way to blame themselves.

"For believing, until now, that his son was, in his own words, 'a vegetable.' For shortening all our visits, for ridiculing me every time I spoke to him. Now, imagine what happens next. Janek musters his courage, even wears a tie to go to the hospital, he leans against the bed, puts his fingertips on David's shoulder, and ..."

Karine chokes up and instinctively reaches for her handkerchief.

"Imagine, Janek asks David to forgive him... Imagine ... David moans and turns his head toward Janek, his mouth open as if about to speak."

Caroline, too, is crying openly. Bemused, the server waits with the warm goat-cheese salads balanced on his arm.

"It's extraordinary, Caroline. It's as if Janek has just brought David back to life. Never mind about Dr Sollers's pencil. I realize that, in reality, we're actually at the same point. The only difference is that, in his father's head, David is alive. And that..."

Karine wrings her handkerchief.

"If he does die, it will be as a living person, do you understand?"

"Completely," says Caroline, sliding back in her chair.

The salad glides under her nose. She eyes it in confusion. She scarcely remembers having ordered it.

Finally standing so light
no more mass.
Before me a cropped field
haystacks like soldiers.
Up there, bell towers balconies slanted roofs
above the last roofs, nothing but mineral, jagged summits wild
and bare.
The grass yields under my heel.

Bertrand has perched himself on a chair to watch the big black cloud threatening to burst at any moment over the parking lot. He's hoping for a nice snowstorm—pure utopia. Caroline, meanwhile, strokes David's hand. His eyes are half open, his features relaxed. She has just helped him to swim; at least, that's what she believes.

Last night, Marie called while their mother was in the shower, giving them a good forty minutes. Her stay in St Augustine is no picnic. "Still, there are the beautiful vestiges of colonial Spain," if you're looking for positives. Otherwise, she feels "inadequate, incompetent, imperfect." She wonders about her capacity to forgive. "Everything looks easy, seen from Tibet, but enlightenment 'on the rocks' is a different kettle of fish." She'll be coming back soon.

The cloud shatters, releasing a horribly loud hail shower. Bertrand squashes his nose against the windowpane.

"You know, Mom, sometimes I'm amazed that Dad can still sleep with all this noise."

"You're right, it's incredible. You know what amazes me?"

"No, what?"

"I forgot to bring an umbrella."

"Doesn't matter. We can run."

"Yes, okay. We'll wait a little while, just to see if it slacks off."

Steve shows up in the meantime. From the way he's standing in the doorway, it's easy to see he has no business in the room.

"Hi Steve," Bertrand says. "Have you looked outside?"

"Yeah, I have, actually."

For someone who always knows what to do, he appears quite hesitant.

"Actually, I wanted to tell you, Laura had an ultrasound this morning, so we traded shifts."

"Cool," Bertrand says, though he doesn't really see why this matters.

"So?" Caroline asks, all at once uneasy.

"So I just got off work, and as soon as I change my clothes I can give you a lift, if you like. We're going in the same direction."

"How do you know where we live?" Bertrand asks in surprise.

Steve answers while looking at Caroline.

"I have access to your father's chart and it includes his address."

"Ah. What kind of car do you have? What colour?"

"A grey Renault. Nothing special."

"That's okay, we'll come with you anyway."

"Yeah?"

"No," Caroline cuts in.

"Hey Mom, you just said you forgot your umbrella."

"No."

"But Mom, you're always talking about ride-sharing…"

"Maybe to the Metro?" Steve suggests.

Caroline arches an eyebrow and repeats:

"No. Thank you."

Steve goes away. Caroline nibbles a fingernail despite the vile polish. A three-block ride in this doomsday weather—did the offer have strings attached? Yes? No? Bertrand tears himself away from the window.

"Can we go now, Mom? I'm hungry."

In a sudden frenzy, Caroline hurriedly gets him into his coat and collects their things. But instead of heading toward the door, she steps up to the window. There are two small, grey Renaults not very far apart in the parking lot. She pulls Bertrand by the hand.

"Come on, we'll scoot down the stairs, the way you like."

"Huh?"

"We'll play a joke on Steve."

Outside, the hail has given way to a downpour. They decide to wait next to the Renault with an 'I Climbed Mount Washington' sticker on the rear window. Bertrand puts his schoolbag over his head.

"It's raining, Mom."

"I know. Steve will take us to the Metro so we don't get too wet."

"Mom?"

"What?"

"I'm already wet."

They finally see him running with long strides between the cars. He's wearing his hospital uniform and rain boots and is carrying a large garbage bag. Some distance away, he fiddles with his keys and it's the other Renault that blinks. Caroline feels silly and considers stealing away, but Bertrand charges toward the car to get there first. When Steve catches sight of him, he joins the race, making sure to lose by a nose.

They settle into the car without a word, all of them dripping wet.

"No kids' seat," Bertrand says after a while, by way of reproach.

"Sit on your schoolbag," Caroline suggests.

"I can't find the seat belt," Bertrand whines, as he struggles with the garbage bag, which takes up two-thirds of the back seat.

"Wait, I'll give you a hand."

Steve steps out of the car, leans in to push aside the garbage bag, finds a cushion for Bertrand, and, with some difficulty, eventually fishes the belt out from between the seat and the backrest. As Steve straightens up to close the door, Bertrand shouts:

"Your bum is soaked!"

"Bertrand, please," Caroline intervenes.

"He's right," Steve says in the boy's defence while he starts the car.

"And, besides, why are you still wearing your hospital pyjamas?"

"Because the person whose locker sits on top of mine let their shower gel leak out. My clothes are all sticky, so I put them in the big bag."

"Oh, that's why it smells funny."

"What does it smell of?"

"A lady."

"A lady, eh? Well, it's someone you know, Bertrand. Guess who."

"Yes! I know! I know!" Bertrand yells excitedly. "It's Nurse Pronovost. It smells of Nurse Pronovost!"

Steve glances in the rear-view mirror.

"You're amazing! It is indeed Nurse Pronovost."

Caroline, clearly impressed as well, turns around and pats him on the leg.

"Well done, my dear Watson."

"Steve, what do you smell of?"

"Well, I dunno. Iodine, I suppose."

"I like that. Why does Nurse Pronovost keep shower gel in her locker? Does she take bubble baths too sometimes?"

"No, she goes to the hospital swimming pool and takes a shower afterward."

"She likes to do laps?"

"It does her good."

"Why?"

"Her legs are always hurting her. She even spent part of last year in a wheelchair."

"A wheelchair! How was she able to push other people's wheelchairs?"

"She took a break from work."

"It must be an almost impossible line of work if your legs are always aching," Caroline notes, recognizing a possible explanation for the chronic surliness.

"I know this may be hard to believe, but apparently it's the only one she likes."

Steve knows a lot about Lucille's mitigating circumstances. Among other things, he knows that she works evenings so she can mind her daughter's twins in the morning, that her husband has been unemployed for five years, and that her youngest son is forever threatening to drop out of school.

"Here's the Metro station. I guess this is where we part company?"

Caroline musters a considerable amount of humility:

"Actually, if we're really headed in the same direction, maybe we could go all the way home?"

Nothing is said during the whole second half of the ride. The lady's scent inundates the car interior. Bertrand can barely see outside. November gradually drains the days of their light and everything is blurred by the torrential rain. Caroline looks at Steve's hands and the leather bracelet hiding the dial of his watch. She notices that when they're together, the silence doesn't feel awkward the way it did before.

He stops in front of their house and leaves the motor running. Their house, the front yard strewn with dead leaves, the darkened windows, the peeling front porch.

December

Bertrand made himself a calendar "to have a better way of waiting for Aunt Marie," and now he draws a pirate on it each morning. He finished the last one today, and, after he got home from school, helped Caroline make the bed and dust off the Buddha. Dinner is ready, the table set.

When he hears the horn, Bertrand runs to the door and opens it just in time to see Sandra and Marie climbing out of the car through the trunk.

"Why are you …"

"Well, you know, bubble gum and bailing wire, that's Sandra for you."

Marie throws herself into their arms.

"You smell of apple pie, Carol."

"What about me?" Bertrand asks.

"You? Chickpeas!"

It's been a long time since the kitchen has seen such cheerful talk. Even the news about David is positive: private room, drawings all over the walls, communication exercises, a third urinary-tract infection successfully treated. Bertrand is able to read him the sports page now. He even turned Martin Bilodeau's awakening into a cause for hope. Marie launches into an account of the adventures of "Lorrie" ("so much cooler than Lorraine"), while peeling off layers of clothing one after another in reaction to her usual temperature spike.

When it's time for the apple pie, she starts to wrestle with her backpack, eventually extracting two packages wrapped in gold paper. Bertrand first unwraps a black vinyl coat fitted with huge shoulder pads, some forty pockets, and snap fasteners.

"Dad will love this, that's for sure."

Caroline silently resolves to throw the contraption in the washing machine or to forget it at the skating rink. Meanwhile, Bertrand has gone ahead and unwrapped the gift meant for his mother. He dumps page after page torn from a fashion magazine onto the floor and finally holds up a gigantic necklace of polished shells. Caroline buries her face in her hands.

"It'll look pretty near the bathtub," Sandra assures her.

"Provided you cut the string," Marie advises.

Last village before the climb
roofs aflame, pink and blue. The roofs of simple, coloured life,
house-church-mill.
The purple sky closes in on them
pulverizes them.
Ahead
several paths—which to choose?
The steepest one, to my right.
Afterward
I know
there will be no way back.

Marie hums as she steps out of the shower. A towel twisted over her hair, another around her hips, bare-breasted, she rummages through her bags for a clean T-shirt. While her sister was away, Caroline often caught herself envying the nook she'd created for herself: the triangle of Indian cloth, the lotus flower, the candle, the Buddha, the patchouli. Almost nothing, and yet totally Marie.

But when it comes to her own house, Caroline finds that it just isn't her. There was a time when she lived in brightly coloured slums and used her books as nightstands. Now her books are piled up in the cellar, her decor is perfect for the sports pages. She would like to retake possession of the place, but she pictures David grappling with motor impairments and faulty memory, in desperate need of familiar markers.

She was waiting for Marie to come back to discuss this with her. Her sister doesn't answer right away; first she applies skin cream to her legs, then discovers a wrinkled blouse she had completely forgotten. She opens it at arm's length to have a better look, blithely exhibiting herself in front of the window.

"We'll start with the paint," she suddenly announces. "Next, we'll get rid of the runner on the stairs—what's underneath? We'll choose new doors for the kitchen cabinets, and you can afford a nicely stripped oak table with a beeswax finish—I know a fabulous antiques dealer. We'll put up shelves for your books, and if we run out of shelves we'll use books to stack other books. We'll put books everywhere. We'll buy bolts of coloured cloth and I'll order real goose-down cushions from Béatrice. We'll hang chiming mobiles in the front hall and glass crystals in the windows that will project rainbows when it's sunny, and we'll win Bertrand over to fuchsia-coloured shower curtains with winged fairies."

The intention is good, but the results disastrous. Bertrand, who interprets the slightest stroke of a paint brush as an erasure of his father, loudly rejects every phase of the operation. Redecorating turns into guerilla warfare. He pours a gallon of paint down the toilet and hides the toolbox in a far corner of the backyard. In the end, Caroline confines herself to changing the shower curtain.

It's too soon for their life to change. They don't really have permission. Everything still happens in the present tense.

The present, they say, is the key to happiness.

Though you still need to find the lock.

Marie then turns her attention to the hospital cafeteria, where the selection of hot beverages leaves much to be desired and the coffee tastes of dishwater. She urges the head of staff to offer Ayurvedic herbal teas or organic barley but comes up against an uncooperative administration. Seeing that the cafeteria is resistant to her radical vision, she resigns herself to bringing her own teabags in her purse.

Tonight she arrived early, coming directly from a sesshin at the Zen Centre. While waiting for Caroline, she walked through the neurological unit, hugging the walls and listening at doors. She has a passion for perching like a bird close to other people's lives. Then she went down to the cafeteria. She's sniffing her Chai when Caroline finally shows up with ruddy cheeks and damp hair, famished from doing laps in the pool, her coat dripping with snow.

"Sorry, I missed the Metro. Have you been here long?"

"Yes, I went upstairs to reconnoitre."

"Ah," Caroline replies distractedly, her blood sugar critically low.

"You know, I think the nursing staff is fantastic. We don't always appreciate their impact on the patients and their families…"

Realizing that her sister's attention is wandering all the way to the dessert section, Marie pulls a crushed cereal bar from the bottom of her bag.

"That's true," Caroline says as she hungrily snatches the bar. "Me too, I keep forgetting to thank them."

"Gratitude, unfortunately, is considered old-fashioned."

"Are you criticizing me?"

"No, no."

"Lecturing, at least?"

"Oh! Would I dare do that?"

"Yes."

"Okay, let's change the subject. I caught a glimpse of Nurse Pronovost before you arrived."

"Oh? And your assessment of the nursing staff hasn't changed?"

"I get the feeling she has issues."

"Apparently she has bad pain in her legs. I must admit, she doesn't take up too much of my mental space."

"I also noticed that the girls do a lot of talking behind Steve's back…"

"The girls?"

"The nurse's aides. They all have eyes for him. It appears that Brigitte, the night-shift nurse, arrives early only Monday to Wednesday, when he's on duty."

"I gather you're specializing in third-floor gossip."

"Not at all. It's just that I think talking to Steve is much nicer than talking behind his back."

It irritates Caroline to realize that this comment annoys her, and she falls into an automatic sequence of unpleasant thoughts: Steve chats with Marie, Steve, like everyone else, finds Marie attractive, even fascinating, Steve invites Marie for a drink, Marie … Stop, Carol.

"He reminds me a little of Christian Rimbault," her sister adds dreamily. "The same calmness, maybe. I think it's worth the effort to get closer to him."

Caroline coughs. An oat flake stuck in her throat. There

you go. Marie has discovered the Québécois equivalent of her Tibetan guru. Predictable.

"In that case, you should get closer," she retorts, nervously gathering together the table crumbs.

"But Carol, I mean you. What have I got to do with it? You can trust him to help you concretely—that's all I'm trying to say."

Caroline rubs her hands together to get rid of the sticky crumbs.

"Got it."

"He also has this latent sadness, don't you find?"

"Very latent, maybe," Caroline answers, and thinks back to the annual appearance of the werewolf.

"He may need help too."

"Aren't you extrapolating a little?"

"Just a little."

Marie smiles mischievously behind her cup of tea. Caroline contemplates her own cup of dishwater.

Dense unfathomable forest no markers. Blackberry thorns rotten trunks. Branches berries leaves roots vegetabledecadence blockedroad. The trees swallow the sky. Ants climb up inside my pants. The ground its sugary rich smell, full overfull.

There's a vision in my blindness.

"Dad, I have something to tell you. Listen up: Mom changed the shower curtain. I don't know where she found it, but there's fairies in a pink sky, it's awful, I'm sorry, I couldn't keep her from doing it. She looks happy, though, she even sings sometimes, like before. I didn't want to change anything. Everything exactly the way it was, Dad, so when you come back you'll have no trouble recognizing our house."

Caroline steps out of the washroom, and Bertrand changes the topic:

"Do you understand, Dad? We may get a white Christmas, or maybe not, we'll see. It'd be a shame if you're still asleep on Christmas Day, because we could unwrap the gifts together..."

"Bertrand," Caroline cuts in, "would you like to go skating soon at the park in Little Italy?"

Bertrand's face lights up like the lanterns in that very park. "Today?"

"Today it's already late, but maybe tomorrow?"

Three knocks on the door. Caroline stiffens. Until now she has reacted to Marie's advice by avoiding Steve altogether. It didn't occur to her that the snow would bring him back with the same offer as before and that this time it would be even harder to turn down.

"Come in, Steve!" Bertrand shouts.

"Are you sure it's me?" Steve asks from behind the door.

"Yes, sure, it's you."

He comes in.

"How did you know?"

"Easy: Laurel and Hardy scratch on the door with their fingernails, Nurse Pronovost walks in without knocking, and you, well, it's just you."

"Okay, that sounds empirical enough."

"Who's M.P. Rickle?"

"Empirical. As in, being observant. I just came to let you know I'm leaving early today because of the storm."

"But you just arrived, didn't you?"

"Lucille heard the weather report and arranged for someone to replace me."

"Lucille?" Bertrand asks.

"Nurse Pronovost," Steve and Caroline answer in unison.

"But Nurse Lucille could have called you on the phone, right?" Bertrand says.

"No, not really. I was already on the road."

"What about your mobile?"

"Don't have one."

"What?" Bertrand, unable to imagine any adult without a mobile phone, is shocked.

"Anyway," Steve goes on, "I can give you a lift, if you like. Public transit is going to be hell."

"Cool," says Bertrand, who would very much like to avoid a bus packed with wet overcoats.

Steve waits for Caroline's answer, but she's busy trying to figure out whether he, too, needs help or not, and says nothing. His calm demeanour makes him hard to read.

"Perfect. In five minutes," she hears herself say as if from a distant shore.

Surprised at having instantly received a positive answer, Steve abruptly leaves the room. He comes back five minutes later and finds them with their hoods on. Bertrand looks him up and down.

"You're funny when you're dressed like a real person."

"Funny how?" Steve asks. He has just a grey hoodie on.

"Like, I dunno, just normal."

"Normal, eh? Thanks, that's nice to hear."

"You think it's normal to go out in the middle of a snow-storm without a coat, Bertrand?" Caroline says.

"Well, at least my hair is dry," Steve shoots back.

"Mom swims nearly every day, I'm a really great swimmer too, how about you, Steve, do you like to swim?"

"I used to, yes," Steve says, without elaborating further.

"What about skating? Would like to come skating in Italy with us?"

"Um…"

"I could lend you Dad's skates."

"Okay, shall we go?" Caroline cuts in, obviously ill at ease.

As they walk past the nursing station, Lily tears herself away from her computer screen. The sight of them leaving together intrigues her, and, after a rather humdrum day, she rushes to share the news with the whole planet. Among her potential audience, she pictures in particular the two little nurse's aides—the pests!—and gloats in advance over their disappointment.

All anyone can see outside are snowflakes swirling in the bright headlights. Steve finds his car almost by accident. While he clears his windshield with a broom and Caroline does her best to help out with the back of her mitten, Bertrand examines the inside of the vehicle. An assortment of objects are jumbled together: snowshoes, a thermos bottle, a hammer, and, whoa, an axe. Is this the Renault of a serial killer?

"What's this in your car?"

"This what?"

"This."

"It's an axe."

"Why are you carrying an axe? In your car?"

"Sometimes I chop wood for my neighbour. She just turned a hundred and two."

"I can count to a hundred and two. One two three …"

Bertrand is still counting when the trusty winter tires finally flatten the wet snow. But he suddenly breaks off because, despite the poor visibility, he glimpses something that sends him into a frenzy.

"Hey! That's Jonathan Louvain, in his father's arms!"

"Where?"

"Right there. Wait, Steve, wait!"

"Bertrand, we're not going back to the parking lot. We just left," Caroline objects. "Anyway, you can't see a thing."

"But Mom, what's the matter with Jonathan Louvain? Why is his father taking him to the hospital?"

"I don't know, Bertrand."

"But why?"

"No idea."

"But Mom, are there other kids from my class in the hospital?"

"Bertrand..."

She spends the rest of the ride trying to allay Bertrand's fears about finding himself in a hospital bed, too; if that happened, would his mother stay with him all night and give him Pringles for breakfast? Caroline, meanwhile, has been thinking she would rather Marie not see her getting out of Steve's car, and is looking for an excuse not to pull up in front of her house. All she can come up with is the suggestion that they stop off at the corner deli for some cake, "a nice piece of bread pudding to cheer up Bertrand." She invites Steve, who declines because he needs to get going before the brunt of the storm hits.

Before she has time to ask where he lives, the deli comes into view. The plow has banked the snow up on either side of the street, so Steve drops them off in the middle of the roadway. They say goodbye, she, displeased with herself for having promised bread pudding an hour before dinner, and Bertrand, pretty happy about how his afternoon is working out. Clambering over the snow bank, they can make out through the deli's misty windows Marie, stuffed with lemon pie, waving to them with a smirk.

That night, Caroline goes out for a walk. The falling snow has turned to powder and melts gently against her cheeks. The swish of tires from the few cars on the road is muffled. The big snowblower's flashing lights tinge the sky an opaque orange. She walks with her head down, her mittens stuffed inside her pockets, her hat pulled tight over her ears. The wind blurs her footprints behind her.

Snow and night.

The bluish carpet, neither dark nor pale, soft as down, covers the sidewalks, stairs, hedges, handrails; it smooths out the bumps, rounds off the right angles. Everything is upholstered in white, like prose sheathed in poetry. Caroline walks slowly, her soles making a hollow sound. A question keeps snapping at her heels, a question she refuses to confront. She has David's scarf on and finds it too tight.

In the morning, Bertrand insists on wearing his big yellow ski goggles to school. He tries in vain to pull his snow pants over his boots and hunts around for his other mitten. His still-damp scarf has slid under the radiator. Caroline finds another, hand-knitted and riddled with broken stitches. They've probably just missed the bus.

"Goddamn country!"

"Mom, don't say that. It's beautiful."

"You're right. Sorry."

He's just found his mitten, but puts it on before zipping up his coat and now he's unable to take hold of the puller. Marie drifts nonchalantly into their field of vision in her dressing gown and has the nerve to complain that the snowblower kept her awake. Of course, she won't be the one to shovel the front walk. Caroline is starting to sweat in her heavy coat.

"Mom, do you feel like pulling me in the toboggan to the bus stop?"

"No, Bertrand, I don't. You weigh almost more than me!"

"Dad pulled me all winter last year."

"You've grown since then."

"Do you think he could still pull me?"

"Um..."

"Well, I think he could."

The zipper snags on the scarf. Caroline is about to lose her temper but manages to get a grip at the last minute. It's not Bertrand's fault that the nagging question followed her all the way to her bedroom, curled up at the foot of the bed, and woke her with a start in the morning.

Who's to blame, then?

No one.

As the days grow shorter, they go by more quickly. The snow stubbornly piles up. It carves hills on the window ledges and mounts impossible obstacles along the sidewalks. Marie keeps a close eye on Caroline, looking for signs and certitudes while waiting for the right moment. One night, as they settle in for a dangerously addictive TV series, she says it point-blank:

"Listen, Carol, I think I've stayed here long enough. I'll be leaving soon."

Caroline, snug as a bug until now, sits up at all once.

"The couch is uncomfortable, right? You'd like to sleep in my room? I should have realized earlier."

"No, no, the couch is perfect. I've stayed long enough, that's all, there's no other reason. You're open-hearted, your son goes to sleep and gets dressed on his own, he cleans up his spilt milk and makes his bed without being asked. You changed the shower curtain. Intensive care is behind us."

"What does that mean?"

"It means that no matter what happens, you'll get through this."

"You think?"

"I'm sure."

"Oh, Marie. When are you leaving?"

"Next week."

"But where are you going? India? Tibet?"

"Brossard."

"The suburbs?"

"I'm going to help Béatrice with her children's clothing project. It interests me. And that way I'll be nearby. I mean, if you ever need burnt macaroni or a runny omelette. . . Don't cry, Carol, you're ready. I'll leave you my Buddha."

"What about your job?"

"I'm giving up my career in felt."

"But you'll be here for Christmas Eve?"

"Of course. I'll even sleep on the couch if you make me a gin and tonic."

"Or two."

"I'll sleep on the couch anyway."

They come together in a long hug.

"Thank you, Marie. For everything. Thanks a million."

Christmas, it turns out, will be not very white, but not exactly brown. The snow melts, blows in again, then melts again. "Whitish," according to Laura. "Shitty," according to Nurse Pronovost. From David's room, the cars in the parking lot seem to be covered with a bride's veil. Thanks to the head nurse's kindness, Caroline has managed to organize a little party in the hospital on the Wednesday afternoon between the office party at the library and the one for the staff in David's unit.

Bertrand has made paper garlands, one for the house and another for David's room, which were linked together in his imagination. He even made sure the sequence of colours was identical in both. There are Christmas songs playing on the CD player. Janek is serving glasses of ginger ale, while Bertrand's ten fingers are deep inside the jar of maraschino cherries. Caroline is showing Marie the greeting card she received from Lorraine, a big lobster with a Santa Claus hat: *Merry Christmas and a Happy New Year. May All Your Wishes Come True.*

Through an unfortunate mistake, Karine slices a piece of Christmas log for David, the one with the plastic axe. She puts it aside for the first staff member who shows up. The lucky person is none other than Nurse Pronovost, who walks in without knocking just as the exchange of gifts gets underway. She reluctantly consented to the whole business without expecting either the merry hullabaloo that greets her or the beribboned package Karine presents her with. Lavender bubble bath, chosen by Bertrand, "to relax her." The nurse lets out a nervous giggle that ends in a grumble:

"Turn the volume down a notch on the noise machine, eh, you're already quite a crowd as it is."

She motions with her chin toward David, who remains impassive.

"He's going to find this tiring."

Bertrand is unintimidated: "Nurse Pronovost, can you tell Steve we have a present for him too? Tell him it was me who chose it."

"He's busy right now."

She leaves them to their exchange. Marie found a large shawl for Karine, hand-woven from pure mohair wool, which cost her a whole pay cheque. Karine, forever sensitive to the cold, wraps it gingerly around her shoulders, twists her body to look at it, and is so touched by this kindness that she decides Marie deserves her Biblical name. She herself chose two newly published novels for Caroline, who, for her part, bought Janek a pair of leather gloves. Janek, after agonizing for an hour or two, wrote Marie a cheque, which amply covers the price of the shawl. They all chipped in to give Bertrand the Lego airport set, and he shuts himself in the washroom to build it then and there.

Steve makes his entrance as Karine obstinately tries to slip a plush giraffe toy for infants, the softest thing she could find, into David's hand. Bertrand pounces on the starry blue package that he wrapped himself at the cost of an entire roll of tape. While Steve, examining it, wonders how to unwrap it without resorting to surgical instruments, Bertrand, bursting with impatience, shouts:

"It's socks for Crocs! For your Crocs!"

"Wow. Thanks," Steve says, noticing at the same time how Janek, at the far end of the room, presses his cheek against David's and gently strokes his hair.

After ripping the paper open with his teeth and trying on the socks, which are a perfect fit, Steve has to get moving. Time is ticking away and he has work to do. But there's a gift waiting for Bertrand, too, from the nursing staff. Steve struggled to win them over to the idea of a baseball mitt, because Nurse Pronovost insisted on sweets. Ultimately, with everyone turned against her, she backed out of the group present and imposed her own. Steve is acting as customs officer; he wants to get Caroline's approval before letting Bertrand overindulge.

Caroline follows him to the Sunshine Room. The decor in the little lounge seems less dreary to her than the last time. It's almost inviting. In a corner of the room, hidden under a large padded armchair, lies a cardboard box overflowing with presents, as if the unit had drawn on a special holiday budget.

Steve crouches down to rummage through the box. Caroline watches the back of his inclined neck, the roots of his dark hair, and realizes she will never walk fast enough, the night will never be cold enough, or the snow white enough for her to shake off this emotion. The Sunshine Room becomes suffused with a pleasant, undeniable, suspicious tension that she'd like to dispel with an innocuous comment, but her mind is blank.

"Your father-in-law seems to be doing remarkably well," Steve says without getting up, his voice muffled by bubble wrap.

"Yes, he's been through a kind of supernatural conversion."

Intrigued, Steve stops rummaging and turns toward her.

"Oh? How do you mean?"

"Bertrand started making strange drawings that convinced Janek that David was trying to communicate with him.

The images, in his view, could only have come from David."

"Really? What sort of drawings, might I ask?"

"They're images from Polish folklore. A story about a drowned woman, covered with weeds, very grim."

"About what?" Steve mumbles, suddenly gone pale.

"A drowned woman. They aren't squeamish, these Poles of ours."

He turns around abruptly and resumes his search with his arms buried so deeply in the piles of bubble wrap that his uniform seams are in danger of splitting.

"I know it sounds a little esoteric," Caroline goes on, "but the main thing is that my father-in-law has gotten closer to David, and Bertrand has gone back to drawing tractors."

Steve stands up with a red package in one hand, a green package in the other, and something dark in his eyes. Caroline is certain she isn't projecting this time. He holds up Nurse Pronovost's amazing find and, with a faraway voice, says:

"Cherry Blossom."

That night, long after visiting hours, the door to David's room opens without a sound. The floor is littered with the scraps of wrapping paper and cake crumbs missed by the partygoers' hasty cleanup. Bertrand laid out his Lego airport and aligned the pilot, flight attendants, and passengers on the rim of the bathtub. He also ran some tests on the control tower in the sink, which was brimming with water. It does indeed float. Still, he left everything lying around when he went away.

It's nearly one in the morning. Steve has finished his shift, given Brigitte an update, and gone to his locker to change his clothes. Now he's sitting in the visitor's chair at David's bedside.

The athletic man who arrived on a stretcher in June is much changed. Steve already knows his most intimate details: the atrophied thigh muscles, the chafed buttocks, the threat of bedsores on the back of his knees, the smell of sweat, the sound of saliva gurgling in his tube, the blood pressure, the contents of his diaper. He knows that, more often than not, the day-shift team stimulates his bowel movements and that his iron constitution has helped him overcome a series of infections even though he has no spleen. But Steve does not know the man himself, or his voice or thoughts. All he has is the description given, in the past tense, by his family: funny and versatile, sociable, sporty. Acrobatic, impulsive, full of contradictions, ready to surprise and be surprised. Devoted, faithful as a dog, playful as a pup. The photos pinned up on the board show him but without revealing much: a young groom in sneakers, a new father looking very emotional, a vacationer luxuriating on a freezing New Brunswick beach. Very blue, laughing eyes, perfect teeth, a sensuous mouth.

For once, Steve is in no hurry. He contemplates David, the workman who found a way into his most painful and closely guarded secret.

How? Why?

Is there a form of communication so subtle that it eludes the average individual? Is he, Steve, somehow hard of hearing?

He touches me, searches for me. I twist my ankle in the hollow of a root.
The dry leaves the needles.
The dead are dead.

Steve slips the giraffe back into the closed fist. Then he slides one hand under the nape of David's neck, where the skull begins. Often, before falling asleep, he pictures himself in a coma and his conclusion is always the same: this is where he'd like to be touched, at the base of the skull. He believes that a warm, compassionate hand, right there, would help him feel supported. It never occurs to him that the support could come to him without the coma. That maybe all he needs to do is ask.

At one thirty, Brigitte, midway through her rounds, jumps when she sees him.

"Still here, Steve?

"Yes."

"It'll be late when you get home."

"I'm used to it."

"I'll leave you my key, if you like."

"No, thanks."

With her long black hair tied in twin ponytails, her lovely green almond-shaped eyes and her thick, almost Asian-looking eyelids, Brigitte, everyone agrees, is straight out of *One Thousand and One Nights*. This is not the first time the Scheherazade of the B Wing has invited Steve to sleep over at her place, and it's not the first time he has declined the offer. She wonders what's stopping him from having a little fun.

"The invitation still stands," she says. "I'll come by later for Novak."

The dead are dead.
The living live with the living.
The man touching me is alive. It's everywhere in his hand, contained to the point of hurting me.
Hurts me where I breathe
right
in
the middle.
He stays a long time. Why? He provides no care
only his sorrow
his wife
the darkness for them both.

Christmas comes and goes, brushing them along the way with its mandatory joy. Everyone plays along. As they leave midnight Mass, the snow is falling in wet clumps, but the presents are sheltered and waiting for them at Caroline's house. Janek paid the equivalent of three Christmases for Bertrand's gifts, by way of compensation. Similarly, Caroline picked a fir tree so tall the top bent against the ceiling. They play cards, pin the tail on the donkey, charades, and realize, without saying so, that David's absence has brought them much closer together. They gather around an emptiness, a family shaped like a donut.

January

In the early hours of New Year's Day, Nurse Pronovost adds a note in David's chart concerning the marked congestion in his breathing tube and his fever. She orders the aspiration frequency to be doubled and places a medicated adhesive strip behind his ear to help keep the tube clear. She recommends a chest X-ray, a secretions analysis, and an urgent medical examination.

A few hours later, the nurse on the next shift notes that his temperature has fallen, the patient is calm, and the tube is normal. She doesn't see the urgency of calling the doctor, especially on January 1st, when the hospital is overflowing from traffic accidents, attempted suicides, and alcoholic delirium. Nor does she think it useful to alarm the family unnecessarily.

Birds rustling resin.
A ruddy path among the spaced-out trunks
the needles crunch a yellow gleam
in
    dusty
      rays.

Leaden legs. If I stop I won't be able to move again.

The forest opens onto a moonscape—
stony hollow amid flared crests
the smooth surface of a dark lake

a cumulus hangs from the sky
reflected
in almost every detail.

Surreal brightness I suffocate.

After a day of skiing at the Olympic Park, skating in Parc La Fontaine, and sledding down the hill in Parc Lafond, Bertrand's cheeks have turned a lovely red. "A pair of apples for my basket," Caroline sings during their merry chase around the house, which ends with tickles on the living room carpet.

But the holidays are over, and going back to school means going back to all their routines. Friday, at the usual time, Caroline steps into the neurology unit.

"Happy New Year, Lily!" she says as she walks past.

"Oh, Mrs Novak!"

The receptionist has an odd expression and, incredibly, has stood up partway from her chair.

"Dr Sollers would like to see you, Mrs Novak."

"Now?"

"As soon as possible. We knew you'd be coming today, otherwise we would have called you this evening."

Caroline straightens up and tugs on her sling bag with both hands.

"What's going on? Has there been a change?"

"The doctor will fill you in," Lily says, ducking the question as much out of professional discretion as from the lack of self-confidence that confines her to virtual relationships.

Her pink head disappears behind the counter while she contacts Sollers's office. Then it pops up again like a Muppet: "He's expecting you."

Dr Sollers is indeed expecting her, but before speaking he clears his throat, not once, but twice.

"An infection, Mrs Novak."

"Another infection? Urinary?"

"Pulmonary, probably. We are waiting for the test results."

"Is it serious?"

"Well . . . your husband is immobile, usually horizontal, he has no spleen, a very vulnerable case, *you know.*"

"But is it serious?"

"The fever is high. We have begun a course of broad-spectrum antibiotics. I have a microbiologist on the case. He will locate the source of the infection. When the antibiogram has been obtained we will go on the offensive with a precise *target*. I have *confidence* with respect to the quality of the treatment."

"Should I repeat my question, Doctor?"

"Nosocomial infections . . ."

"Excuse me?"

"Hospital germs are robust, Mrs Novak. But we have caught it *early* and we are doing everything possible and, therefore, yes, his chances are good."

Caroline struggles to stay calm, but her hands worry at the canvas bag. For months, she has been preparing herself for an exchange like this. All to no purpose, it turns out.

Dr Sollers, meanwhile, knows that he has not yet delivered the knockout blow. It's at times like this that he is most afflicted by his chronic anglicisms. If only he could frame things with a well-constructed sentence, everything would be fine.

"Mrs Novak? Our *guidelines* are clear. I must inform you. If your husband loses respiratory autonomy, we do not put a respirator on him. Also, we do not reanimate a patient in a vegetative state."

"Why?"

"Because the foreseeable quality of life will probably be poor."

Of course, he refrains from mentioning the lack of personnel and available beds, the budget restrictions, the fact that a comatose patient costs nearly a million dollars a year. The strap on Caroline's bag gives out a squeak.

"In regard to visits, the unit is flexible in such cases. However, you must consider his need for rest. You as well, and your in-laws, *you have to take care*. This is important."

"Yes."

"Regarding your son—remind me of his name again…"

"Bertrand."

"I know he has special permission, but I advise you to limit his visits."

Diagonal
  descent
      the ground c r u m b l e s.

Below
on the lakeshore a child sits
arms wrapped around knees.
He sees me, stands
pitches pebbles in the water.
The surface receives them with long thick concentric shivers
like molten metal.

> *You were waiting for me?*
> *Tak.*
> *I'm coming up.*
> *Tak.*
> *Are you coming with me?*
> *Nie.*

Why?
Musisz iść sam.

I must go alone.

Why were you waiting for me?
Zostalem aby sie pożegnać.
Goodbye?
Tak

Tak. Tak. Pain, pain, pain.
Breathe, breathe how?
In slow, thick, concentric ripples.
The wind rises
carries words far away
          the stones constantly tumble down erase my steps
  make me
go back
          open sky
                    low-hanging fog
          cold damp clinging
  legs hampered heavy
          heavy hampered
          a road far too
  far too
                    hard.

David has a pneumococcal lung infection, a fairly common occurrence among patients with no spleen. His fever remains high, his pulse is rapid, his breathing tube sputters and whistles, he's shivering.

Caroline takes two days off and spends them at the hospital, shuttling between the café near the main entrance and the room on the third floor. She prefers to visit David briefly but frequently. She comes in masked, gloved, and over-caffeinated; she finds him pale, restless, and out of breath. She no longer knows what to hope for, or how.

After checking his temperature while constantly clicking her tongue, Nurse Pronovost bluntly explains that the fever leads to excessive sweating, which leads to a reduction in urine, which in turn can lead to another urinary-tract infection. A urinary-tract infection can of course require yet one more antibiotic treatment, and it's well known that repeated recourse to antibiotics makes the organism resistant to their effects, and hence more susceptible to further infections, which represent one of the main causes of death among comatose patients.

"I prefer to make things clear, Mrs Novak, as you've probably noticed already. There's no point in kidding yourself."

Caroline listens without flinching. Either way, with or without Nurse Pronovost's input, the anxiety has come back. Not just when she wakes up, but the rest of the day, too, and a good part of the night.

> *Cave.*
> *Crawl there*
> *mouth full of dust*
> *lungs full of gravel*
> > *I'm not going to croak before reaching the highest peak.*
> *Drained.*
> *The fight. Against what?*
> *A black, viscous, impregnable stain.*
> *Dying doesn't frighten me.*
> *Losing my life?*
> *Not now.*

"He hardly opens his eyes anymore," Caroline says behind her mask. "He's as stiff as a board."

"The coma is very deep right now," Steve answers.

"Do you believe he wants to live?"

"He's responding well to the treatment, anyway. Very well, actually."

"He's made of steel."

"Not just steel, I suppose?"

"No. Velvet too, obviously. But do you think he wants to live, or not?"

"Ask him, Caroline."

I breathe.
That's all.
I last one second at a time.
I breathe—
   badly.

"When can I go see Dad?"

"Soon, buddy."

"Is he all right?"

"I've already told you. He has a bad cold and needs to rest."

"Is it my fault?"

"Oh, Bertrand! Why in the world would it be your fault?"

"I don't know. You don't take me to the hospital anymore. Do I keep him from resting?"

"Of course not. I just want to make sure you don't catch his cold."

"I don't mind having a cold."

"You'll see him again soon, I promise."

"It's already been a week."

"How about pizza tonight?"

"All dressed?"

"Yes."

"Extra-large?"

"Yes."

"Even so, Mom, it's been a week."

At the far end of the cave another cave still another
*   round narrow smooth soft*
my side against a wall. A monstrous mass crushes me
*   —a bear—*
where is the way out? The light? The air? Where is the air?
The bear weighs, weighs a ton of stifling heat.

"Our Father who art in heaven, do not let David suffer.

"If he must live, let him live in tranquility; if he must die, let him go in peace.

"Protect Caroline, protect Bertrand.

"Help Janek to understand himself.

"Our Father who art in heaven, I do not ask You why.

"Why You are taking David back so soon, in the middle of his life.

"Why You are acting like a thief.

"I know that is not the right question.

"I know, because You never answer it.

"I beg You to just lighten our burden.

"To accompany us.

"To clearly show us the road we must follow to heal as quickly as possible.

"Because it hurts, Lord. It hurts very much.

"You, too, lost a Son; you know what I am talking about.

"Don't You?"

Karine crosses herself, convinced she has been heard. Today, she did not go through the Black Madonna. For the sake of speed, she thinks, though in reality a doubt gnaws at her. A doubt about the Virgin's true power of intercession, even though it was, she thought, acknowledged and documented.

She genuflects one last time, the signal Janek was waiting for to put his cap back on.

My bear sits on me like a hen.
I am folded all tucked in and warm.
Tiny miniscule needle point
>   *cell.*
The cell grows twofold.
The cell multiplies.
Time exists space exists—I exist
the heart beats.
The skin closes over the secret of the organs
in this secret another hides
>   *that of the*
>   *void*
>   *from which I came*
>   *that:*
>   *of my immaterial matter.*
I would like to remember.
It is forbidden.
The skin is ready, somewhat tight, the envelope for a fragile,
fragile shipment
>   *do not fold ne pas plier*
>   *I will be born.*
>   *I will forget everything.*
>   *Almost everything.*
>   *Unless.*

Caroline serves Karine her cup of Assam tea and Janek his glass of Budweiser. They've come especially to see her, and called ahead three hours ago. Janek has gone so far as to wear a tie. Wide and brown. Not being one to renew his wardrobe, he wore the same tie on his wedding day. Caroline thinks back to Roger Pitt's jarring necktie, the day they discussed the compensation process. It looked for all the world like the hangman's noose. Today, Janek. Why?

Faced with her in-laws' silence, she announces: "The fever has gone down. But he's agitated. The staff are constantly popping in to drain his tube."

There's a lull, which is rapidly saturated by Janek's unease. Karine comes to his rescue:

"Caroline, Janek has something he'd like to ask you."

Caroline eyes her father-in-law. It's been ages since he last spoke to her directly; Karine dutifully played the part of carrier pigeon. But this time the feathered friend has left the message on the doorstep. Janek swallows a mouthful of beer; the amber bubbles cheerfully rising from the bottom of the glass in blatant contradiction to his state of mind.

"In the event . . ." he begins. "If he were to . . ."

"Yes," Caroline says engagingly.

"About the headstone . . ."

His heavy, choppy accent makes things even worse. What comes to mind are plow horses laboriously digging furrows to plant words in. He talks to his Bud:

"I was wondering if we could write the name he was christened with on it."

Caroline doesn't quite understand the request. What else do you put on a gravestone? The name burns Janek's mouth as he explains:

"Dawid Nowakowski. With all the w's."

"Ah?"

"It's important for me."

When he looks up at her with his eyes full of childish hope she is taken aback. Tormented for months by the tragic namesake, he has finally decided to acknowledge it for what it is. A mistake, perhaps, but one so meaningful as to earn its place on the stone.

"It's his grandfather's name. My father's."

"Of course," Caroline says, more than ever mindful of the baggage of grief the Novaks lug behind them. "Your father, what was he like, Janek? Does David resemble him?"

"My father? He was ... er ... hard-working."

With this brutal statement he sums up the whole, complex life of a man who had been steamrolled by the last century. His memories of him are sharply conflicting. On one hand, he sees his father sitting him all bundled up in a sled, adjusting his scarf and pulling him along Nowa Huta's snow-covered avenues, as white and broad as the sky. His father's upright bearing inspired boundless confidence. Yet later on, the same person kicked over a stack of books, which he then threw into the stove without even looking at the titles. Immersed in an intensely private drama, he inspired sheer terror in Janek.

The last thing he remembers about his father is especially confusing for Janek. Leaning both elbows on the crumpled tablecloth, his nose plunged into a glass of vodka, he'd muttered: "Listen, Janek. Listen." Janek hated his drunken voice. "At Zakopane, I dreamed of climbing Rysy."

A boozer's ravings.

"The highest peak in Poland."

Janek wanted to leave the kitchen. Dawid, his head resting in the crook of his arm, appeared to have fallen asleep. But no; "In our country, Poland, Janek. Free Poland."

Couldn't he instead say something father-to-son, something Janek could take into adolescence, into adulthood?

"Listen, Janek," Dawid insisted, slurring his words, "I should have. I should have gone up, because it was my last chance. After that, everything was always dragging me down. The bottom, the muddy ditches, are for frogs. Tadpoles. Janek."

To this day, Janek has no idea what that rare confession meant. Besides, delirium tremens came soon after. Hence the peaks, the frogs, the tadpoles. What's there to say about him?

Caroline waits for a more substantial story, some flesh on the bones, images that would allow her to better understand her David. And Janek, too, would like to elaborate, but nothing comes to mind. He takes another draft of beer and just repeats:

"Yes, that's it, hard-working."

His glass strikes the table like the pronouncement of a sentence, terse and definitive.

Through exhaustion
everything goes away
except the transparent centre
where
we are bound
together
by the roots.

Eventually, the antibiotics work their miracle. The temperature drops, the other symptoms abate. Caroline asks herself why her anxiety isn't following the same curve. Everything troubles her, even the empty messages on the answering machine. They are so regular that she wonders if it might be a burglar checking to see if someone is home or a maniac planning to assault her in the street. Each morning, on waking, she tells herself that sooner or later she will have to sort out David's clothes, clean up the garage, give away his tools; the logistical and emotional enormity of the task keeps her from getting up. When she finally does go out, she focuses all her attention on the thick, insulated, non-skid soles of her boots.

To her great despair, since the onset of the pneumonia, only Steve's presence affords her some relief, and he works part-time, never lingering more than a few minutes. He notes the vital signs and temperature. Or he drops in simply to see how she and Bertrand are getting on. Every time he leaves, she has a moment of panic.

He's there today, to administer the antibiotics. He has connected the little transparent pouch to the intravenous catheter, adjusted the drip rate, noted the time in the chart. He's already about to leave. She hasn't yet spoken to him, and he confined himself to a discreet nod of the head. She looks at his back, his shoulders, his arms, his solidness. If only she could lean against him for a while, like a tree trunk, and not spoil things. He's on his way out. Her panic rises. It rises to the point where, without thinking, she intercepts him:

"Are you taking your break soon, Steve?"

"Once the infusion is done, in twenty minutes or so. Why?"

"Could I offer you something to drink? During your break?"

"Do you know Dieter Verkest?" he asks strangely.

"I have a Post-it by him," she answers just as enigmatically.

"A Post-it? Ah."

"See you in the cafeteria?"

As soon as the infusion is finished, Steve swings by his locker. For several weeks, Dieter Verkest's book *Touching the Beyond* has been waiting there for Caroline, right below the famous quote drawn from it.

When he finally shows it to her, she responds like a true Montreal public-library professional, flipping through it with her thumb, stopping at a random page, scanning a paragraph, skipping to the back cover and the inside of the dust jacket. The author photo takes her aback: bon vivant, glowing skin, crooked teeth, a sizable proboscis. She goes to the table of contents, which is annotated in the margin. Out of a sense of decency, she avoids reading the dedication on the flyleaf.

"Can I borrow it?"

"If you're interested."

He has never seen her smile so broadly; her features open up, her cheeks redden, a pretty dimple dents her right cheek.

"Actually, my supervisor put it on the order list," she says, tapping the cover. "We'll be getting it soon. I was planning to take it out. But I'd rather have your used copy. It reminds me of the sofa in the Sunshine Room."

"I've read it three times."

"Three times? Why?"

"It helped me get through a difficult patch."

"Oh?"

"A long and very difficult patch."

Caroline waits, hoping he'll be more forthcoming, but he stops short, as if at the edge of a cliff. He retreats to his cappuccino, and she notices how the froth quivers. The king of the tourniquet, the syringe, and family support, astronaut Steve Austin loses his cool because he let the shutter covering his private life open a crack. He was always endearing without realizing it, but now, with his trembling, he transcends the drab cafeteria.

"Give me your hand."

He looks up at her. He hesitates, barely a second, and slides his hand, palm up, across the pale-yellow Formica. Caroline places her hand in his. She noticed Steve's hands long ago; for a long time she has found them balanced, attentive, assured; for a long time she has tried to guess exactly how warm they are.

"Thank you," he says.

But Caroline pulls back, suddenly aware of the absurdity of the setting, the coldness of the table, the little bags of powdered milk, and Lily standing at the cash, loaded up with a mountain of carbohydrates, refined sugars, and saturated fats. Aware, too, that Steve's break has just lasted sixteen minutes.

I was going somewhere.
Wasn't I?
I was going up.

Laura stays in the blue room longer than she usually does. She pensively studies Bertrand's drawings, of which there are so many that they overlap. He kept his promise: they will indeed have to buy a new wall.

"Are you okay, Laura?" Caroline asks.

The nurse strokes her belly, whose bulge threatens to pop the buttons off her XXL shirt.

"Lots of vehicles," she says.

"Yes, lots. With a predilection for fire trucks."

"Hey, that's true."

"You look sad, Laura, am I right?"

"It would be tactless of me to talk about it."

"Well, you know, when it comes to tact ... I'm beyond that now."

"It's just that ... Do you sense something special when you come into the room?"

"Like what, exactly?"

"You feel ... What's the word? Suspension?"

"Suspension? No."

"I should keep quiet. Sorry. Let's drop it, all right?"

"No, Laura. Why leave suspension in suspense? Which suspension, for starters?"

"There's no scientific evidence."

"I'm beyond that too."

"It's just an intuition."

"You mean death? Is that what you sense?"

"It's more like ... what's the word? Distance."

Laura gives Caroline a very candid look.

"You know, there's nothing negative about it. On the contrary, it's very peaceful. Enveloping."

"So why are you crying?"

"I was looking at Bertrand's drawings. I was thinking of Bertrand."

Caroline bites her lip. Laura ventures to put her hand on Caroline's shoulder, then she steps slowly toward the door. She stops for a moment, says nothing, and leaves.

I sing for the dead, says the voice.

My syllables are hoarse—naked peaks under a merciless wind. The wind is me, the song is me, and the peaks and the passage.

The dead sometimes ask to be resuscitated. I don't allow them to linger. Muscles are made of earth, they return to the earth. Blood is made of water, it returns to the water. Oxygen returns to the air and bones to stone. All just compostable matter on loan.

And consciousness?

Its path is secret, but my song prepares it.

After that, I shut up.

Once again, Nurse Pronovost was right; she should have been a clairvoyant. The urinary-tract infection flares up just as the lung infection was taking its leave. Again, the fever, the shivers, the drastic decline in the volume of urine along with its dark colour, shot through with blood. The antibiotic treatment is duly readjusted. Dr Sollers comes to let Caroline know. While not alarmist, he makes a point of being realistic. You need to call a spade a spade and a patient at risk a patient at risk.

Back at David's bedside, she gently massages his temples. His hair has gone curly at the ends, a first. Should he wake up now, he would demand a pair of scissors. But he's not about to wake up. He is descending the Glasgow scale, one rung after the other, and fighting infections one after the other. Nothing is impossible to a willing heart.

"Give me a sign, David, please."

Nothing. Nada. Zilch.

She tells him she loves him. She has eroded the words through repetition and dried out his skin by stroking his forearm. She asks him if he wants to go. If he's too tired to go on.

"We would tell each other everything, David, remember? Will you tell me if you want to live or die?"

Caroline has been sleep-deprived a long time. Exhausted now, she dozes off in spite of herself. She wakes up with a start and a stiff neck, and immediately drifts off again. In her half-sleep, a memory takes shape, hazy at first, then more and more distinct. David is in their poorly heated garage with his knee on a board and a drill in his hand. "Come to dinner!" She has already called him three times. He had promised to do the cooking because it was Sunday, but she replaced him at the stove due to his ongoing project. She storms into the garage.

"David, it's ready, dinner is served, it's getting cold, we're waiting for you. Are you coming or not?"

"I'm almost done."

"You've been saying that for the last two hours. You'll finish up later."

"I'm almost done, Caroline. You know me, eh? When I start something I have to finish it. Go ahead and eat without me."

She had slammed the door behind her, stomped her heels all over the floor, let David's plate go cold, and avoided speaking to him until he found a way to make her laugh.

She jumps.

"You know me, eh?" She had the impression of hearing him from down there, from the land of his coma. "When I start something, I have to finish." Even so far away, even so faint, she's certain he has kept that trait, which so enraged her back then.

"Take your time," she whispers, stroking his hair. "Please, let me know when your time is over."

January draws to a close. The days grow imperceptibly longer; you have to trust them. In the cubicle at the library, where Marie has come to spend the lunch hour with Caroline, Dieter Verkest's book turns up. Marie wipes her fingers on her jeans before picking it up and gives it a slightly suspicious once-over.

"*Touching the Beyond*, eh?" she says between mouthfuls of tabbouleh.

"Leaf through it," Caroline coaxes her. "It smells of wood-fire."

"Woodfire? So, where does Steve live?"

"No idea."

"And it's full of annotations, too."

Indeed, the margins are filled with stars, brackets, lines, arrows, question marks, exclamation marks, ellipses.

"He's really a criminal."

"You said it. The library's number-one enemy."

"Is he copy-editing or something?"

"No, just reading closely, I guess. Two or three times."

The appreciative note isn't lost on Marie; she looks hard at her sister as she tries to dislodge a piece of parsley from her teeth with her tongue.

"Did you notice the dedication?" Caroline asks.

Marie finds the flyleaf and reads aloud: "For S., a reachable beyond, from the seeker." She whistles.

"A very nice turn of phrase. 'The seeker'—who is that? His girlfriend? His ex?"

"Again, no idea."

Caroline shrugs, pretending to be nonchalant. She knows nothing about Steve, or so little.

"Have you read it?"

"Some of it."

She read only the annotations.

The room the walls the hands. The window?
Washed-up.

They hit my back bend my legs pierce my arm massage my
calves fill my stomach wet my mouth, I float.
I was going somewhere.
I'm out of time.
The first hour the last minute.

"I have all the results," Dr Sollers announces as he arrives
at the nursing station. "*He's clean.*"

Laura smiles.

"*Sparkling clean,*" the doctor adds.

"He certainly has a lot of grit."

"We brought out the heavy artillery."

Sollers prefers to give credit to the treatment. He consistently prefers the quantitative over the qualitative, which may
be one reason his marriage failed. He has pondered it at times,
but since the hypothesis itself is qualitative, he tends to dismiss it.

"*In any case*, you can tell the family that he has come
through once more."

"Yes, Doctor."

"But keep an eye on him. *You never know what comes next.*"

February

an
insolent
perfectly
vertical
rock
face

Prompted by an interlude of mild winter weather, Caroline has offered to bring the bicycles up from the cellar and pump up the tires for her and Marie. After adjusting David's seat to her height, Marie follows behind her sister on the bike path until a cyclist in professional gear streaks by and splashes them with mud.

They decide to stop for a while by the edge of the pond in Parc La Fontaine. Ripples lick at a thin margin of ice, the white sun lights up the surface with blinding reflections, the lapping water whispers its secrets. Ever since David's pneumonia, Caroline sees beauty everywhere. To her, life has taken on the appearance of those transparent leaves found in the spring, their network of veins still intact, a masterpiece so fragile you dare not touch it.

The sunbeams have ended their show. The pondwater grows dark, quivering at the surface, all at once opaque. Marie suggests some hot chocolate. There's no lack of choice among the icy tables on the terrace of the nearest café. No other customers, aside from them, have come to invoke the spring.

"Marie?" Caroline says, shivering and clasping her cup like a hot-water bottle, "Would you think I'm a monster if I told you a big part of me has already let David go?"

Without giving her sister time to answer, she continues:

"We've been living without him for months, and I spent all of January saying goodbye to him. If he ever wakes up, we'll have to reinvent everything. The history that we had—I've already lost that. When the fever was at its worst, Laura asked me if I had anything I still needed to say to him. The answer is no."

She dips her finger in the chocolate drink.

"I'm going to tell you something. The day he fell, he left in a bit of a hurry, he was late. Vidal, who'd come to pick him up, wouldn't stop honking. David was holding his lunch box in one hand, a brownie in the other, and his keys between his teeth. He was overloaded, so I opened the door for him. . . I opened the door. I took the keys out of his mouth to kiss him. He wrapped me in his arms. He said, 'See you tonight, beautiful.' I answered, 'I love you, gorgeous.'"

She presses the cup against her heart through her windbreaker. She has replayed the dialogue in her head a thousand times, and the lines have been worn down. But recounting the scene brings back all its power.

"'I love you, gorgeous' . . . It helped me so much to have said that to him just before he left. It was the last thing I said to him that I'm sure he heard. That's what he took with him. Don't cry, Marie. Marie? Come, don't cry. For once, the story ends well."

The hollows the protrusions my fingers my toes
everything fits
I throw my shirt down to the bottom of the cliff
it opens like a parachute
sleeves deployed buttons shining in the light
in free fall
free
I no longer know where I end where the rock begins
the shirt down below blends in with the ground.

Is this still a dream?

Yet there he is, he really is there, in their bedroom, at the foot of the bed. Caroline slides down next to him. Unaffected, he's preoccupied with packing his trekking knapsack. He stuffs it with an incredible number of silly objects, including his baseball bat, a bilingual dictionary, and a box of muesli. She calls him but he doesn't hear. She asks him where he's going, he doesn't even raise his eyes. She offers to help him, and he finally looks at her. That's him, that's his smile. Calm, happy. He swings the sack onto his shoulder, opens the closet wide, and disappears. Caroline follows him as best she can, tangled up in the dresses and shirts. The hangers clink in her ears and hook into her hair, a shelf collapses and a pile of sweaters drops onto her feet. David reaches his hand out to tighten a light bulb. The closet is brutally lit up and Caroline discerns a door she was unaware of. He opens it. He turns around and smiles again, but it's not his smile anymore. It's a blissful expression, almost a radiance. The expression of one who has descended into the abyss and come back immortal.

He leaves.

Caroline wants to follow him. She struggles to extricate herself from the hangers, the shirtsleeves, and the sweaters, whose stitches unravel, the wool twisting around her thighs. She can no longer find the door. This somehow reassures her—there never was a door here. Meanwhile, the light bulb blows out. Total darkness. Actually, there never was a light bulb.

She wakes up all at once. A dream, of course.

Her heart pounding, she waits for the anxiety to well up. She feels it lurking somewhere in the middle of her belly, where it usually nests, but what wells up surprises her: relief.

She dare not move. David is very near, she's sure of it. She wonders if the nearness means that he is in fact very far away. After all, the far side of the world lies at our feet.

The peak in sight
just one more sheer wall
I am naked
just my skin
I climb.
Life passes through me
like a thread through the eye of a needle
I feel it pass pass
alive
it really is so simple
maybe too simple.

This is the third break that Steve and Caroline have devoted to talking about David's vital signs, Dieter Verkest's career, and Mrs Blouin's Day-Glo Cutex. Between breaks, Caroline started to weigh somewhat obsessively the pros and cons of them getting closer. The truth is, the pros win out, and she would like to find a way around the sixteen-minute time limit. She does have an idea, one she has analyzed day by day in such fine detail that she's turned it into a research project. Now she can't hold back any longer.

"Steve," she finally dares to ask, "is it proper to invite a nurse's aide for dinner?"

"Depends. Which one?"

"The big guy there, with a banana muffin."

"When?"

"If he were free on a Saturday ..."

He gives a muted smile that secretly contains another, radiant, smile.

"Not this week. Next week, I think he could."

Below way down there
Summer, winter
David's growth
on one side
his decline on the other.
Around, all around
grey dry jutting points, the brittle rust of the veins of rockslides.
Memory of the earth's crust
flows of lava, of glaciers
furrows of rain, folds of squalls
and gravity clenching everything in its fist, everything
but the royal eagle.

In the mailbox, wedged between two flyers from the same Greek restaurant, Caroline finds an envelope from the construction company. David's T4 income-tax slips. Naturally, she neglected the fact that his income-tax statements had to be filled out. For the federal and provincial governments, he remains a taxpayer, with a date of birth, a social insurance number, an income, a dependent child, a spouse, and even contributions to the pension plan. There is, however, a new line to fill out this year: *Amount for a Severe and Prolonged Impairment in Mental or Physical Functions (Consult the Guide).*

She thrusts the envelope into her bag and goes off to work. The T4s from the library shouldn't be long in coming either.

The peak, finally.
Finally at the summit of the highest summit
yet I raise my head again
it is there
          the eagle
it circles
          it reigns
its flight
          is absolute.
In the end, I will die.

When Bertrand goes away to his grandparents' on Saturday morning, Caroline already knows what will happen. She sees herself cleaning the house from top to bottom, leafing through a recipe book, doing some extra shopping, renting a film just in case, choosing a pricey wine, changing her skirt three times, putting on makeup then removing it, taking the orange tablecloth with burgundy polka dots, used only for parties, out of the sideboard, setting the table, and then deciding it's a bit over the top.

She sees herself putting everything away except the table-cloth, preparing a candle, two, three, four candles. Dispersing the candles so she can forget the kitchen, the whole house, its history. So she can create a den smelling of vegetables au gratin and pie, with subdued lighting that lets her imagine herself as free and new and available.

In the bath, she pulls out the stainless steel plug and leaves it beside the cold water tap.

In the end, you always die, but for me it will come soon.
The experience is quite simply over.
The ball, Bertrand? Who's going to throw you the ball?

Steve arrives at six o'clock sharp. So sharp, in fact, that Caroline is convinced he was waiting in his car for twenty minutes with a stopwatch. He has on a pair of jeans and a woolen sweater softened from wear; he's holding a paper bag. She foolishly didn't expect him to be out of his hospital uniform.

"I like the colour of your sweater, apple, or ... What colour is that?"

Steve pulls on a bit of his sweater and glances at it. In the light of the streetlamp he isn't too sure anymore.

"Green?"

"Green. It's a green that suits you. Your eyes."

She stands there clutching the door handle.

"Can I come in?"

"Oh, sorry! You'll catch cold. Forgive me, it's just that ..."

"It's just that you'd prefer to see me in my uniform."

"No, not really, no, not at all in fact, it's just that ... nothing. Come in."

As soon as Steve steps through the door, Caroline regains her composure. This is precisely what she was afraid of. What she was hoping for. No, what she was afraid of. It's as though Steve had always lived in this house, with his green sweater, his jeans, his disarming equanimity. He blends with the decor so naturally that it verges on the surreal.

He hands her the paper bag.

"White chocolate? Good idea. Thanks. Shall we go into the kitchen? Would you like something to drink? Tea? Coffee? ... Beer, wine, port? Juice? Orange, apple? Even raspberry?"

"A nice glass of water would be fine, for now."

"A glass of water. Okay."

Caroline is disappointed he doesn't provide her with an excuse to start in on the bottle of wine (or beer or port). As she fills the glass with water, she feels she can see David everywhere in the kitchen. She left the T4 slip lying about on the counter, but she doesn't need the T4 to conjure him up reading *L'Actualité* over his toast crumbs. Or washing the dishes with the dishrag slung over his shoulder, or putting his arm around her waist, or wiping up spilt milk and scowling at Bertrand. She sees him changing the garbage bag, which was leaking onto the floor; he tries to slip it into a new bag but fails, the bloated bag splits open, a chicken bone rolls out, Bertrand protests—who's been eating chicken? He eyes the bone, brings his index finger close, but dares not touch it. We don't eat animals here, Dad. WHO ATE CHICKEN? And David, the one who ordered out from the St-Hubert rotisserie so he could snack in private during a hockey game once Bertrand was in bed and Caroline off to the movies, David caught red-handed, pinches his lips not to laugh. Yes, it would have made more sense to change the cupboard doors. Buy an oak table. The kitchen as is lets David move about, move the way David moved, with ease, coordination, move the way he won't move again, ever, now that he looks less like himself than that rigid chicken bone.

Steve seems to be looking for the switch. Holding a box of matches, Caroline precedes him and lights all the candles except the solitary one perched above the sink. Was she right to invite him? Her dilemma resurfaces, intact. Without realizing it he comes to her rescue:

"It smells good here. What is it?"

"You'll see. I hope it's okay. I tried a new recipe."

Steve motions toward the counter.

"I have an espresso machine just like yours. A gift from my mother."

"Oh?"

"Yes. I was wondering what sort of coffee maker you used."

"Really?" she asks in surprise.

"I always have questions like that when I meet people, you may think it's a bit silly..."

"No, no."

"No?"

"Not at all. I've got the same quirk."

Caroline blushes.

"So, ask," Steve prods her playfully.

"...Dog or cat?"

"Rabbit."

"Rabbit?"

"I have a niece with Down's syndrome who adores rabbits. Her name is Amélie. The rabbit's name is Custard. I look after my niece every second Sunday, so my sister can get some time off. She's a single mother—not easy."

He steps forward to take the glass of water, which Caroline might otherwise hold on to all evening.

"Carpets?"

"Wood. Rough-hewn."

"Doesn't need sweeping. City or suburb?"

"Country. The Eastern Townships."

"The Eastern Townships? How long did it take you to get here tonight?"

"An hour and a half, give or take."

"But ... Why do you work in Montreal?"

"I did all my internships at the hospital, then I applied for a position that had opened up, they hired me, time passed. I also do a little work at the town clinic."

Momentarily out of questions, Caroline crouches in front of the oven and pretends to make adjustments.

"Do you like fish? I probably should have asked beforehand."

"Fish is perfect."

"I figured you'd rather avoid meat. I mean, you must have a good reason for choosing the cafeteria's veggie tourtière. We avoid meat too, ever since Bertrand visited the Granby Zoo. He saw a lot of living animals and put two and two together, you see."

"He's sharp as a tack, Bertrand."

"Yes, for better or worse. What about the windows? Curtains or blinds?"

"Nothing."

"What do you mean, nothing?"

"I live two kilometres from my neighbour, Mrs Lemieux, the hundred-and-two-year-old lady."

"And Mrs Lemieux is no peeping Tom."

"Mrs Lemieux is as short-sighted as a mole."

"What do you see through your windows?"

"The woods on one side, the lake on the other. A small pebble beach."

"It must be very pretty."

"It's pretty, but fairly neglected. In fact, I'm staying there next week to do some repairs before everything falls apart. After that—have you heard?—I'll be on the day shift. We've reorganized to accommodate Laura's maternity leave."

"You'll miss Nurse Pronovost…"

"She's moving to the day shift as well. We're inseparable."

"I see… And you stay in Montreal when you work at the hospital?"

"I sleep at a friend's place."

Steve plunks his glass down on the counter. He feels he's talked enough about himself.

"Is it my turn to ask questions?"

Caroline sweeps her hand around to indicate the house.

"Curtains, city, carpets. As you can see."

"But what does your week look like?"

"Ah, my week ... School, library, school, home, bath, supper, beddy-bye. Monday, Wednesday, Friday—hospital. Weekends, it depends. But always in town. Just in case."

"Of course."

"Would you like a glass of wine now?"

"Only if you're having ..."

"Would you like a glass of wine, please?"

"Okay."

"I've got a nice dry white here. Is white good? Dry?"

"Excellent."

Caroline dives into the refrigerator and reappears with a bottle. Soon, the cork makes a loud pop followed by the cheerful gurgle of wine spilling into the glasses.

"What do we drink to?" she asks.

"To Bertrand."

"To Bertrand and Amélie."

"Bertrand, Amélie, Custard."

The first sip finally relaxes Caroline, as if allowing her to be someone else. Someone who could be herself. Herself at this very moment.

"The country, the bare windows, Mrs Lemieux—I wasn't expecting that. I'll have to review my list of questions."

"More questions?"

"Yup. The review's all done. Hiking shoes or sneakers?"

"Crocs."

"You *drive* wearing Crocs?"

"Well ... yes."

"Is it legal to drive with Crocs ?"

Steve shrugs.

"Were you wearing Crocs when you drove us here?"

"No."

"Why not?"

"You were with me. I was afraid you'd say it was illegal to drive wearing Crocs. Especially with a child on board. I wore my rainboots, both times."

Caroline studies his face for a moment. The first time, she refused to get into the car. She said no, a big no with a stainless steel O. Then why did he wear his boots anyway? Was he so intuitive that he guessed she would change her mind? She decides to let it go.

"Why keep a pair of boots in your locker?"

"Because I help out in the garden from time to time."

"The hospital has a garden?"

"Right now there's a sort of muddy patch full of holes, while they wait for funding or for someone to donate saplings. You're surprised? It's posted all over the corridors. *Do you have a green thumb? Do you long for nature in the city?* And so on."

"I must have missed it," says Caroline, who would rather not talk about the hospital. "Your stove? Gas or electric?"

"Gas."

"In the living room, an old couch or wicker stuff?"

"Hammock."

"Wonderful. Bath or shower?"

"I prefer the shower. You?"

"Bath. Which reminds me, the trout must be ready."

She serves him a gargantuan portion and serves herself a tiny one. She's not hungry. At all.

"This supper of yours—really good."

"I think I've asked all my questions."

"Are you sure?"

"What do you mean?"

"While we're at it, Caroline. We covered locations, kitchen, living room, bathroom …"

The way he holds her gaze leaves no room for doubt. Or retreat.

"All right. Mattress or futon? Single or double?"

"Mattress, double."

She takes another sip of wine, immediately followed by two more.

"Alone?"

"Alone now, yes."

"She went away?"

"She went away."

"Far away?"

"Yes."

Caroline pours more wine and goes to light the neglected candle over the sink. When she sits down again, Steve has already drained his glass. A miniature storm has overtaken his eyes, like that day in the cafeteria when she asked if he had children, like the day she told him about Janek's conversion. She refills his glass.

"Tell me about her."

He brushes his hand across his forehead, stares at a spot on the ceiling as if summoning his memories, selecting them.

"Half Huron... Energetic, smart. Painter. Skier."

"How long were you together?"

"Eight years."

"Happy?"

"It was ... extreme."

"How so?"

"As in, 'I'm going to trek across the Appalachians and eat nothing but seeds for all twenty-eight days of the next lunar cycle.'"

"Wow."

"Or, 'I'm planning a series of portraits in the palliative-care wing, I'm sure it can be cathartic for dying people and their families.'"

Steve raises his glass and examines it like a crystal ball. The pricey little dry white wine has a lovely, bright colour. He drinks it a little too fast.

"And . . . she followed through?"

"Oh, yes. Sometimes she would come home completely demoralized. Shattered."

"That must have been hard."

"It was a case of take it or leave it. What can I say? I loved her."

"You still love her."

"Still."

"You wanted children?"

"She wanted seven."

"And you?"

"Maybe just six."

"And?"

"She miscarried three times in a row. The third time we went for tests, both of us. Fertility, genetic compatibility, blood count, family history, diet, the works."

"And?"

"Nothing."

"It drove you away from each other?"

"No, it brought us closer together, I'd say."

He smoothes the tablecloth with the flat of his hand.

"I think it drove her away from herself. She began to do strange things, let's say stranger than usual. Like strolling naked by the lake in the middle of the day, or burning her canvases on the beach while singing at the top of her lungs. . ."

"She sank into a depression, you think?"

"Probably. But she refused to see a doctor, a shrink, someone. For her it was a sort of initiation rite, and nature would help her if she learned to hear it better."

"Did you insist on the medical approach?"

"No. Given her personality, she was right. The cure was in seeing, in listening. In any case, she had to find it herself."

"And you?"

"What about me?"

"It was hard for you too, wasn't it?"

"Yes. I suppose, yeah."

He hesitates. Caroline waits. She senses that the words are getting harder and harder to enunciate, as though he were moving a huge pile of rocks.

"One night, she began howling at the edge of the pier. I was at the clinic. Mrs Lemieux called the police. She may be short-sighted, but she's not deaf. And sound carries on the lake."

He drains his glass, bends his head down.

"Officer Brébeuf was snoozing. He prefers the night shift precisely because he can snooze, it's a well-known fact. By the time he arrived at our place I had already calmed her down."

He rummages in his jeans pocket and pulls out a small white bone that reminds Caroline of the chicken leg, and Bertrand's fierce indignation. She stops breathing; even her breath seems too heavy for the fragile terrain ahead of her, a thin sheet of black ice where the wrinkles of the newly captured current are still legible.

"It looks like a bird's leg."

"It is a bird's leg. She wore it as a pendant."

Leaning over the table, Caroline can make out the minuscule hole at the tip of the bone, barely large enough for a thread.

"She gave it to you?"

"In a manner of speaking."

He places the bone in the centre of the table, as if he needs more distance to tell the rest of the story. He even pushes his chair back to arm's length.

"I came home from work one morning. I heard the phone ringing as I opened the door. I was expecting her to answer, but it kept on ringing. It was Mr Gagnon, on the far side of the lake. She'd just landed on the beach with our canoe. She was stretched out in it, high and dry in every sense. She'd let herself drift all night."

He runs his fingers through his hair; it falls back on his brow as tousled as before.

"It was cold?"

"Freezing. I rushed over to Mr Gagnon's place. It's a long drive around the lake. He'd sat her down in an armchair near the fire wrapped in a heavy woollen blanket with a hot-water bottle in her lap and a large glass of rum. Her face was very white, very distant . . . very . . ."

"Very?"

"Her lips were blue and her eyes . . ."

He pauses, looking distraught.

"Her eyes scared me. Too intense, too dark. The rest of her face was completely impassive. Like a funeral mask. Demented . . . She ended up in the psychiatric ward."

"Is she still there?"

"No."

Steve's fingers skim across the bird's leg.

"They sapped all her strength, and I let them do it. After seven months, they sent her back to the brush like a little lost animal. The next night, she did it Virginia Woolf-style."

"She did what?"

"Filled her pockets with stones. Half of our beach ended up at the bottom of the lake with her. She left the little bone on her pillow, right next to me, while I slept like a fool, believing I still had my arms around her."

"Oh, no, Steve."

Caroline is about to stand up, but he motions for her not to.

"It has been two years, you know."

"And you've been dealing with this alone for all that time?"

"I haven't talked about it until now."

"It's the candles?"

"Not just the candles."

"The wine."

"Not just the wine."

He slips the bone back into his pocket and says:

"Anyway, to answer your question, a double mattress."

For a long time they say nothing, smooth the tablecloth, fidget with the gratin.

"Steve, I'm sorry for asking that question."

"I insisted that you ask it, Caroline."

"I still feel guilty."

"I've noticed that tendency of yours."

She waits a little, and then, ever so slowly, she starts to serve the triple berry pie. He volunteers to prepare coffee with the famous espresso machine. Decaffeinated for Caroline, given her insomnia, caffeinated for him, since he can sleep whenever it suits him. They nibble on the pie without speaking. The silence hovers, genuine and weightless. A naked silence of uncurtained windows. Steve, his beautiful hands resting on the tablecloth, finally looks up at Caroline with all the candour in the world, a candour laden with pain, strength, and desire. Especially desire.

He will not be the one to make the first move. He knows he has no right to make that move, and he won't.

Caroline is fully aware of her own emotion, such as it is, irresolute and insoluble. Here, tonight, at this moment, looking at the pie crumbs, she feels exhausted from swimming against the current. Her heart is racing, her mouth is dry, her hands are clammy. Her skin calls out violently to the hands placed on the tablecloth in front of her. That's the truth, pure and simple. And unsayable.

She has no wish to ask for anything, no wish to take anything, no way to receive anything. She's shaking. The first move must come from her and each second more of waiting adds to its imminence. It's unavoidable. It's bigger than her. She leaves her chair and steps toward Steve. She stops in front of him, he stands up. She places her hand on his sweater, keeping him at a distance while bringing him closer, a gesture as ambivalent as her own intention. Touch him, don't touch him. She breathes in his smell, a mixture of wool, almonds, and woodfire.

Then, like a compass needle finally stopping at north, she abandons herself all at once to her impulse. She pushes him toward the living room, pushes him with her head and hands, and he obediently walks backward until he's sitting on the couch. She puts her knee down beside him and kisses him with a sort of desperation. He responds in kind. He clasps her hips and draws her toward him. Their grieving bodies awaken simultaneously, abruptly, imperatively, kindled by the powerful urgency of healing within each other. Caroline weeps. Her fists tug at the wool and her head is thrown back. Steve licks her throat, licks her tears.

He lays her down on the couch. He slowly glides his hand under her clothes and removes them one by one. He undresses her without her quite being aware of it. How long. A long time, a short time, it hardly matters. Wherever he touches her he sets her ablaze; he touches her everywhere. He caresses her as though her body were already familiar to him, as though she were the one he'd been healing for nine months. His eyes are closed. When he opens them again, what she sees there is fear.

The wind blows on my forehead
cuts through it.
Big white snowflakes fall on my skin
vanish before they melt.
The surrounding sky pushes and pushes, wears me down
soon I'll be nothing but the path of the light.

She brings blankets and they fall asleep on the couch, entwined and in constant danger of dropping to the floor. Yet their sleep is uninterrupted, dense, and immobile. When dawn slips in between the curtains, Caroline rubs her eyelids. Steve's breathing grows lighter, his fingers glide over her thigh.

"I couldn't invite you into my bed," she whispers without turning around.

The large warm hand settles on her belly.

"I know."

"The kitchen table, not my specialty."

"That's all right."

"The floor, that's David's."

"Okay."

He draws the blanket over their shoulders and sighs:

"There's something unprofessional about all of this."

"What do you mean? I think you were fabulous."

"You know very well what I mean."

"Yes, of course: Steve Austin, Nurse of the Year."

"Exactly."

"Too bad."

"What about you?"

"Me? The semi-widow? I've thought about it a lot."

"And?"

"Slippery slope. Makes it hard to think."

She sits up on the edge of the couch, brushes her hair away from her face. He stays stretched out on his back with his hands behind his head. Actually, his head looks funny in the morning, the shaggy hair, the puffy eyes, the conspicuous beard. His mouth looks different, too, more animated somehow.

"I'm hungry," Caroline says. "Breakfast?"

"Tell me the truth."

"What?"

"This is a sofa bed, right? You can open it?"

She flashes him a wicked smile.

"Do you want to open it?"

"No, no," he assures her with an identical smile.

She gathers her clothes up from the floor and starts to dress. He watches her with an inscrutable expression. She feels

271

slightly awkward, taking care to hide any unwanted rolls of flesh. He, on the other hand, sees nothing that isn't desirable, but he dutifully turns away, followed by the blanket, which leaves him half-naked. She pauses with one arm midway through a sleeve. He's even better-looking than she expected. What with chopping wood for his hundred-year-old neighbour, lifting inert patients, and keeping his cottage from falling apart, he's acquired a degree of physical perfection obscured by his ill-fitting uniform.

She heads to the kitchen. Two of the candles are still burning. Their flames are unpoetically reflected in the toaster and the empty bottle. The barely touched pie, the sticky plates, and the dry cups have been left lying on the stained tablecloth. Caroline puts the dirty dishes in the sink and pours two large glasses of orange juice. She drains half of hers in one go, she's that thirsty.

"Orange juice?" she calls toward the living room.

"Thanks."

He's standing in the doorway, stock still and barefoot. He keeps his hands in his pockets, as if to prevent them from straying too far. And because he generally uses them with such great assurance, this detail transforms him.

"A penny for your thoughts."

"I think you're beautiful."

She gives herself a once-over: tangled hair, rumpled skirt, bare feet.

"You do?"

"Yes."

"Would you like a slice of pie? We could have pie for breakfast."

"It's a relief to tell you that, Caroline."

"What?"

"That for months I've been thinking you're beautiful."

"At the hospital? With my bloodshot eyes, the shadows under them, my chewed up fingernails?"

"And all the rest, yes."

She finishes her orange juice.

"Thank you, Steve. It does me good to hear that."

He eats his piece of pie standing up. She doesn't sit down either; in the daylight, images of David have returned to putter around the kitchen. They proliferate, fill up the space, clash with reality. David hands Bertrand a wooden spoon and they gobble up half the raw cookie dough. He purges the kitchen-sink pipes, promising to replace them soon, when the next pay cheque comes in, before Christmas anyway, guaranteed. She sees him—oh, this is pitiful. She sees him changing the outside lightbulb over the front door, bare-chested in the middle of October. The muscles of his forearm neatly intertwine as he unscrews the old bulb and screws in the new one. He makes fun of her:

"Interesting, eh, watching someone change a lightbulb?"

"I think you're gorgeous, that's all."

"You do?"

"Yes."

"Wait. I'll be right there."

Caroline shakes her head to chase away the rest of the memory, but there's no stopping it. She sees David towing her into the bedroom, laughing as always when he "parades around in all his splendour."

Steve draws her out of her thoughts:

"You're not doing too well, eh?"

"Not really, no."

"Are you sorry?"

"No no no. No, Steve. No. Why sorry? Just ghosts, that's all."

"I know all about ghosts."

"What do you do about them?"

"They mostly haunt the places they know. Would you like to go to the deli for breakfast?"

"This ghost spent a lot of time at the deli. Especially when my mother was in town."

"So what would help?"

"I'm going to take a shower. Do you want to take a shower? How about a shower?"

"But ..."

"I changed the curtain."

"Ah. Well, okay."

Steve goes away in the afternoon. The next day is a Sunday with Amélie. Caroline doesn't have time to feel lonely. Less than a half-hour later, Bertrand, back from his grandparents', blows in like a tornado, full of stories to tell. He talks non-stop, during supper, in the bath, on his pillow, and Caroline, her head spinning, goes to sleep early in her big deserted bed.

March

David opens his eyes just once or twice a week now. He yawns less, moans more often. Sores have developed on the fragile skin over his sacrum, protective cream has been replaced by a medicated ointment—not the first time—and he is responding well. The physical therapist who mobilizes his joints every day finds him somewhat stiff.

Caroline, who never hid anything from her husband, is afraid of their next one-on-one. As a couple, they had mastered the art of transparency, the ability to say: "You're getting on my nerves. Why? Because of this and that. Okay, I'll make an effort." So what now? How will she be able to look him in the face? His silence will act on her like an accusation, his vulnerability will fill her with shame.

When the time comes, she stays rooted to the spot in front of the bed. The outline of the curled-up silhouette is apparent through the sheet. The mouth is open, the lips slack, a thread of saliva is about to trickle down the chin. Even so, it's still him. She'd like to own up to everything. To admit: "David, it's too hard to wait without knowing, the endless months, the pneumonia, Bertrand's questions. I think you'd like him, Steve, that is. You'd trust him. He's there, he's solid, forgive me."

She'd like to tell him that, she'd like to know he hears her.

Unbound, confident.
Something has changed.
To touch my wife
To touch her.
To utter a syllable
just one.
Leave.
It resonates unendingly, from one peak to the next.
Leave, Caroline.
Leave.
Leave.
Leave.
Live.

The following Monday, there are three knocks on David's door, and Caroline blushes crimson. Steve, whom she hasn't seen since their night on the couch, steps halfway through the door as though waiting for permission. He has just finished his first day shift and has already changed his clothes. Bertrand rushes to his schoolbag to show off the gold star with which Mrs Létourneau has graced his arithmetic exercise book. Caroline looks at Steve bending over Bertrand's workbook; she watches his hands and imagines them doing something very different. She faintly hears him suggesting Bertrand trace the numbers on David's arm.

"This is a hundred, Dad. Then one hundred and one ... one hundred and two ..."

After each number, Bertrand waits for the reaction. No reaction—it doesn't matter much; he's learned to do without. At least his father is there, he's breathing, and he's gotten over his bad cold. Bertrand grows bored and starts to jump up and down, asking if he can go to the vending machine to get some C7s. Caroline gropes in her bag for change, and he dashes away.

"If Lucille catches him ..."

"I know. He's got so much energy to burn."

"It must be exhausting at times."

"Someone always has to be around to keep him moving. If Marie is on hand, she steps in and takes the opportunity to do her jogging. Otherwise, I go get his friend Maxime and they play in the park at the corner of the street."

Caroline thinks back to Élise's candid advice: clearly, Bertrand needs a man in his life, too.

"I'm heading out soon," Steve says. "Can I give you two a lift? Do you want more time? I still have to run an errand downstairs."

This simple question ignites a Bengal light in Caroline's belly. To be outside, to spend twenty minutes with him, en route to a normal life, to leave behind the hospital together— what a lovely mirage.

When they arrive at the car, Bertrand immediately notices the booster seat.

"It's my niece's," Steve explains. "I left it in the car, just in case."

"In case of me?"

"Come on, get in," Caroline urges. He doesn't move.

"But Mom ..."

"What?"

"The seat. It's pink."

"Put your coat over it."

Once inside the car, Bertrand soon forgets the colour of the seat and begins to suck his thumb while leaning his head against the window. He likes to see the streets stream past and abandons himself to a multitude of small wonders: a dog the size of a rat wearing a coat, a house that has kept its Christmas decorations, a limousine as long as a city block, a boy lifting off his skateboard and landing back down on it.

In the meantime, Steve and Caroline think nothing but suspect thoughts and therefore prefer to leave them unspoken. He puts on some music, which happens to be Fred Pellerin's "Silence." He's very fond of this song; still, he reaches out to change the CD. Caroline touches his arm to stop him. The contact stirs their emotions. The song even more so. He drives slowly.

When they reach their destination, he leaves the motor running. The drive was a bit too quick. This may be the last time they see each other this week, and Caroline still hasn't dared to ask him for his phone number. Nor has he offered to give it to her. All at once, she glimpses the sum of the days that remain to be strung together, just like the months that have just ended, an endless horizon of lowering clouds.

"Bertrand," she says while handing him the keys to the house, "go ahead and show us how you're able to unlock the door all by yourself."

He doesn't need to be coaxed. He bounds up the porch's peeling stairs holding the key so tightly in his fist that it leaves red marks. With his back to them, his tongue sticking out, and his ten fingers joined together to take aim at the lock, he doesn't notice that neither his mother nor Steve are paying attention.

"What are you doing next Saturday?" Caroline asks.

"I don't have any plans."

"Would you mind coming back to the city?"

"No. Not at all."

"But, Steve, I've been thinking."

"What about?"

"About the slippery slope."

"And?"

"Could ... could we see each other without ... without ..."

"Of course."

"You're sure?"

"Very sure."

"Thank you."

She ought to get out now, but doesn't want to.

"Would you like to stay for supper?"

He mulls it over with a lopsided smile and glances at Bertrand, the true cause of his indecision.

"So? Is it yes or no?"

"It's yes no. Some other time."

Bertrand, meanwhile, has opened the door only to realize that no one witnessed his victory. He protests loudly.

"Hey! Mom, Steve! I unlocked the door and you haven't even gotten out of the car!"

"Coming!" Caroline shouts as she opens the car door.

She has barely closed it when Bertrand starts to drag her toward the house by the already frayed strap of her bag. The grey Renault moves off and blends into the street and the onset of night.

"What's for supper?"

"Macaroni."

"Steve doesn't like macaroni?"

"Why do you ask?"

"Oh, I dunno. It looked as if he wanted to stay, but then he left."

Caroline places her hand on her son's head. What else does he know? What has he figured out? Everything going on around him is beyond his ken. His life is like a film for grown-ups that she took him to see by mistake. Too complicated, too painful. She ruffles his hair. Its texture increasingly resembles that of his father. In a word, horsehair. Good, dirty-blond horsehair.

She doesn't talk about Steve to any of her friends. Does she still have friends? Hmm. They can be counted on the thumbs of one hand. And Marie? Is she a sister or a friend?

Anyway, how would she justify herself?

She could say that to go on loving David and being the mother of his child she needs to feel alive.

She could say: imagine you've spent the whole day slogging through sleet, your muddy boots weigh a ton, your legs are frozen, your cheeks have turned white. You take a hot shower. The water pours down the nape of your neck, down your back, over your belly, and you know everything will be alright now, that, in the end, everything will be all right.

Then the girls would say, yeah, fine, so the attending male nurse, cute guy, single, sure, you need to fill up the time, find a reassuring presence, naturally, you must feel so alone, an affair, after all, can make sense under the circumstances, you forget about your troubles—who could be satisfied just with visits to the hospital? But then again, poor David. In any case, don't get too attached, and what about Bertrand in all of this? And this nurse guy, can you trust him? He wouldn't by any chance be taking advantage of the situation a bit, would he?

Élise of course would broach the subject of contraception, Adèle that of successful grieving, and Simone would get into feelings. Sandra would make a sincere effort. But the truth is that Caroline does not want either to share Steve or expose him to reality. Or even to Marie, come to think of it. So long as he exists in the realm of the secret, nothing can happen to him, neither insult nor conflict. Nor a bad fall.

He came into her life in spite of the circumstances, not because of them. He detracts nothing from David. On the contrary. How can she explain faithful infidelity to the others? Ramified love? Desire . . . that doesn't exclude sadness, happiness that doesn't exclude insight, the unsuspected potential of a double sofa bed? David himself comes under the heading of the inexplicable, a husband neither dead nor alive, a man both mysterious and unchanging.

And what about her? Who could understand her? A hazy identity, hopes and fears in suspension. A woman, nevertheless, at this very moment. Serene whenever she is in the moment, but unable to grasp the landscape as a whole. The panoramic view, or any notion about the future produces a sensation of vertigo that she avoids at all costs.

The living need the living
skin needs skin
in a world of
tension, contortion, expansion, contraction
the energy the mountains put into being born
is devoted each day to being alive.
I remember.

In the park where they fed the squirrels for much of the afternoon, a beautiful sun slants through the naked branches. Steve is slumped on a bench next to Caroline with his head bend back. He worked late the day before in his local clinic and has been dozing off in spite of himself. She looks admiringly at his profile, which is strong and well balanced, like the rest of him.

"Steve?"

"Hmm?"

"Do you intend to give me your telephone number some day?"

"That depends."

"On what?"

"Do you want it?"

"Yes no."

"That's what I thought."

The sun grazes his long eyelashes and lends him a kind of fragile radiance, as if his presence depended on this passing ray.

"Unfortunately," he goes on, "I'm working at the clinic all next weekend. I tried to get out of it but it's impossible."

"Could we see each other the following week...?"

"Would you be offended if I offered to repaint your porch?"

"Should I take that as a metaphor?"

"Only if it suits you."

"Would you change the colour?"

"Same answer."

Caroline ponders his offer. Steve repainting the porch—what will the ghost say? The neighbours—who cares? They can talk as much as they like. But will the image of, say, David *building* the porch keep intruding? The nails, the boards, the drill, the sandpaper. Especially the nails. Tap tap. The hammering.

"It was David who built the porch."

Steve straightens up and turns toward her.

"Caroline, David built your whole life, yours and Bertrand's."

"True."

"You think he wants your life to fall asleep along with him?"

"No."

"Listen. I'll be free that Friday, no clinic. Saturday too. Sunday I'm with Amélie. If we do the painting, fine. If not, we'll do something else."

"We could play backgammon."

"Scrabble."

"Stealing Bundles."

She slides along the bench until her thigh touches Steve's. He would have liked to move closer much earlier, but she's not his wife. He feels her flowing, burning through his veins. She's taking up more and more space and he must learn about love again from scratch. It frightens him. Another man's wife, another-man's-wife. In his own way he hears the hammering too.

They head home, their hands buried deep in their pockets, without speaking. The texture of the silence between them has changed once again. It's the silence of them both now; they inhabit it together.

Encouraged by signs of an early spring, Caroline is won over to the porch project. She gets out the sander, seals up the holes and cracks, buys rollers and paint, a blue-grey duly approved by Bertrand despite the slightly different shade. She takes Friday off. Yet it's a risky undertaking. You can easily go from short sleeves to snowshoes in this country; it might snow tomorrow on the fresh paint and the final coat could freeze overnight. It's too soon, but it's also too late because Caroline has made up her mind. In fact, it's now or never.

The weather is still fine on Friday morning. Strangely warm, actually. Tonight, Bertrand will be sleeping over at Maxime's, who has just received an iguana as a gift. They plan to put it on a leash and walk it around the garden. On Saturday Mr Giguère is going to take them to a hockey game and buy them sundaes. Everyone is happy with this arrangement, except the reptile no doubt.

In the knapsack that he's brought to school, Bertrand has packed his favourite pyjamas and a scarf "that smells of Mom." He grips her hand tightly and is in no hurry to join the other children, already seated in a circle.

"I want to ask you a secret, Mom. In your ear."

Caroline leans down. She already knows what he'll ask; this has become a ritual.

"You're not going to have an accident while I'm away, eh?"

"No, I promise. I'll be at home. I'm going to bake apple crumble for you."

"Okay. You'll look both ways before crossing the street, eh, Mom?"

"Yes, Bertrand, I promise."

She kisses him.

"Mom?"

"Yes?"

"You think everything will be okay at Maxime's?"

"I'm sure of it. Are you taking the iguana to the hockey game?"

He lets out a cascade of crisp, beautiful laughter.

"No, Mom!"

Leaving the schoolyard, she chats briefly with another mother, unbuttons her jacket, and looks not once but twice before crossing the street. The grey Renault is already parked in front of her house, but Steve himself seems to have vanished. She quickens her pace. She leaves the door open behind her and goes upstairs to change her clothes. From her room she hears the door closing, footsteps on the ground floor, the kitchen sink faucet. She goes back down in an old, oversized T-shirt, a pair of jeans ripped at the knees, and sneakers already splattered with beige paint.

She finds Steve starting up the espresso machine and dressed exactly like her, except for the lemon-yellow splatters.

"I see you've dressed up in your finery," she says by way of a compliment.

"Likewise. I went to get bagels, they're still warm. Want one?"

"I must admit, I'm not very hungry."

"Me neither, to tell you the truth."

Caroline's stomach shrinks whenever Steve is nearby. This may be a symptom they have in common.

"Cups?"

"In the cabinet on the right."

He opens the cupboard and the Dieter Verkest Post-it jumps out at him. He stands there, unable to follow through with the cups.

"The red cup is mine," Caroline says.

They both anticipate what will happen next. They've each been thinking about it, separately, all week. Each of them, separately, has methodically pulled arguments in favour of Platonic love out of the hat. The hat is empty.

The good, strong espresso, barely two mouthfuls, provides a somewhat short pause. The empty cups leave them face to face in their identical clothes with an almost tangible discomfort sitting between them on the floor tiles.

"I'm thirty-five years old, but I feel like fifteen," Caroline says.

"Thirty-seven, fourteen," Steve replies.

He doesn't budge. He struck a deal with himself about making the first move. But Caroline steps closer, close enough to hear his breathing turn erratic. She raises his T-shirt and puts a hand on his lower back. She pulls him toward her and tastes the coffee on his lips. He greets her mouth but hardly understands what's happening. He is aflame, consumed by an unknown desire and at a loss for what to do with it.

They must have moved without realizing, because now her bum is pressed against a drawer handle. He clasps her tightly with one arm, as if wanting to bring her inside his skin. He's removed his watch and flung it on the counter. He tries to remember, but everything is a jumble. Not the table, or the floor, or the bed. Where?

"Where, Caroline?"

"Here."

She flips her shoes off with her toes, he pulls off her jeans, scarcely grazing her thighs, and lifts her up. The red cup flies up and smashes on the floor, Caroline laughs, he enters her, still laughing, the laughter is transformed and the transformation unmoors him, the sound of it carries him to a place very white and remote; only a tiny corner of his mind stays aware that the counter is too high, too uncomfortable, and it must be even worse for Caroline, with the edge of the cupboard against the back of her neck, yet he feels her clasping his ribs, and everything accelerates. He'd like to slow down, but it's close to a panic, she's on the point of capsizing, he hears it in her voice, he would like to wait, it's too quick, too strong, but just in time she lets out a cry, because he's lost, completely lost.

They don't stir for a long time after. Breathless, leaning his whole weight against the counter, Caroline's hair entangled in his fists, he hugs her, his head resting on the cupboard where the Post-it stands guard: "We are too weak to look love in the face."

She sinks her face into the T-shirt, wraps her legs around him. She's crying. Her warm, peaceful tears, soaked up by the cotton, finally douse the embers. He's going to cry too, maybe. At last.

> The upthrust of blades of grass
> the spark of hearts
> the power of a birthing
>   who can eye the sun unshielded?
> Love, to be contained, is plunged into the flesh.
> Later, to recover it,
> we hold it up, arms straining, in the arms of another.

They finish the first coat just before twelve, despite the diversions of Mr Ouellette, a retired neighbour, who comes three times to let them know that March is much too soon. A big cloud drifts in from the north, as if it were going down the street determined to burst when it reached the porch. But it sails right by and lets the premature spring, which convinced them to get out the brushes, shine on. To Caroline's great relief, the nails David hammered in remain undisturbed.

She goes in to make lunch. Steve stays outside to examine the tread of a creaky stair. The stair turns out to be flawless, but he comes away with a bad splinter. He heads directly to the bathroom and stays there forever. The grilled cheese sand-wiches are already cooling when he joins Caroline.

"I'll give you no more than a two for your medicine cabi-net."

"Two out of…?"

"Ten."

"That's harsh."

"You get points for the peroxide, that's all. The dates on everything else are past expiry."

"Not the toothpaste, inspector. Or Bertrand's syrup, which I just bought."

"Two and a half."

Steve stops short. It suddenly occurs to him that David's stuff has been sitting around for almost nine months. The anti-inflammatories, the ointments for sore muscles, the deodorants, the after-shave. The badly rolled Ace bandages alone take up an entire shelf. He's wrong to judge the medi-cine cabinet of someone in absentia.

"Was that a quarrel we just had there?" Caroline worries aloud.

"I hope not. You think we quarrelled?"

"No. Would you like to take a peek at the pantry before you sit down? You know, the best-before dates…"

"I'm too hungry."

They're both hungry, but after just a single bite of grilled cheese, their stomachs contract again.

"Do you feel like sleeping here tonight, Steve?" Caroline asks, toying with the cheese. "We could … rent a movie?"

"Okay."

"I think about you, sometimes, weekdays in the evening. Monday, Tuesday."

"You do? Wow."

"That friend you stay with, where does he live?"

"Stéphane? He's three blocks away."

She raises her eyebrows in surprise.

"Too close . . ."

"Yup."

They leave the grilled cheese sandwiches almost untouched and go out to rent the film. When they return, they decide to do the second coat right away, in case the temperature falls during the night. Caroline is busy stirring the paint with a stick when the telephone rings. Automatically expecting the worse, she drops everything and rushes inside.

Steve takes the roller out of the plastic bag he stored it in and pours the paint into the tray. Through the half-open door he can hear Caroline laughing more and more loudly. He has never heard her laugh. She was about to, this morning, when the cup fell on the floor, but he interrupted her. He wants to see her. He absolutely wants to see her laugh. He leaves the roller on the porch, wipes his hands on his jeans, removes his shoes.

He finds her leaning on the counter, at the very spot where they stayed welded to each other for such a long time this morning. His watch is still lying there with the strap turned up. Caroline, holding the receiver away from her ear, wipes the corner of her eye with the back of her finger. Close at hand is an unwrapped bar of dark chocolate. Still grinning when she sees him resting against the doorpost, she shakes her head.

"But in the end, did the police come?"

The answer sets her off again. She laughs so hard that she feels she ought to apologize to Steve, who, arms folded, is watching her and laughing too.

"Oh, the indignity! The sheer indignity! Stop, Marie, stop! Where's her car now? . . . Pointe-aux-Trembles? . . . Oh, no . . . she's going to what? To give it a *funeral?*"

More laughter. It comes from her belly, from a part of her belly that Steve unknotted for her; still holding the receiver, she steps toward him proffering some chocolate. Then she stops abruptly. Marie has just thought to ask her how she was.

"Fine... Yes, I mean it, *really* fine... In good company, yup... Yes, probably who you think ..."

She casts a sideways glance at Steve.

"Exactly, yes, we're doing some repairs and touch-ups. .. Hmm ... Marie, please, keep it yourself. I'll call you later... Me too, big kiss."

She hangs up, shaking her head.

"So?"

"Listen to this. A friend of ours, Sandra ..." she begins.

"I saw her at the hospital, I think."

"Oh, yes, that's right. Early on ... anyway. She drives an old car that's been slowly dying on her, one door at a time. Even the windows got stuck. Up until recently she could still use the trunk, but it jammed too, in the Adirondacks. Marie was with her to go hiking, they spent the whole day trying to get out of the car, finally they had to call the firemen. They arrived with the siren wailing... Do you like the chocolate? Organic, fair trade, and all."

"Know what?"

"No."

"We should have rented a comedy."

"True. So why did we choose a psychodrama?"

"Occupational conditioning, in my case."

"Projection, in mine."

"We'll go back and exchange it."

"Yes, that's it, Steve. Exactly. We'll exchange it."

The eagle soars
far far higher than the highest peak.
In my palm a handful of dry earth tiny pebbles somewhere
between sand and rock

rough granular they slip through my fingers.
Dry crumbly earth ready to spill
just open your hand.

I want to fly.

The second coat of paint is finished in no time; the matter of the porch is finally settled. From time to time Mr Ouellette pushes the curtain back to supervise the work. He examines the porch, checks the sky, shakes his head, raps on the window, gestures, lets go of the curtain. Steve finds this very funny; Caroline, quite annoying. They clean the rollers and brushes, store the leftover paint in the garage, return to the video club, take a shower. Steve realizes he has no clean clothes, refuses to borrow David's bathrobe or, even worse, Caroline's, supposedly because "it's pink." He spends the evening in his old Cirque du Soleil T-shirt.

They order Mexican food, eat in the living room watching the romantic comedy, let themselves be distracted by each other, lose the thread of the story, come back to it just as the credits appear, and end up falling asleep on the sofa bed, which they've taken the trouble of opening this time. They sleep in a tight embrace under the white quilt, and as they sleep their breathing blends together to the point that, if a ghost happened to be in the room, it would take them for a single, perfectly relaxed body.

Sunday, March 25
Day 4

The next morning finds them in the same position. Caroline's hair tickles Steve's cheek. He wakes up. The breast in his hand takes him a little by surprise. Through the curtain he sees the shifting silhouette of the maple tree standing amid its rotting leaves. He feels calm, a calm so deep it makes him wonder. It's as though a massive, taxing weight left him overnight and now he can enjoy a large, airy, unknown space of freedom. For the first time in a long time he has the feeling he could fill his lungs to their utmost capacity. Yet he doesn't dare. Not as long as Caroline stays suspended, waiting. A hiatus. Above all, don't move in during a hiatus. The cool breast burns the palm of his hand.

Caroline stirs. She stretches, yawns, turns toward him and smiles without even opening her eyes. She tucks her head in the crook of his neck, and the already familiar scent of almonds fills her with an ethereal joy.

The telephone rings.

She stiffens all at once, her blood freezes. She instinctively checks the clock. 7:02. This time she knows it will be no laughing matter.

She reaches the kitchen by the third ring. The floor is cold, the room steeped in a greyish, meaningless atmosphere. The heating will need to be turned back on; the false spring is over. At the fourth ring she looks at the telephone but doesn't touch it. At the fifth she picks up the receiver.

Steve listens from the living room. He didn't dare follow her. The hospital rules are all too familiar to him: call early in the event of a dramatic change, but not at night, if possible.

"Yes, I understand," Caroline says, and he can tell just from her voice that her face has gone pale. "Doctor who?... Ah. This morning? At what time?... Yes, I'll be there... No. No, that's all right... Yes, I know. Thank you."

He goes to her. He puts his painting gear back on and brings the quilt. She is slumped in a chair, her face hidden in her hands, and when he covers her she's like a small, compact mound of snow. He pours two glasses of orange juice, sits down in front of her, and turns his eyes from the glass that she's ignoring to the telephone that she pushed to the middle of the table.

"Talk to me."

Nothing.

"What's happened?"

She glares at him.

"Can't you guess?"

"I'd rather you told me."

She bites her lip, nearly drawing blood.

"Has he had a relapse? What are the symptoms?"

In her head, she reviews the little she knows: alarming fever, severe drop in blood pressure, heart rate off the charts, respiratory distress.

"Caroline?"

"They think it's septicemia."

Steve sinks back in his chair. Caroline tightens the quilt around her chest, her hands curled up like David's.

"The doctor wants to see me asap."

"Sollers?"

"No, someone else."

"Ah. Morel."

"I'm going over there right away."

"I'll come with you?"

"With me? In ripped jeans? On a Saturday? *With me?*"

"Why not, Caroline?"

"It's a sure way to lose your job."

"At least let me drive you there."

"No."

It's as if he's come up against barbed wire. He'd like to move closer, but doesn't dare. There is no way to read her, to understand what might help. His hands are empty, the worst possible situation for a nurse, a health-care specialist.

Suddenly, she cuts him a furious look.

"You and me, Steve, we killed him. I killed him."

"The opposite is probably true."

"What's that supposed to mean?"

"You may have freed him."

"You're pleading your own cause."

"I've seen a lot of people dying."

"So?"

He needlessly run his fingers through his hair.

"Nothing. You're right. Whatever I say, it'll sound like I'm justifying myself."

"I'll bet he sees us, besides. He comes and sits in the armchair where he'd watch TV, but instead of the sports news, he sees us fucking on the couch."

"We don't fuck, Caroline, he can't have seen that."

"Oh, come on, Steve."

"I caress you, I discover you. That's what David sees, if anything."

"Not much difference, seen from outside."

Steve suddenly looks worried.

"Do *you* see a difference?"

"Yes."

"Do you want me to wait for you here?"

"No."

"You'd rather I went away?"

"Yes."

"Can I do something before I leave?"

"What?"

"Anything?"

"No."

She shakes her head. For some reason that escapes her, she has an urge to hit him and, at the same time, to latch onto him as though he were the last piece of the real world. Behind the barbed wire, her soul is raw.

"Caroline . . ."

"No, no, no."

There is no other word left.

The light always-everywhere
comforting vital blinding with truth
the structure of a living heart.

"Mrs Novak? I'm Dr Morel."

He looks like a middleweight who's just taken a punch. Flat nose, white scar on the upper lip, brush cut, dark complexion. Stocky, hardly taller than Caroline, he wears black jeans and a grey shirt open at the collar, stretched tight over his biceps. She could easily picture him on a Harley-Davidson; in a word, she feels she can trust him.

"Where is Dr Sollers?"

"On sabbatical. I've taken charge of all his cases."

"He could at least have said goodbye."

Dr Morel opens his hands to indicate there's nothing he can do about it. He offers her a glass of water. The water cooler sounds more like a geyser as it fills the small paper cone.

"I'm sorry to have to meet you in such difficult circumstances. Would you like to sit down?"

"No, not really," she answers even as she settles into the sadly familiar chair.

Something is not quite right in the office. It takes her a moment to realize the stifling scent of musk has evaporated. In fact, the window is open in spite of the cold. The middle of the desk is dominated by a cardboard folder nearly as fat as an old phonebook, full of pink and blue sheets. The corners of the pages stir in the breeze. The doctor places his stubby-fingered hand on it.

"I've gone over your husband's chart with the microbiologist, the intern, and the head nurse."

Caroline stares at the brown folder containing the details of every hour of the last nine months.

"Under the circumstances, I wanted to see you alone. Otherwise, it would feel too much like a committee meeting. What do you know about septic shock, Mrs Novak?"

"Nothing."

"Okay. Simply put, septic shock is caused by the presence of micro-organisms in the blood, usually Gram-negative bacteria. It can be due to complications from a respiratory disease, even after a period of latency. The micro-organisms trigger a systemic reaction. First, blood circulation is distributed abnormally, meaning a poor supply of oxygen. The lack of oxygen entails the gradual failure of all the organs. In other words, without drastic, immediate treatment, it's fatal."

The inexorable chain of causes and effects, made graphic by the doctor's hand gestures, leaves Caroline speechless and horrified by the image of the organs liquefying one by one.

Why not boiled in oil, while we're at it? Meanwhile, she wonders if there might be another cause for effects like this. Might David, by any chance, have finished doing what he needed to do? Does the clear signal she asked him for bear a resemblance to Gram-negative bacteria?

"Although it's not yet a permanent coma," Dr Morel continues, "the vegetative state—you know this as well as I do, probably better—has persisted for quite some time."

"Yes."

"If he had already passed the twelve-month mark, the situation would be more clear-cut. But, either way, the chances of him returning to a normal life are nil. You know that too."

"Yes."

"Based on his chart, he's shown a remarkable level of physical resistance on several occasions."

"That's true."

"Still, I think it's legitimate to ask: are we talking about living or surviving? Are we talking about necessary support or unreasonable obstinacy?"

"Those questions have already been preying on my mind, Doctor."

"I understand. We took emergency measures last night, but you have the final say on where to go from here."

"What about the law? What does the law say?"

"In a case like this, the protocol is quite vague. We're obliged to act according to the principles of beneficence and 'do no harm,' which leave a lot of room for interpretation. We also need to consider any wishes expressed by your husband before the accident. Nothing on paper, am I right? As a rule, it would be in his chart."

"No, nothing on paper."

"Did you ever talk with him about the possibility of something like this occurring?"

"No."

"In your opinion, which way would he lean?"

My God, Caroline is thinking, *are we choosing a car? Ford or Nissan?* She sighs. David always leaned toward life. But, in the meantime, the definition of "life" has changed. She hears herself answer with frightening neutrality:

"David would hate futile therapy."

Dr Morel nods in approval, visibly relieved. There's nothing worse than struggling with the family, their beliefs and wishes, when everything argues for surrendering. He would do anything in his power for a patient like David, still young, a father, if there were the slightest hope of improving his situation. That hope doesn't exist.

"In light of his current quality of life, his repeated infections, the severity of the sceptic shock, and future possibilities, the law stipulates that the decision whether or not to keep him alive belongs to the family and medical staff. In this case, me."

"You, whom I'm meeting for the first time."

"Yes, I'm afraid."

Dr Morel's style is direct and casual. Once again, Caroline pictures him in the boxing ring. She prefers him by far to Sollers, so aloof. Too bad he's arrived so late.

"We absolutely need the consent of a proxy," Morel goes on. "You're first in line, Mrs Novak."

She is short of breath. She'd like to set the icy cup of water down somewhere, but it wouldn't stay upright.

"I guess you'd like to take some time to think it over..."

"No. I already share David's view."

She is shivering, frozen to the bone. He goes to shut the window.

"There are also your in-laws," he says. "They have to be consulted."

Caroline imagines the scene: Karine hiding her face, Janek chewing on his moustache.

"You get along well, I believe?"

"You've made inquiries?"

"Seems to me it's the least one can do."

"The least for some goes beyond the most for others."

Dr Morel brings his lower lip up over his scar. No doubt a way of keeping from criticizing his colleague who just flew off to Europe with his precious research grant.

"And, informally, we need to get the nursing staff's input as well."

"Why?"

"To agree on the best way to proceed."

"What does that mean, exactly?"

"There are a number of possible approaches, Mrs Novak. On one hand, we can decide to stop the interventions already initiated, such as antibiotics, oxygenation, irrigation of the vital organs, volume expansion, and so on, I'll skip the details. On the other hand, we could also choose to suspend various forms of daily support, such as providing food and water. We need to find the middle road between futile therapy and no therapy."

Caroline sits up. All at once, the blood has returned to her face.

"You'll let him die of hunger? of thirst?"

"It's more complex than that."

"I want David to feel supported in his final moments, Doctor."

Morel pushes the palms of his hands out as if to fend off an assailant.

"That goes without saying, Mrs Novak. But, one way or the other, we're looking at a compromise. If we keep your husband's strength up, the natural decline of his vital functions will be drawn out. Outright agony is to be avoided."

"We have to find a way of finishing him off, Doctor, is that what you're telling me?"

"Mrs Novak, *finishing him off*, as you put it, is still illegal. So that's out of the question. Personally, I'm inclined to keep hydration at a minimum. Listen, I understand how difficult this is for you."

"Oh, really? And how can you be sure you understand?"

He hoists his palms again; it's a reflex.

"Would you prefer to talk about this again this afternoon, with your in-laws? Would you like someone from the nursing staff to be present, someone you know well?"

"No. Thank you. Exactly how much time do we have, Doctor?"

"It's impossible to say."

"But are we talking hours or weeks?"

"It's a matter of days. At most."

She bends her head.

"I don't want to overwhelm you with details. But it's my duty to help you choose the most respectful way forward for your husband. We could wean him off gradually. Keep his mouth properly moistened, which is what matters most in terms of comfort. We have good reason to believe that gradually reducing internal hydration allows a kind of physical desensitization to occur. A sort of natural analgesic, if you will. We can also soothe him, up to a point, with appropriate medication."

"Up to a point, meaning what?"

"Meaning we must avoid provoking his death with excessive doses. Morphine depresses the respiratory system. You have to go easy."

"Would you necessarily give him morphine?"

"Not necessarily."

"I've seen David refuse to take aspirin when his shinbone was broken in two. 'Ice, just ice,' he said. He said, 'It's my body, I'll put up with it...'"

She squirms in her chair. For David, lucidity was priceless. Are they going to deprive him of his death by taking away his suffering? And, for that matter, *is* he suffering?"

"Nothing hallucinogenic," she finally says.

"Excuse me?"

"I'm drawing the line for him, Doctor. Nothing hallucinogenic. I'm certain David wants to be present at his own death."

This seems to make a strong impression on Dr Morel. Beads of sweat appear on his temples. He nods yes. Sometimes people move him. After all these years spent in the hospital arena, people still move him.

"You must know by now, Mrs Novak, that we can provide support for the family, psychological, or even ... religious support?"

The questioning intonation of the statement betrays the doctor's atheism; as for Caroline, she finds his offer ludicrous.

"Dr Morel," she says, changing the subject, "David signed an organ donation form. A long time ago."

"Yes, it's in the chart. Unfortunately, given the length of the vegetative state, his organs no longer meet the criteria for a transplant."

She looks up at him; her eyes are like a sky that's too vast. There's a lull in the conversation, and the doctor lets it go on. You don't lose the love of your life twice. Only one thing offers comfort in face of the intolerable: compassion. He sizes her up and decides to venture into more hazardous territory:

"You know, Mrs Novak, oftentimes our patients slip away when they sense that their loved ones are ready."

"Ready?"

"When they feel safe, well supported. At peace with themselves. Already engaged in the grieving process."

Caroline chokes up. That's what Steve tried to tell her his morning. Clearly, Dr Morel is not pleading his own cause. His cause consists of people who are dying or revived and whose fate is largely out of his hands. They hold each other's gaze for a long while, and the vastness of the sky in her eyes becomes habitable again.

"I don't want to pry, Mrs Novak, but is that true of you?"

"For your statistics?"

He cocks his head to one side.

"It would help me refine my perception of things."

"Yes, Doctor, it's true of me."

She sits back in her chair. She is not going to explain to this stranger the long period of coming to terms with an intangible presence, or the reinvention of everyday joy, or the reunion with her own body as created by David, as left by David, the hot blood, the pounding heart.

"Can I ask you a personal question, Doctor?"

"Why not?"

"Do you believe that consciousness is the product of chemical processes?"

He scratches his chin. Caroline hears the heavy beard under his stumpy fingers. He must shave twice a day. He smiles, and the scar disappears.

"No."

"Then what is it, in your view?"

"You know, Mrs Novak, I'm just a neurologist. There are points where science must be humble enough to raise a white flag."

He leans both elbows on the massive desk.

"However much we pretend to know everything, the truth is, there's mystery at both ends of life. And in between, too, though we tend to forget that."

do they feel it when they touch me
the light
do they see it

I have nothing else to give them

Caroline has spent the whole day at the hospital, bent over David's greyish skin, alive to Janek's silence, Karine's prayers, and Morel's plan, supported in every way by the staff on duty, whom she doesn't know very well because it's Saturday.

When she goes back home with Bertrand, it's dark. So very dark. She walks with slow, measured steps, his little hand in hers, not speaking. For him, she rehearses in her head different versions of the unacceptable. He's frowning. Her grip is too tight, for starters. And then there's her listlessness, her lateness, the darkness.

"Mom, did you bake crumble for me?"

"No, I'm sorry."

"Why?"

"Tomorrow."

The light bulb over the porch is on. She spots it from a distance. She would never have thought to turn it on before leaving this morning. She chased Steve away, but he still found a means of waiting for her, somehow. The light gives her a precise marker, such that she can almost count the number of paces before she arrives at the newly painted porch. The dark, inhospitable expanse of the street offers something of a reprieve, but as it gradually diminishes a sour taste rises in her throat. She shivers when she slips the key into the lock. The grating of metal on metal sends chills up her spine.

In the hallway, she kneels down in front of Bertrand to do the things he long ago learned to do by himself. She lifts the backpack off his shoulders. She opens the Velcro fasteners of his coat, removes it, and hangs it on a hook. She unties his shoes, carefully places them side by side. She takes the pyjamas and stuffed toy out of his bag. Then she stands up and holds her hand out to him.

"Let's go, buddy."

They go upstairs. She kneels down again and brushes his teeth. He doesn't understand. What's going on, Mom? The question spins around in his head. It seems to him that his mother lingers over each gesture. Squeeze the tube of toothpaste. Turn off the cold-water tap. Smooth out the crease in the bath mat. It seems to him that as soon as her hands stop touching things, she'll collapse like a house of cards. Now her hand grazes his cheek. He can't stand it. He decides to pee.

"Would you like to sleep in my room, Bertrand? With me?"

"Why, Mom?"

"I want to talk to you a little. After that, I'd like for us to be together."

He walks into her bedroom ahead of her. He sits down on the bed without pulling the covers back. His face is serious, almost mature.

"What did you want to tell me, Mom? Did I do something not nice?"

"No, no," Caroline says anxiously. "No, not at all."

He exhales in relief. A respite, just barely.

"It's about Dad."

His face, curiously, lights up.

"He woke up?"

"No, Bertrand, that's just it. He isn't going to wake up."

"What do you mean?"

"I mean, ever."

His small fists pull at his pyjama pants.

"He's dead, isn't he?"

"No, but he's really very sick."

"The doctor can heal him, like the last time. He must have some mercu . . . some mercu . . ."

"No, Bertrand. The sickness is in his blood."

"Why, Mom? Mom?"

"His body is very, very tired now, Bertrand."

"But, Mom, he's always sleeping, he's not tired!"

"He's so weak inside, he doesn't have the strength to fight."

"But the doctors can press down a bit on his heart, like Martin Bilodeau. Can't they?"

"The doctors think it's better to let him rest for good."

"For good, what does that mean?"

"Forever."

She's going to cry. She doesn't want to cry.

"Dad is ready to die, Bertrand."

"But, Mom! How can you know that Dad…? That…?"

"It's complicated, Bertrand."

"It can't be true, Mom. I was waiting for him, I …"

"I know, my darling."

He screams:

"Mom! I want to understand, Mom!"

She wraps her arms around him, he wriggles, hits her, hurts her.

"Me too, Bertrand, me too. I'd like to understand."

He keeps on thrashing about, and she tries not to panic. A dizzying hole is opening up in her child's life, a hole that nothing will ever be able to fill. She does not know how to comfort him for such a profound heartache. He eventually wears himself out and grows limp. He buries his face in the crook of his mother's neck and rubs against her skin to smell her, like a small, hunted animal in search of its den. Kneeling on the carpet, she rocks him, wondering if her arms are long enough, sturdy enough, soft enough, warm enough.

"We have to accept it, even if it's hard…"

"I can't, Mom. I never will. Never never never."

"Get into my bed. Here, with me."

They huddle together under the quilt, but they're cold, both of them. Bertrand shakes like a leaf. She strokes his hair. He'll fall asleep, sooner or later; he's a child, after all. An endless hour later, his breathing finally changes. His body relaxes. He grows very warm. He smells of fresh baking.

Caroline, however, can't sleep. She'd rather not, anyway. While David is still alive. To be with him, here on earth, for as long as possible. To feel his remaining minutes go by.

Monday, March 26
Day 3

Around two in the morning, Caroline opens the closet door wide. She does a mental calculation of the number of bags she'll need to take David's clothes to the Salvation Army. She tells herself she ought to keep something for Bertrand. Maybe a belt. Certainly the watch. Then, all business, she promises herself she'll call the Quebec Federation of Labour to hand David's final tax report entirely over to them.

At dawn, she decides to make herself some herbal tea. Maybe listen to some music. She goes downstairs in the dark and stumbles over Bertrand's school bag, which she shoves aside with her foot. In the kitchen, she lights just a candle. The quivering flame reveals a piece of paper lying in the middle of the table. A telephone number with the Eastern Townships area code .

soon
the energy freed from the body's mass
                    finally
released into space

available anew

if they think they're losing me
_   they haven't understood_

we have never lost each other

She calls at seven sharp.

"Caroline," he answers.

His telephone voice is even fuller.

"Am I waking you?"

"No."

She hears sparrows chirping in the background.

"I'm sorry, Steve."

"For what?"

"For yesterday."

"Come on, now, Caroline."

"I could have treated you a little better."

"I've seen worse."

"Exactly."

The birds happily fill the ensuing silence.

"Are you, by any chance, drawn to difficult women?"

"Difficult? . . . No. Complicated, maybe."

"Bionic man looking for complicated woman."

"Has a pretty nice ring to it, I think."

"Granted."

They fall silent again. Caroline's neighbour sets to work in the garden with his power saw.

"How's Bertrand?"

"It's hard."

"Take him out to play ball."

"Yes."

"Get him running."

"I'll try."

"Have something to eat too, maybe."

"Maybe."

"Please. Have you seen David?"

"Yes."

"Morel?"

"Yes."

"Do you want to talk about it?"

"No."

"And your in-laws?"

"It's horrible for them."

"You'll tell me if there's anything I can do."

"I promise, Steve."

Silence, sparrows, saw.

"It's a little early for a power saw, isn't it?"

"He does this to us every other Sunday."

"I'm sure it's illegal."

"You can tell him that."

"If you like. I'm driving down to Montreal tonight. Do you want Stéphane's phone number?"

"No. Get some rest. See you tomorrow?"

"Caroline?"

"Yes."

"Nothing. See you tomorrow."

She hangs up, but her hand stays on the receiver. Her eyelids are burning. The tiredness wraps her in a dense, even comfortable fog. Emotions come to her muffled, as does the noise from next door. After an eternity, she stands up; her legs are numb. She opens the bag of bagels and inhales. She's not hungry.

Behind her, the shuffle of Bertrand's slippers, the rustle of his flannel pyjamas, feathery sounds. She thrusts her hand into the bag. He likes bagels.

"Mom, why did Dad's blood get sick? What kind of sickness?"

love
nothing but love
>*the rest already vanished*

become the eagle now
>*fly*

>*fly*

The catheter was removed from his stomach. The one on his arm was left in place for partial hydration. On the other arm, a butterfly needle was installed for analgesic injections. A transfer to palliative care was planned, but the floor team opposed it, given the good relations they had developed with the family. The idea of depriving them of a familiar space at the very last minute seemed counter-productive.

Dr Morel gives the nursing staff a lot of latitude and was won over by their arguments. When dealing with a patient unable to communicate, he finds they're in a better position than anyone else to decode symptoms, read signs of discomfort, and even decide on dosages. For their protection, however, he requires a detailed report on the administration of analgesics, including the reasons for it; he wants to avoid accusations of euthanasia.

A film of sweat covers David's face, while his dry lips let out the raspy sound of very rapid breathing. His hands are cold and marbled. His closed eyes move quickly, alive to the images he will take away with him.

The chart still dominates the foot of the bed, ready to collect data on a natural death, measured according to objective parameters and dictated by the body's chemistry and mechanics.

From one piece of data to the next, the narration of a failure.

gravity opens its fist I rise up

"Mrs Novak, hello."

"Hello, Nurse Pronovost."

"You can call me Lucille."

"Lucille? But … Okay. Fine."

Caroline is struck by the irony of the situation. Why is Nurse Pronovost making an effort to be on more familiar terms now that the story is coming to an end? Chances are that, after next week, she'll never see her again.

The same is true of several of the health professionals who've been revolving around David for nine months. She got to know only a fraction of the actors involved in this drama and is meeting them now as they leave the stage. The dietician, the day-shift orderlies. The physical therapist, who comes in to say a few words to her, nearly apologizing for not stepping in, for not bending and unbending her husband's limbs, for not tapping him on the back or opening his fingers.

"You work Sundays now, Lucille?"

"I'm filling in for someone," Nurse Pronovost answers, rolling her eyes because this person has a tendency to disrupt everyone else's schedule.

At this point, she abruptly picks up the chart, scans it over the top of her glasses, and puts it back on its hook, shaking her head in disapproval.

"What's the matter?" Caroline asks.

"What?"

"I get the impression something is bothering you."

"Hmm."

"What is it?"

Nurse Pronovost gives her arm a vigorous rub.

"… It's … the gradualness."

"You mean the hydration?"

Lucille glances at David. She shouldn't be discussing the plan in the absence of her colleague and in the presence of the person dying. But, then, oh well.

"If a body decides to pass away, I think we need to ensure they don't suffer, that's all, and not to keep them down here. What we're doing with your husband is giving with one hand and taking away with the other."

"That's pretty much what Dr Morel said to me."

"Dr Morel wants at all cost to avoid any association between his actions and a death. Reduce the intake while eliminating as few tubes as possible."

"Why?"

"You want my opinion?"

"Yes."

"My honest opinion?"

"Yes, Lucille."

"He's afraid of death."

"But…"

"Like all doctors, actually. Why do they become doctors in the first place? Eh, Mrs Novak?"

"Well…"

"Right. That's my view and I don't mind sharing it."

"I gather that you yourself, Lucille, aren't afraid of death."

"No."

"Could I ask a favour of you?"

"Such as?"

"Could you explain to me how things will go for David?"

"Explain what? The visceral consequences?"

Nurse Pronovost, always so brusque, so hurried, so blunt, gives herself an uncharacteristic moment to think, something she apparently can't do without worrying at her glass frames.

"I'll spare you the distinction between the hyperkinetic and hypokinetic phases, if you don't mind, and jump ahead to the consequences."

"Okay."

She takes a deep breath before starting in.

"Well now, the process is more or less as follows: in response to the presence of bacteria in the blood, right from the start a cardio-circulatory disorder sets in. The impact on the lungs is immediate, as you saw yourself. After that, the lack of oxygen triggers various anomalies. The liver has trouble filtering and detoxifying the blood, which prevents it from performing its immunological functions and, as you can imagine, this sets off a dandy of a vicious cycle. The digestive system is affected—let's skip the haemorrhages and necrotic lesions. Eventually, there's an acute kidney deficiency and added to that are hematological anomalies with a risk of thrombosis due to the reduction of coagulation factors. In a word, the collapse of one organ impacts on another and so forth. It's a carnival of failed systems. I'll skip the brain damage. At this point, as far as your husband is concerned, there's no need to elaborate. In sum, it's hardly a pretty picture. Everything falls apart, piece by piece, and each new problem is itself potentially fatal. You can see why it would be unfortunate if it dragged on."

"Yes. Thank you, Lucille."

"You're welcome."

"I think I'll go get a breath of air."

"You do that, Mrs Novak."

I   rise

   up

     I hover above

waterfalls gorges
a river
a lake

empty space
my wings

I   glide

the sky with no roads paths obstacles

I'm flying at last
I'm flying

leaving no trace

They all tilt their heads up at the very same moment.

Marie marvels at the return of geese in the sky over Brossard.

Steve propels Amélie into the air and catches her against the sunlight.

Nurse Pronovost notices, far beyond the hospital parking lot, the black smoke of a fire.

As she hangs her freshly washed curtains back up, Karine is surprised to see a solitary cloud shaped like a pierogi.

Janek shakes his fist at the pigeon that just fouled the windshield of his Honda Civic.

Bertrand is fascinated by the intersecting vapour trails of two airplanes. They drift toward each other, meet, and drift apart. He can't take his eyes off the point where they touched.

In her search for fresh air, Caroline has come out onto the hospital's fallow garden. To shield herself against the repulsive sight, she looks up at the sky. So blue. So pure. So vast.

"We always fall into something bigger," Marie would say. Maybe, she thinks, that is the point David has reached, the point where all that's left to fall into is infinity.

heaps of water on the frothy walls
chamois on the steep slopes

the earth rolls beneath their hooves
below everything
clumps together
everything
melds comes apart melds again

here
I
soar

pure power
without snags
or injuries
or fear or error

calm joyous true
strength

free and orderly
resolved

When the phone rings at ten p.m., Caroline is afraid it's to notify her of David's death and her heart sinks into her boots. Which is why, on hearing the all-too-familiar voice at the other end, she lets out a howl:

"MOM!"

"Yes, it's me. My poor poor Caroline."

"You spoke to Marie?"

"She filled me in. You might have called me yourself, darling."

"So, to top it all off, I get a complaint."

"No, no, don't take it the wrong way. I just wanted to tell you I'm thinking of you."

"Okay."

313

"And I'm thinking of Bertrand too."

"Yes."

"I called you several times, but you never answer the phone."

"...Oh?"

"I didn't dare leave you a message, you understand. I didn't want to bother you."

All those anonymous calls, then, were Lorraine's handiwork... Troubled by this realization, Caroline answers testily: "You should have."

"I'll keep it mind in future. Would you like me to come to see you? Do you need anything?"

"No, no. Thank you."

"Okay. In that case, keep me posted."

"Yes."

"Okay... Bye?"

"Bye, Mom."

"Bye-bye. Err ... take care of yourself."

"Yes."

"All right. *Take care, darling*," she says in English.

"You too."

Caroline hangs up. Is it too late for the two of them? Perhaps. Lorraine seems more distant from her than ever. On the other hand, Karine has grown closer. In a certain way, the constellation is holding together.

Karine is alone with Janek for the extreme unction. She wears a black dress with a stiff collar and over-polished patent leather shoes. She has been rehearsing the last rites in her mind for a very long time, but she always pictured them as her own and not her son's. She wonders what will happen afterward. Will she be able to laugh, take an interest in mundane things, focus on a recipe? Will she be able to feed herself or have to live on communion wafers?

She stands upright, bolt upright. Dignified, restrained. She suspects she looks like an old branch tormented by winter. Something inside her was pared away during the very slow countdown of the last nine months, an undeniable process of erosion. Watching her son all that time, she came to recognize the infant in the grown man. She remembered how, in the very beginning, each minuscule toe, each unpractised muscle seemed to her to enclose a small parcel of the sublime. It's in the sublime that she recognizes him. In the persistent miracle of existence.

Her view of death has changed. She now sees its function clearly: to distinguish the eternal from the ephemeral, the profound from the superficial. She regards her grieving as a shortcut to the portion of the divine granted her in this world, and she is determined to climb that steep road even if it means losing the last few kilos that keep her standing.

The priest, free to absolve the dying man without hearing his confession, proceeds quickly. He sprinkles holy water and mechanically recites the prescribed phrases, laying bare the ritual's banality when detached from its inspiration. Karine is disappointed by his performance. As she makes a mental note to mention it to her spiritual support provider, something warm suddenly interrupts her train of thought. Janek has slipped his hand into hers.

She is filled by a memory made up of ferns and innocence. All in all, life goes by in a flash.

Tuesday, March 27
Day 2

At Marie's suggestion, David's bed was turned to face north, in keeping with the instructions of Padmasambhava, author of the *Tibetan Book of the Dead*. Nurse Pronovost found this complicated because of the machines and electrical outlets. Still, since David will be neither resuscitated nor aided by a respirator, she took the initiative, while she was at it, of muting the instruments so the family could engage directly with the dying man, without distractions or intermediaries. After all, it's now or never.

Bertrand was let off school and Caroline has taken a leave of absence. Together with Janek, Karine, and Marie, they've organized an uninterrupted vigil much like a relay race. Sandra has offered to be their taxi driver using the old Jeep Cherokee she purchased and has apologized for not doing more due to her fear of hospitals.

She just took Bertrand to the Chinese restaurant. Janek decided to come along but disliked the way she gesticulated while driving. Karine declined the invitation due to an appointment with her spiritual support worker. Marie, seeing a chance for Caroline to enjoy a rare moment of privacy, excused herself on the pretext of an urgent need for camomile.

David is panting, mouth agape, skin drawn, pale, bluish, almost mineral. When he gasps for breath, his heart races so fast it can be seen throbbing under the sheet. At times he stops breathing for long intervals and appears already dead. But then all at once he rallies, sounding like a Metro train.

Caroline has finally left behind the memory of what he was and her preoccupation with what he will be. She watches over him, such as he is, with no future, and thus no past, and, in contemplating him, experiences a joy equally profound and out of place. She finds him beautiful, still and always. He resembles the essential David that nature intended when it carved his skull and gave him bones. She lets herself be pervaded by the space he has entered and which draws him farther and farther away. She no longer speaks to him, but touches him constantly. She thinks as little as possible.

The suspension that Laura referred to enfolds her momentarily, and when it does, Caroline plunges into an almost unbearable clarity, a distant eternity, as if death had already come, but without birth, as if elsewhere had always been the true place. There are very brief moments when she touches an immaculate sky, a perfect peace.

Ultimately, without saying a single word, David will have been her best teacher. She knows she will spend the rest of her life searching in others for an intangible magnitude, an insoluble mystery. She thanks him for leading her there, so close to a new kind of truth. For creating a final memory in the shape of an absolute shelter.

Bertrand didn't touch his imperial roll or his chop suey. Back at the hospital, he finds the nurse in charge of support for children, the same one who met him at the intensive-care unit immediately after the accident. It was Caroline that asked her to step in. Ever since she found the Italian soccer team T-shirt in the kitchen trashcan, she's been at a loss for how to respond. Lily arranged the meeting, and the nurse is waiting for Bertrand so she can tell him the fairy-tale version of the facts: the stomach and kidneys go to sleep, the blood starts to flow very slowly, the brain starts to dream... Her version is as fluffy as Nurse Pronovost's was blunt.

Bertrand has worn a frown for three days. While the lady narrates, he studies his father's rigid hands, listens to his laboured breathing. All his courage these last months rested on the conviction that David would wake up. He bet all his chips from the very start, was at times the only one to hold up the torch of optimism, and now the defeat comes as a crushing blow. The visceral consequences give him a stomach ache.

"Can you tell me what would help you right now?" the nurse asks, admitting the limited impact of her involvement.

"I want to see Steve."

"Steve? Why?"

"Because."

"Okay, I'll check to see if he's available."

Steve does not keep them waiting. Caroline lets him in, but Bertrand doesn't bother to turn around. Steve steps into his line of vision on the far side of the bed.

"Hi, Bertrand."

"Hi."

"This is hard, eh?"

"Hmm."

Bertrand steals a glance at David but, as if seared by what he sees, quickly comes back to the sheets.

"He looks like he feels bad, Steve. Can you do something to stop it?"

"We've just given him something."

"Will it make him feel better?"

"Yes."

"You're sure?"

"Positive."

"How do you know?"

"I know it, Bertrand. It's my job to know it. Trust me."

Bertrand gives him a skeptical pout and grips the sheet in his fist.

"Would you like me to show you a special part of the hospital?"

"Special how? I don't like the hospital."

"It's a place especially for kids."

"When?"

"Now."

As he follows Steve along a maze of corridors, through doors that open by magic at the touch of his magnetic card, Bertrand notices that his leather watchband is speckled with drops the same blue-grey colour as their new porch. He's struck by the coincidence. Ordinarily, he would greet this with a shout, but he's in no mood to marvel today. They come out in a wing full of colours, clashing sounds, barking, mewing, cooing.

"What does 'animal therapy' mean?"

"You'll see," Steve answers, and ushers him toward an exotic aquarium.

"What's 'pilot project'? Can I see the pilot?"

A young therapist skips toward them, her blond ponytails bouncing on her shoulders.

"Steve!"

"Hi Sophie. This is Bertrand."

"Hi Bertrand. Are you here to see the animals?"

"The what?"

"Come. This is a good time. It's quiet. I'll show you Custard's sister."

"My rabbit," Steve explains. "I adopted him here."

Bertrand lets her steer him to a room painted apple green

and canary yellow with gym mats covering the floor and a large cage shaped like a castle. Sophie picks out an angora rabbit with red eyes that jiggles its paws excitedly.

"It tickles!"

"Hold her underneath. That's it, excellent. You can pet her, she's really nice."

"Her fur is soft. What's her name?"

"Alice."

Bertrand strokes Alice's back while she nibbles at his wrist. He lets himself get completely engrossed, his hands full of warm, wiggling life. The big slab of reinforced concrete pressing down on his lungs starts to soften. Steve's break goes by, stretches on, finishes. Though reluctant to do so, he must break the spell.

"Bertrand? . . . We have to get going now. We'll come back if you like."

Bertrand sniffs loudly and wipes his nose in Alice's fur.

"We'll come back. Eh, Sophie? Can we come back?"

"Of course."

No sooner has he put Alice down on the gym mat than she springs toward the corridor with Sophie chasing after her. Bertrand slowly straightens up, all the while wiping his nose on his sleeve. He keeps his head down, worried that Steve might see he was crying. But as soon as he comes alongside him, he wraps his arms tightly around Steve's thigh. Steve leans over and hoists him up. It's been a long time since anyone lifted Bertrand up; they all say he's too heavy now, that he's grown too much. He curls up in Steve's arms and bursts into tears.

They're about to step back into the neurology unit, when Nurse Pronovost heads them off.

"Hey, Leclerc!" she roars, arms akimbo.

"Who's Leclerc?" Bertrand asks.

"That's me," Steve answers, unfazed.

"Go inside to your mother, little fella, you know the way," Nurse Pronovost instructs him.

Bertrand scampers away, anxious to avoid the lava flow. Speaking in a whisper, Nurse Pronovost sounds even more threatening:

"You disappear while you're on duty with the son of a patient, you bring him back with his cheeks on fire, teary-eyed, and holding your hand to boot. It takes just one rumour for you-know-who to whip out the code of ethics."

"Come on, Lucille . . ."

"Don't give me that come-on-Lucille line, you know exactly what I mean."

"We're allowed to be human, aren't we?"

"Watch yourself, Steve, that's all I'm saying. People are already chattering. As if they weren't all running after you, on top of everything else."

"Back off a bit, Lucille. Put yourself in his shoes for a moment. Besides, I couldn't care less about the gossip the girls are spreading."

Nurse Pronovost puckers her lips, straightens her blouse, and strides away toward the cafeteria, intent on buying herself a diet Pepsi. Steve stays put. He is shaken, but Lucille's warnings play no part in his unsettled state of mind. Whereas the fact that Bertrand, who's been as taut as a wire these last three days, felt free to break down in his arms has sent a shock wave through him. A child's trust has always seemed the most precious thing of all to him. This child's trust fills him with both gladness and fear.

Despite being late, he dashes over to the nursing staff's kitchenette. There's something he must do, something he doesn't want to put off for even a second. He opens the drawer, ferrets around in it a little, picks out a knife with a serrated edge. He slips it under the strap that has obstructed his watch for four years but that, surprisingly, never came apart.

It takes the small, unsharpened steak knife a while to split the leather. Long enough for Steve to hear the lapping of the lake and the song of the cicadas, to taste the maple-sweetened bottom of the dark water; for the tapered, gleaming, nearly blue locks of the woman knotting the bracelet to graze him one last time. He sees her smile with delight. He sees himself putting on his watch to go to work, noticing that the strap will obstruct the dial and deciding to keep it anyway, for as long as possible.

The steak knife prevails, and the frayed, faded, paint-stained piece of leather drops onto the counter. Steve stuffs it in his pocket. When he gets home, he'll burn it. He knows exactly where. He knows exactly in which direction the smoke will take it, and why.

Martin Bilodeau learned that David was dying from Roger Pitt, who heard it from the mouth of Diane Simon, a receptionist at the Quebec Labour Federation. Diane Simon was told by Caroline herself. Sitting at the very back of the Pie-IX bus, Martin constantly makes sure the multi-blade Victorinox is still in the pocket of his windbreaker. He feels nervous. He doesn't expect to see either David or his family. But even so.

Nor does he expect to see a pink head emerge from behind the reception desk of the neurological unit. Lily gives him an inquiring look; she senses a spam. Martin fumbles with the zipper of his pocket and takes out the penknife, which he has cleaned, oiled, and rubbed like Aladdin's lamp.

"Is this where David Novak is?" he asks, blushing.

"Visits are restricted to family members," Lily answers, surprised at the arrival of a new visitor at this late stage.

"Yes. But I have this ..."

He opens the hand holding the knife; Lily takes a step back. One more argument in favour of metal detectors.

"It's ... it was David's. I wanted to leave it for Bertrand."

As Lily says nothing, he adds:

"Bertrand, his son? His name is Bertrand, right?"

Lily takes the utensil with her fingertips and drops it into a Ziplock bag, which she seals tightly.

"You'll give it to him, eh?"

"Yes, yes. I'm sure he'll be pleased. *Poor little sweetie.*"

Feeling the same sense of relief that comes after he positions a ledger, Martin retraces his steps to the elevator. He waits for a long time and finally gets in. The elevator stops at the second floor. The other Martin Bilodeau, his namesake, is on his way back from a rehabilitation session. He steps inside, leaning on his cane, and the Martin who saved David's life moves back to make room for him. The elevator starts to descend and stops at the ground floor again. A clown armed with two dozen helium balloons quickly fills the remaining space. Martin Bilodeau pushes a balloon away from Martin Bilodeau's face as he struggles with his cane while attempting to squeeze into a corner. They exchange slightly embarrassed smiles.

Dr Morel watches David's decline with admiration. He finds him tough. He believes that, against all odds, considering his failing respiratory, kidney, and liver functions, David will get through the night and, maybe, part of the next day. Caroline decides to go home. It's better for Bertrand. Janek and Karine will keep watch at the hospital, on the cot Hattie has set up and fitted with a feather pillow in a Lion King pillowcase, Nurse Pronovost's contribution. If things take a sudden turn, Brigitte will call.

Back home, in preparation for bed, Bertrand has peed, had his story read, been cuddled; he is wearing his pyjamas with the monsters. He tells about his meeting with Alice, Custard Leclerc's sister, three times. Caroline is stretched out beside him. She contemplates his profile in the glow of the nightlight, the down of his skin, so fine it looks powdery, this miniature

David who goes on living and growing each day. Bertrand lets out a prodigious yawn.

"Mom, the sandman isn't coming."

"No?"

"No, he really isn't."

"You want a song?"

"No, a story."

"Another story?"

"Yes."

"Which one?"

"The story the lady told me today at the hospital. You know, the one about Dad's lungs."

"Oh . . . yes. That story."

"I didn't understand all of it. The lungs go to sleep, and then?"

"The blood changes, it gets weaker."

"And then?"

"Then the kidneys go to sleep too."

"And the heart?"

"The heart too. Everything goes to sleep."

Bertrand nestles against her. He is thinking.

"You know, Mom, there are things in my head. A whole bunch."

"Yes."

"Is it like that for Dad, too?"

"Yes."

"The things in his head, do they go to sleep too? Or do they go somewhere else?"

"That's one of life's secrets, Bertrand. Even grown-ups ask themselves that question. All we can do is imagine what the answer is."

"What do you imagine, Mom?"

"A big, open sky," Caroline decides, thinking maybe David does have mountain sickness after all. "A really big sky. What about you?"

"A lot of warm light."

"Ya? Light?"

"Warm light."

Bertrand yawns. Caroline hugs him, maybe a little too hard.

"You want a song now?"

"No, thanks."

"Good night, buddy."

"Mom?"

"Yes?"

"Stay with me tonight, okay?"

"Okay, Bertrand."

Janek let his wife have the cot and assigned himself the chair. He aches in his lower back, between his shoulder blades, in the nape of his neck. Most of all, he's waiting to hear, behind David's laboured respiration, the peaceful breathing of Karine's sleep. He gets up. He lays his head on his son's pillow. He would give anything to be dying in his place. That would be in the order of things, it would follow a natural sequence. As it is, the situation revolts him. All he can do for his son is utter the words he has prepared. The words. They absolutely must come out of his throat before tomorrow morning. This is hard for him, almost superhuman.

"Dawidek…"

He does not like the sound of his voice, mixed together like this with the death rattle. But he perseveres; he must spit it out no matter what:

"I wish you a beautiful new land, Dawidek… Free, new. A beautiful land, that's what I wish for you."

He kisses the damp, fevered forehead.

"Will you forget us? Eh? I will not. Ever."

Then Janek wonders how he'll manage to stand up again.

Wednesday, March 28
Day 1

The floor is still asleep, the lights are dimmed, sounds are rare and muffled. Steve arrives a six a.m. and collects what he needs without running into anyone else. He decided to come here after a particularly uncomfortable, restless night on Stéphane's futon. He's about to do an orderly's job, and why not? Besides, this isn't the first time he'll be working outside his schedule.

He wants to wash the man whose wife he loves. He wants to touch him on this, his last morning, barehanded, without the mandatory gloves.

"It's me, David, it's Steve."

He turns him over to open the gown. Everything is simpler without the tubes. He undoes the diaper, which is perfectly dry. He dips his hands in the soapy water, wrings out the luke-warm sponge, and rubs down every centimetre of skin. He applies ointment to the back of the knees and under the heels. He massages the blue fingers. On the swollen abdomen, the long scar writhes like a snake in time with the fitful breathing. He refreshes the temples and feels the pulse coursing along the throat. He presses a damp towel against the lips. He combs the hair. He shaves the beard. With the back of his thumb he gently smoothes out the eyebrows.

peace peace peace
    peace

Steve arrives at the station just in time for the morning handover. Brigitte, her face drawn, her ponytails slack, clutches a cup of filtered coffee. Nurse Pronovost adjusts her blouse.

"So, did Mrs Guérin leave you be?"

Brigitte shrugs.

"Same old, same old."

"Meaning what?"

"Meaning she rang seven times for piddling things."

"She's being transferred today and is probably feeling stressed," Nurse Pronovost suggests. "What about Sleeping Beauty?"

"He's really congested, I gave him subcutaneous scopolamine at two-thirty. His blood pressure is almost undetectable, pulse over 90, temperature 39.2°. He's at the end of the line."

"I just saw him. He looks really peaceful," Steve chimes in.

"What do you mean, you just saw him?" Brigitte asks in surprise.

"I washed him. We can check that off on the to-do list."

"What do you mean, you washed him?" Brigitte snaps.

"I wanted to wash him."

"What is your problem with Novak, Steve?"

"I wanted to wash him, I washed him, end of story."

"Honestly, now, what is your prob …"

"We're allowed to be human," Nurse Pronovost cuts in decisively.

She, too, did some pre-dawn thinking. She has known Steve for a long time, since he first started in pediatrics. She

328

regards him in a way as her son, which is why she is liberal with her scolding. Over the years, she has seen him happy and she has seen him miserable. She saw him struggle, visibly waste away, pull himself together, steady himself, and keep going. From the subtle signs that perhaps only an old, arthritic nurse can discern, she senses he is coming back to life now. "Why get in his way, big Lucille?" she asked herself in her lavender-scented shower. It wasn't through want of trying, but she couldn't come up with a good reason.

Dr Morel holds his stethoscope in both hands, and there's something solemn in his second of hesitation. Then, in a tone of voice he keeps as neutral as possible, he declares:

"It's a matter of hours."

The statement reminds Caroline of the pointless encouragement she got from the gynecologist in attendance at her delivery. Then, "hours" seemed like an infinite stretch of time. Now, "hours" are like table crumbs, scarcely enough for the sparrows.

Janek puts his arm around Karine's shoulder, while she hides her face in her long hands, worn out by nocturnes. He can put up with Chopin, but has vetoed the *Funeral March*. To summon up his courage, he thinks of the countless armies that brought his country to its knees, even erasing it from the map three times. Razed its villages, pillaged its coffers, slaughtered its women and children. He thinks of his Poland deprived of natural boundaries, a doormat for Germany and Russia, who never had any qualms about entering without wiping their big boots. His Poland that nevertheless rose from its ashes each time: the only acceptable version of a resurrection.

Placing his son's death on the broader horizon of a collective destruction and redemption brings him a little solace. The ordeal of communism left him with the capacity to view himself as a small part of a whole, and his own suffering as a drop of vinegar diluted in a large glass of water. He tries to project onto David's emaciated profile the symbol of an indestructible nation: an eagle, wings spread wide, wearing a crown. Yet his historical perspective can't stop his moustache from trembling.

"In terms of pain control . . ." Morel begins, speaking to Karine rather than Caroline.

"The criteria remain the same, Doctor," Caroline interrupts.

"The final hours are necessarily gruelling, and I must ensure that he is as comfortable as possible," the doctor insists. Having come to the medical profession because of the violence he endured at home as a child, he finds the suffering of others hard to bear.

"But look at him," Caroline objects. "He's perfectly calm."

Morel has to acknowledge this. The ragged breathing could be a sign of distress, but there's no other evidence of this. The patient's tranquility contradicts all his predictions. He concludes that Novak's brain injuries, further aggravated by the septicemia, have completely disconnected him from his physical experience.

I see I see everything I hear
I hear

I see them, them
    at last. At last

Caroline has grown thinner
the old purple coat she's so fond of
is too big

my mother has aged my father's hair turned white
close very close to each other

where is Bertrand
show me Bertrand
I want to see Bertrand

"Marie? It's me. . . Listen, it's almost over. Can you bring Bertrand? Is he still asleep? Take a cab…Marie? Could you try to get him to speak to David?…Thanks. See you in a bit. What would I do without you?"

Caroline puts the telephone down on the small coffee table in the lounge; with the tip of a frayed fingernail, she scratches vaguely at the peeling varnish where countless cups have left rings.

he has grown
a lot

his face isn't that of a child
it's the face of a man
down in a trench

Bertrand grips the sheet tightly in his fist.

"Aunt Marie, the way he's breathing scares me."

"I know, it's troubling."

"He's got a funny colour, don't you think?"

"That's because his blood isn't circulating well. Would you like to talk to him a little?"

"No."

"Why?"

"I don't know what to say."

"You know, Bertrand, you haven't spoken for quite a few days."

"Hmm."

"I understand, I realize it's hard. But this is the right time to tell your father things that matter."

"Like what?"

"Things that are in your heart."

"Why?"

"When you grow up, you'll be glad you told him all those things."

"You think?"

"I'm sure of it."

He is on edge as he thinks it over.

"Would you rather I went out?" Marie asks.

"Yes, I would."

She kisses him on the cheek and leaves, pulling the door shut so he can clearly hear it. Only then does he raise himself up on tiptoe. He touches David's earlobe with the edge of his lips.

"Dad…"

He strokes his hair.

"I didn't want you to go away."

David's moments of apnea are increasingly prolonged. Every time his chest sinks down it seems less and less likely to rise again.

Janek can't take it any longer. He goes outside to smoke. He gropes around in the inside pocket of his jacket. Turned soft by the warmth of his chest, that of a living man, the pack of cigarettes nauseates him.

Karine, exhausted from her night on the cot, has gone down to the chapel to nap for half an hour, no more.

Marie and Bertrand go looking for the animal-therapy wing, to no avail.

Caroline is here.

Caroline is here
that's her scent
that's her clear voice that's her voice

she says: You gave us so much happiness.
she says: I love you, David. I wish you a peaceful journey.

Quite suddenly, she is gripped by hunger. She forgot to eat breakfast. Come to think of it, she also forgot to have supper last night.

Karine should be getting back from her nap momentarily.

Just a quick run down to the cafeteria to buy a sandwich and she'll come back to join her.

Nurse Pronovost takes advantage of the family's absence to check vital signs. She steps toward the patient, but something stops her; the room seems very bright to her. She turns her eyes up toward the fluorescent lights, they're off; she turns her head toward the window, the curtains are drawn. She adjusts her glasses and goes out, forgetting why she came.

he breathes in
draws me in

he breathes out
empties out

.

.

.

.

expels me

the tunnel
the rasping song the naked peaks below the wind without pity

all
is
open

June

With the sun beating down, two workers, each with a long streak of sweat down his back, unroll the turf. Bertrand, meanwhile, puts down his new shovel. He has nearly finished covering the roots of his contribution to the hospital garden. He pulls out of his pocket a letter folded in eight, and kneels down to place it near the sapling. He takes a handful of cool, rich, black soil from a large plastic bag that's been ripped open, and sprinkles it on the paper. He repeats this until the message has completely disappeared.

He stands up, wipes his hands on his shorts, smiles with satisfaction, and picks up his shovel again to finish the job.

Dear Dad,
it's me who pict out your tree.
It's a red maple like the one in frun of the house.
It loses it's leafs in the fall but they come bak after.
For real, every year.

Bertrand shakes the tree to make sure it's solidly planted. A leaf comes loose and slowly drifts down toward him, so slowly that his catch is effortless.

Acknowledgements

This book was written with the financial support of the Canada Council for the Arts.

A number of health-care professionals also made essential contributions to this project. For their rigour, patience, and availability, my heartfelt thanks go to Linda Roy-Huneault, Lise Huard, and Dr François Marquis in Québec; Élisabeth Jacq and Maryvonne Roussel in France; Michelle Church and Fiona Branch in the UK.

I wish to thank Lazer Lederhendler for the talent and sensitivity he has brought to the translation.

My fondness for Poland owes a great deal to a memorable afternoon spent in the company of Marta Jaciubek-McKeaver, and to the friendship of Wioleta and Szimon Jarosiewicz.

Many of my questions about building sites were answered by the perfectionist construction worker Nick Healing.

I am indebted, as well, to the inspiring work of Amy and Arny Mindell, who pioneered "coma-work," a great source of knowledge and hope for comatose people and those close to them.

I am deeply grateful to the friends and loved ones who read one or more versions of the manuscript—I won't name them, they know who they are.

Finally, thank you Alan and Élie for making life so precious, every day.

About the Author

Born in Montreal, Pascale Quiviger studied visual arts, earned an MA in philosophy, and did an apprenticeship in print-making in Rome. She has published four novels, a book of short stories, an essay, a young readers series, and a book of poems, and has written and illustrated two art books. Her novel *The Perfect Circle* won the Governor General's Literary Award for Fiction in French, and, in English translation, was a finalist for the Giller Prize. *The Breakwater House* was a finalist for the Prix France-Québec, and *If You Hear Me* was translated into Spanish.

A resident of Italy for more than a decade, Pascale Quiviger now lives with her family in Nottingham, England.

About the Translator

Lazer Lederhendler is a full-time literary translator specializing in Québécois fiction and non-fiction. His translations have earned awards and distinctions in Canada, the UK, and the US. He has translated the works of noted authors, including Gaétan Soucy, Nicolas Dickner, Edem Awumey, Perrine Leblanc, and Catherine Leroux. He lives in Montreal with the visual artist Pierrette Bouchard.